Red Ruckus

Pinnacle Westerns by Brett Cogburn

The Morgan Clyde Series

SMOKE WAGON

CALL ME LONESOME

RED RUCKUS

The Widowmaker Jones Series

WIDOWMAKER JONES

BUZZARD BAIT

GUNPOWDER EXPRESS

THIS SIDE OF HELL

Western Titles

PANHANDLE

DESTINY, TEXAS

ROOSTER

Brett Cogburn

Red Ruckus

A MORGAN CLYDE WESTERN

PINNACLE BOOKS
Kensington Publishing Corp.
www.kensingtonbooks.com

PINNACLE BOOKS are published by

Kensington Publishing Corp.
119 West 40th Street
New York, NY 10018

First Pinnacle printing: September 2022

ISBN-13: 978-0-7860-4813-7
ISBN-13: 978-0-7860-4814-4 (eBook)

10 9 8 7 6 5 4 3 2 1

Printed in the United States of America

CHAPTER ONE

Denison, Texas, Southern Terminus
of the MK & T Railroad, June 1874

The sheer volume of the screaming coming from somewhere down the street, coupled with the fact that the voice's high pitch told it came from a woman, brought Morgan Clyde down the street at a dust-stirring clip that even a long-strided horse would have been hard-pressed to keep up with. The flat brim of his black hat was tilted down in a determined rake to the point that the only thing visible of his face was the stub of a cigar jammed in one corner of his mouth beneath his mustache.

The woman down the street screamed again, followed by the sound of screeching nails and busting lumber. Another voice, this time distinctly male, shouted some warning, followed by the boisterous laughter of several other unknown male participants.

Morgan leaned into his march even more, cursing the pair of freight wagons parked in front of the general store and blocking his vision of whatever was taking place on the boardwalk beyond them that warranted all the noise and excitement. The bottom of his black frock coat flapped at his waist and up about his elbows in the stiff breeze, and the open front of that unruly garment occasionally revealed the flash of the tin badge pinned to his wool vest and the pistol holstered at a cross draw on his left hip bone.

People had gathered on the opposite side of the street to take in the scene, some of them watching whatever was taking place in the alley between Hogan's Mercantile and Klein's Feed & Seed, and others more interested in the looming arrival of their deputy city marshal then storming down the wheel-rutted, potholed thoroughfare in a manner that said he was likely on the prod.

More onlookers appeared before Morgan when he rounded the lowered tailgate of the last wagon. A half-ring of men was gathered in the mouth of the alley, some jeering and catcalling and others giving ribald advice to whoever was screaming within the alley. Morgan shoved through the crowd without so much as an "excuse me," or a "beg your pardon," and the shove he gave one especially big farmer dressed in a tattered straw hat and patched overalls two sizes too short for his overgrown frame caused the man to stagger aside most indignantly. But none of the crowd complained, not even the giant farmer with fists the size of Morgan's hat, not with Morgan's hand resting on that big pistol and his jaws chomping on the cigar like an overheated work mule slavering at the bit in its mouth.

"What's going on here?" Morgan said.

Nobody answered, but the crowd moved back a little.

Morgan took a step closer to the alley and peered intently into its shadowed depths for whatever calamity had caused him to leave his breakfast half finished on the boardinghouse dining table, and his coffee only half drunk and growing cold in his mug so early in the morning.

Now that the crowd was hushed, his hearing was only then registering that along with the woman's shrieks there was the unmistakable sound of pigs grunting and squealing back in the alley, and lots of knocking and banging. What's more, the woman he couldn't see wasn't only shrieking; she was screaming one of the most profane, creative strings of cuss words he had ever heard man or woman utter. And that was saying something, since he had heard some pretty talented profanity artists from docks of New York City to tobacco-spitting bullwhackers in Kansas and saddle sore and half-drunk cowboys up the trail from Texas. And not a one of them could hold a candle to the barrage of shameful oaths coming out of that alley, a fact that caused the town's one and only Methodist preacher standing in the crowd to go a little red around the neck.

"I said, what's going on?" Morgan repeated.

In answer to his question, a rather large red shoat charged out of the mouth of the alley at a dead run, aimed straight at him. He barely managed to take hold of the plow handle of his Colt pistol before the red shoat struck him in the shins.

The impact from one hundred pounds of charging young swine knocked Morgan's legs out from under him and would have sent him to the ground if it hadn't been for the lowered tailgate of the freight wagon just behind him. He caught himself there with a wild grab, but that precarious perch was short-lived. The red shoat's momentum carried it underneath the team of mules harnessed to the wagon. The mules promptly panicked and bolted away in a dead run with the bounding, rattling wagon building a dust storm behind them. That sudden removal of the wagon tailgate from beneath Morgan dumped him most unceremoniously into the mudhole at the end of the leaky water trough Mr. Hogan had built in front of his porch.

Morgan propped himself up with one elbow of his black frock coat buried in the muck of the mudhole and tried to shove his disheveled hat out of his eyes while the braying of the runaway mules faded into the distance. He stood and slung the mud from his hands.

No sooner had Morgan righted himself than more swine began to appear out of the alley. There were white pigs, black pigs, spotted pigs, and everything in between. There were grown pigs and half-grown pigs, and even one enormous sow with swaying rows of milk-swollen teats hanging under her and an entire litter of her little piglets darting and weaving among her legs. To say "pigs" is to imply some type of domesticated, gentle farm livestock of the swine persuasion, but these animals were the farthest thing from tame. More properly, and in the local vernacular of Texas, they were simply hogs.

Hogs or pigs, unlike the red shoat that had preceded them, they didn't exactly charge out of the alley, but rather sauntered at a trot, not afraid and almost oblivious to the crowd of onlookers. And behind them came Mrs. Klein. She was an elderly, petite woman, but she swung the broom she brandished with the sprite and strength of a young giant, all the while continuing to curse.

"Clyde, I swear I'm gonna kill that Hogan if he don't quit letting his hogs get in his whiskey mash," she said when she took a moment to quit swinging the broom and take a breath or two.

At that very same moment, while Mrs. Klein glared at him, it came to Morgan that she was right. Hogan's hogs were definitely drunk. And not simply regularly drunk, but drunk to the point that they didn't even seem to notice Mrs. Klein's broom swinging at them. And their grunting pig talk was more lethargic than anything. The old sow flopped down in the mudhole in front of him and appeared to be about to go to sleep. A smallish black gilt, with a bottle nose two hands long, was so inebriated that when it made a halfhearted attempt at a staggering, weaving trot it fell on its side and didn't get up. Another of the hogs, a young red boar with black spots down its sides, wanted to root under the feed store loading dock, but couldn't seem to figure out that the gap between the porch boards and the ground was too narrow to allow its bulk to pass. Instead of giving up, the boar butted its snout against the lumber twice, and then stood and stared at what had brought it to an abrupt stop, as if perplexed.

Hogan's hogs usually ran in the post oak forest and creek bottom thickets about town, foraging mostly at night. Their only claim to domestication was to be bayed by a pack of Mr. Hogan's mean dogs once or twice a year in order to have their ears notched with a pocketknife to maintain Hogan's claim of ownership. To add further insult to injury, and what normally added to the hogs' skittish distrust of humans, was Mr. Hogan's penchant for castrating most of the young boars with the same pocketknife and to pen up a few of the plumpest hogs for feeding and fattening that would see them end up one day as bacon or a fine slice of salt-cured ham in his skillet.

But there Hogan's hogs were, right in the middle of town acting like gentle pets. Hogan's other business was likely to blame for that, for in addition to his mercantile venture and his pork farming (if you could call it that) were the whiskey stills he was rumored to operate in the very same creek bottom thickets where his hogs ran—the very same whiskey Hogan wholesaled to every saloon in town. And apparently, as Mrs. Klein claimed, Hogan's hogs had developed a taste for the leftover mash and leavings that were a by-product of Hogan's whiskey making, for a more content bunch of hogs were never seen than those that came out of the alley.

"I tell you, Deputy," Mrs. Klein said, "you do something about his hogs or I will!"

Mrs. Klein said more, most of it vile and profane references to the grunting porkers surrounding her, but it all blended together so fast that Morgan couldn't follow half of what she said. But apparently, the Methodist preacher had understood some of it, for he gave out a gasp and mumbled something about the Lord forgiving her as he took leave of the crowd.

"You tell him to keep his livestock penned up like civilized folk do!" Mrs. Klein's attention had shifted from the hogs to the near corner of the long porch fronting Hogan's store.

Hogan himself had sauntered out to lean against a porch post with one hand tucked in his waistband, and picking his teeth with a sharpened matchstick.

"Drunk, good for nothing, stinking hogs," Mrs. Klein said and shook her broom in a threatening manner at the storekeeper. "Just like their owner."

Hogan gave back nothing in reply to that statement, but he did smirk a little.

"Now calm down, Mrs. Klein." Morgan held up his muddy palms as a peace offering, but inadvertently took a step closer to her.

Instead of appeasing the woman, she must have thought he meant to steal away her improvised weapon. She shifted the broom to point at Morgan.

"Don't you try and coddle me like I'm feeble-minded," she said with a shake of the broom for emphasis. "That saloon trash on Skiddy Street might be scared of you and that pistol, but I ain't."

A fight on the streets with a little elderly woman was the last thing Morgan wanted, and he took a deep breath and tried to think his way to a happier ending while he kept watch on the broom. More than a year wearing a badge in Denison, seeing it born from an end-of-the-line railroad camp to something resembling the beginnings of a town proper, and yet he had few dealings with Dorothy Klein other than to see her occasionally frowning at him through her store window when he passed. His guess was that the widow was every bit of eighty years old, but she had a reputation for not letting her age and withering body get in the way of her disagreeable nature. She and her husband hung out their shingle within a few days of the MK & T Railroad, or the Katy as it was called by most, spiking down the last rail. The husband had quickly run for mayor, and just as quickly died of pneumonia before the election could take place. The only conversation Morgan could ever recall having with Mrs. Klein was for her to relay quite proudly that her husband had gotten twenty-six votes, despite being in a pine box twelve hours before the polls opened.

"I'm sure Mr. Hogan will pay for any damages his hogs might have caused you," Morgan said.

"Like hell I will," Hogan said.

Morgan looked at the storekeeper. While younger than Mrs. Klein by about twenty or thirty years, falling somewhere on the tail end of his middle years, Mr. Douglas Hogan could be equally difficult to deal with. And despite the storekeeper's apron he wore and the pair of wire-rimmed glasses perched on his nose, Morgan remembered seeing the old army musket Hogan kept leaning in the corner at the end of his counter. It was kept loaded, according to what Hogan often boasted to his customers, in case he had to run any sassy, carpet-bagging Yankees out of the store.

"Them hogs knocked a hole in my storeroom floor and et up a hole tableful of tater eyes I had laid out for drying," Mrs. Klein said. "And they scattered three sacks of oats besides scaring off my good paying customers."

"You ain't had a paying customer all morning," Hogan chimed in. "Everybody's probably sick of you gouging them with your prices."

"You're one to talk, you old highbinder," Mrs. Klein threw back.

"Let's keep the peace here. No need for hard words from either of you," Morgan said.

"You tell him to keep his hogs penned, or maybe you do your job for once and shut down his whiskey making." Mrs. Klein managed a fake smile, obviously pleased that she might have scored a blow against both Hogan and the deputy city marshal.

"It's open range," Hogan said in his Mississippi drawl. "No law says I've got to pen anything."

"My business premises ain't open range," Mrs. Klein said with her voice getting a little more shrill and crackly again. "And if there ain't a city ordinance against running your hogs on the street, there ought to be."

Hogan didn't give Morgan a chance to cut in. "I don't need you or this Yankee policeman telling me what's in the city ordinances, since I wrote most of them."

The jab at Morgan didn't go unnoticed, and he took another deep breath, reminding himself that it wasn't the first time that Hogan had wisecracked about where he came from, nor would it likely be the last. And Morgan also reminded himself of one of the oldest rules of law enforcement, that the man in the middle often risked getting hit by both sides.

"You two have been business neighbors for a long time now," Morgan willed a kindness and patience in his voice that he didn't feel at the moment. "And you've always gotten along fine."

More than a few in the crowd knew the two shopkeepers well enough to snicker at the outright falsehood of that statement. The two shopkeepers had never gotten along.

"Mr. Hogan will pen his hogs and pay for whatever damages they've caused," Morgan continued.

"Didn't you hear me the first time?" Hogan said, straightening from the porch post.

"I'll take it to the justice of the peace," Mrs. Klein snapped.

"You take your moldy oats and your rotten spuds wherever you want to, you old hag," Hogan threw back. "Been nothing but complaining and griping since you nailed up that shack you call a store beside me."

Mrs. Klein's temporary calm ended right there. The broom wasn't long enough to reach Hogan up on the porch, and the nearest target for her fury was the sow lying in the mud. She reared back and swung the broom with both hands, with Morgan lunging to stop her. Only, Morgan wasn't quick enough, and Mrs. Klein's aim was off. Instead of the sow, she hit one of the piglets standing around their momma. And the piglet immediately began to squeal with fright.

Morgan didn't know much about half-wild Texas hogs, and even less about drunken ones. But he did know enough to realize that a squealing baby wasn't a good thing with so many of its larger kindred around to hear its distress.

"Back away, Mrs. Klein," Morgan said.

At first she didn't respond, and even reared back with the broom to strike again. Then she noticed what everyone else noticed. First one of the grown hogs gave a loud woof of alarm, and then another. The drunken beasts may have been still sluggish and heavy with the effects of Hogan's mash, but the piglet's squealing had awoken their instinct to protect one of their own. In an instant, the sow stood and snapped her jaws twice in threat, and the rest of the hogs shuffled to her side, forming a ring around her and her litter and looking at the crowd as if the townsfolk had them bayed and were about to make bacon of the lot.

Morgan grabbed hold of Mrs. Klein's arm and yanked her towards the crowd. Hogan had disappeared off his porch and was somewhere inside his store.

"Step aside and make a way for them!" somebody called from the crowd. "Don't let them feel like they're hemmed up or they're going to get on the fight!"

"Don't let them hogs gnaw on me!" Mrs. Klein begged, finally seeing the danger her temper and her broom had led her to.

The piglet quit squealing and consoled itself on one of its mother's muddy teats. The rest of the hogs still faced outward, *en garde,* but seemed to have calmed somewhat.

"Back away." Morgan tugged Mrs. Klein with him as he eased away, unwilling to take his eyes from the threat in front of him.

Morgan's Colt pistol slid out of its holster and balanced before him in his right fist. He still wasn't sure that one or all of the hogs weren't going to charge him, and he had no doubt what those razor-sharp tusks could due to a man's legs.

"Unhand me, you big oaf," Mrs. Klein said when they reached the crowd.

But she went willingly when Morgan passed her through its ranks and off the front line of danger.

Morgan watched the hogs in the mudhole and was beginning to believe that they had calmed enough to no longer be a threat. But at that very moment one of the piglet's siblings shoved it away from its milk, and the youngster, already with its feelings hurt from the brooming it had received, squealed again. And no sooner than it squealed than a deep, threatening grunt came from somewhere back in the alley.

Morgan's pistol swung that way just as a large black boar stepped out of the alley. It snapped its jaws rapidly several times, making a loud popping sound, and the ivory white of its tusks plain where they curled its leathery lips on each side of its snout. The adult male stood almost as high as Morgan's waist, and its hide was covered in coarse, black hair, thinning over the thick, plated hide of its shoulders. It was as ugly and formidable a beast as Morgan had ever laid eyes on.

Despite all the jeering and bold talk that the onlookers had put to effect earlier, they fled in multiple directions at once, everyone looking to get out of reach of the boar. Only ten feet separated Morgan from the enraged beast, but there was no place for him to go without turning his back. The .45 revolver in his hand suddenly felt small and inadequate.

The boar came at him at a dead run with its mouth gaped open to bite, and there was no time for Morgan to aim his shot. He simply extended the pistol barrel at the boar's head and squeezed the trigger as he lunged out of its path.

The roar of the pistol sounded at the same instant the boar closed on him. The boar went to its knees from the impact of the bullet, but was up again as if it were never hit. It lunged forward and barely missed taking hold of Morgan's leg with its mouth. Its shoulder collided with Morgan, knocking him aside and down on one knee. In that instant before the boar could wheel back, it was broadside to Morgan and at point-blank range. He thumbed the hammer back on the Colt and extended the pistol's barrel once more, pointing at a spot directly behind the boar's front shoulder.

The impact of the soft lead bullet once more knocked the boar to its knees. But again, it fought for life, shaking its head and slinging blood with its back legs still churning and driving in an effort to turn its body to come head-on at Morgan. It swung its bony head and Morgan felt something hard and sharp dig through his left forearm. He fell onto his back with his boot heels scrambling in an attempt to push away from those slashing tusks and biting jaws, but the boar staggered after him.

The boar was so close that Morgan could smell the stinking musk of it and the sour mash on its breath. The boar loomed over him, blotting out the sky, and then its jaws latched onto the boot top above his ankle, shaking him with violent jerks of its head. Morgan thrust his pistol towards the boar's head and pulled the trigger when he felt the barrel press into the soft flesh of one of its ears. The gun roared and the boar went limp and fell atop Morgan's legs.

Morgan shoved against the boar with his free hand and fought his legs from under the pressing weight until he was back on his feet. He couldn't shake the notion the boar would rise again and come at him, and he stood over the downed hog and fired twice more into its skull before he was sure it was dead.

He was still standing over the dead animal when Mr. Hogan appeared back on his porch. The storekeeper was holding his long-barreled Richmond musket.

Morgan gave Hogan a glance and then looked down at the ripped left coat sleeve on his frock coat. That hand was bloody, either from the boar's wounds or his own, but it seemed to work fine when he flexed his fingers. His left ankle ached a bit, but he could see nowhere that the boar's bite had punctured through his boot top. He was a man that appreciated good clothes and well-polished quality footwear, and the sight of a forty-dollar pair of fancy, high-topped riding boots ruined with scuffs and gouges was almost worse than the pain of his wounds.

He wiped the worst of the blood from his hand against his pants' leg and bent and picked his black hat off the ground, examining it closely for damage before he put it back on his head. He worked his pistol's ejector rod and shoved the empty brass cartridge cases out of the cylinder chambers while he watched the crowd slowly filtering back to him. Most of the onlookers had climbed up on Mrs. Klein's loading dock, and some of them were still leery enough of the enormous dead boar that they stayed there. The rest of the hogs seemed to have run away during the fight.

"That was about as surly of an old acorn rooter as I ever did see," Mrs. Klein said behind Morgan's left shoulder. "Thought he had you there a time or two."

Morgan turned and looked down at her. "Mrs. Klein, I think it best that you go inside before I say something that I ought not say."

She started to reply, took a closer look at him, and then

thought better of it. She mumbled all the way to the steps leading up to her feed dock, looking back and frowning more than once.

"You go on now," Morgan said. "Mr. Hogan will pay for your damages."

She stopped once up on the feed dock to look at Hogan and give him a distasteful frown before she went through the front door and closed it behind her.

"What are you going to do with that musket?" Morgan said to Mr. Hogan.

"That's my boar you killed," Hogan said.

Morgan took a fresh cartridge from his vest pocket and slid it in his pistol, then took another one out and paused without loading it. "What are you saying?"

Hogan's knuckles went white where he held the musket across his chest, and it was plain that he had spoken without thinking it through. Now it was hard to take it back with everyone watching him to see where he would go with it.

"I figure you owe me five dollars for him," Hogan said.

Morgan loaded the last cartridge and closed the Colt's loading gate with a snap. "You do, do you?"

"You had no call to shoot my hog." Hogan's voice was a little louder, and a little more gruff. "There wouldn't have been any trouble if that old hag had any sense."

There was sweat on Hogan's brow, and a belligerent sway to his posture that Morgan hadn't noticed before. It was likely that the storekeeper had been sampling some of his whiskey.

"I'll tally up Mrs. Klein's damages and take them to the judge," Morgan said. "He can decide what you pay to settle with her. Make your case to him if you have a complaint."

"You think you're something, don't you?" Hogan sneered.

"I don't see any difference in you and any of them other carpetbaggers getting off the train every day and playing the high and mighty."

"Go inside. This isn't the time to try me."

"You're dumber than you look if you think I'll pay one red cent to either you or that old hag."

Morgan shoved the Colt hard into his holster and started around the end of the water trough towards the porch. Hogan shifted his grip on the musket and leveled it at Morgan's chest.

"You don't take another step, damn you!"

Morgan grabbed the Richmond musket by the barrel and gave it a hard yank. Unwilling to let go of his weapon, Hogan came with it and landed headlong in the same mudhole Morgan had left earlier.

"You blue-bellied son of a bitch!" Hogan sputtered while he scrambled for a purchase in the slick mud.

Morgan leaned the musket against a porch post while he watched Hogan trying to right himself. No sooner than Hogan got his hands under him and was about to stand than Morgan put a boot to the seat of his pants and shoved him back down.

"Let's see." Morgan pulled a stub of a pencil and a small tally book out of his vest pocket. He walked around the mudhole and stood over the hog once more. He scribbled something and then tore a sheet loose from the book and threw it on top of the dead boar. "Drunk and disorderly. Five-dollar fine."

Hogan looked up at him from where he sat in the mud. "What? I ain't drunk."

"Your hog was drunk."

"You're crazy . . ."

Morgan wrote something on another page and ripped it

free. He threw it at Hogan, who swiped at the lenses of his muddy eyeglasses and grabbed at it feebly.

"Livestock loose on the streets. Five-dollar fine," Morgan said with his voice hard but never raising in volume or changing tone.

"There's no such ordinance!" Hogan growled.

Again, Morgan wrote and threw a page at the storekeeper. "If there isn't there ought to be. Disturbing the peace. Five-dollar fine."

"You'll wish you never . . ."

Hogan never finished because Morgan put a boot sole against his forehead and shoved him back. He flung another sheet of paper at him. "Reckless endangerment of the citizenry. Five-dollar fine."

Hogan came up out of the mud swinging his fists. Morgan ducked a wild blow aimed for his chin, caught the storekeeper by the collar of his shirt, and flung him on his face. Hogan looked back up in time to see another sheet of paper fluttering down to stick to his slime-coated face.

Morgan looked at his torn coat sleeve and then at his shredded boot. "Fifty dollars property damage."

"You . . ." Hogan sputtered. "You can go to hell."

Morgan put his tally book away and gave Hogan another kick in the rump. "Walk in front of me."

Hogan got weakly up on his hands and knees. "What . . . ?"

"You're under arrest."

"For what?"

"Resisting arrest and threatening a sworn officer of the law with a firearm."

"I'll have your badge!"

Morgan took hold of the man again by the back of his shirt and helped him to his feet before he shoved him along the street towards the jail. The townspeople gathered around parted to make way for them. Morgan and his prisoner were several yards along their way when another man wearing a badge intercepted them. He was as tall as Morgan, wearing a white shirt under his vest and his brown duck pants tucked into the top of his boots.

"I could have used your help a bit ago," Morgan said.

City Marshal Jesse Helms stopped and put both hands on his hips and surveyed the crowd and the dead hog beyond Morgan. "I was busy over on Skiddy Street and headed this way when I heard the shooting."

"How much of it did you catch?"

Marshal Helms cocked one bushy eyebrow and nodded his head at the muddy storekeeper. "I caught enough."

"I've been shot at twice and cut once since I took this job, but I never thought I would almost get killed by a hog," Morgan replied. "Glorious profession, isn't it?"

"Well, you've played hell this time."

Morgan looked back at the dead boar and all the tension seemed to leak out of him in one exhale. "Yeah."

Hogan pulled away from Morgan's hold on him and stepped close to Marshal Helms. "You arrest this man right now. I want him fired, and I want him locked up."

"He pulled a gun on me," Morgan said.

"I never," Hogan said. "I only had it when those hogs got on the fight. I never even cocked it."

"You pointed it at me, I guaran-damned-tee you I take offense at that every time." Morgan took a step closer to the storekeeper and felt the pressure building in his head as quickly as it had left only moments before.

Marshal Helms stepped between the two men. "Mr. Hogan,

why don't you go on down to my office and we'll talk about things in a bit."

Hogan gave Morgan a hateful, gloating look, then hobbled down the street towards the jail.

"Morgan, you let your temper get the best of you this time," Marshal Helms said when Hogan was out of earshot.

Morgan started to argue, but realized how ragged his breathing was, and it wasn't because of exertion.

"There's times when you aren't the only one who would like to knock a dent in Hogan's head. I've considered it a time or two myself," Helms continued. "But damn it, he's on the city council. You ever think about that?"

"He was making trouble."

"What? Did he jab you about wearing the blue again? I'd think you would have gotten used to that by now."

"He pulled a gun on me."

"That old musket of his? I doubt it's had a fresh load in it since the war. Its bore is probably rusted solid."

"A gun is a gun. A bullet from a fool like Hogan will kill you just as dead as one from some badman down on Skiddy Street," Morgan said. "A man pins on the badge, he had better learn quick not to take chances. You know the game."

Helms cocked his eyebrow again, and Morgan realized that his own voice had grown too loud.

"Take it easy. I'm only saying that maybe you could have handled it differently," Helms said.

"Kinder and gentler, huh?"

"That's a thought."

Morgan was unable to keep the passion from his tone. "In case you haven't noticed, this town is about at the tail end of hell. Last I counted there were twenty-two saloons, five dance halls, and too many brothels and bawdy houses to count. And only one church."

"It's changing. Won't be long until Denison is a city proper. The rough stuff won't hold with those that matter. We need to play by the rules if we want to be respected as the law. Think things through, you know."

"You mean the city council?"

"I mean the good folk that sign our paychecks and trust us to keep the peace."

"Where were the likes of Hogan when you and I walked into the El Dorado that night after those gamblers killed Deputy Putman? Where were they when every train in here was dropping off another dozen hardcases and tinhorns and every one of them with a pistol on their hip or a straight razor hidden in their boot?"

Marshal Helms rubbed at his cheek with one hand while his other rested on his pistol butt as if the weapon was holding him up. He looked weary, if anything, and Morgan realized that he was what was making Helms that way.

"I'm saying that this town still has a long way to go, but every day there are more and more arriving that want to see it grow. It won't be long before there are as many of them as there are the bad element. We have to be able to recognize between the two."

"The law is the law."

"It's how we enforce the law that I'm talking about. You bend a pistol over the head of those down on Skiddy Street when they need it, but up here on Main Street you walk soft and smile and tip your hat at the gentle folks."

"Are you firing me?"

"No, I'm trying to get you to listen. You're a good lawman,

Morgan, but you've spent too much time in the wild country and following the railroad camps. It's put you on edge."

"I don't think this town is ready to hand over to the preachers and schoolmarms, yet."

"Just think on it." Marshal reached inside his vest pocket and pulled out an envelope that he held forward. "Almost forgot. This came for you in the mail this morning."

Morgan tore one end of the envelope open and took out the letter. It was short and to the point, but he read it a second time to make sure he had the full gist of the message. He put the letter back in the envelope and tucked it away in his own vest.

"If it's any of my business, what's it say?" Helms asked. "I saw that MK & T letterhead. Can't help but wondering what the Katy wants with you."

"Business up in the Indian Territory," Morgan replied.

Marshal Helms must have guessed that Morgan wasn't going to give any more information on the matter, and he turned to look up the street where Mr. Hogan had reached the front door of the jail. "You let me talk to Hogan. He's a stubborn fool, but he knows we need policemen to keep a lid on his town. You take the afternoon off, and I'll saddle a horse and go drag that boar off to make Mrs. Klein happy. Best you have that arm looked at, too."

Morgan shook his head and unpinned the badge from his wool vest. He handed it to Marshal Helms.

"You quitting?" Helms asked as he looked at the cheap piece of shiny tin in his palm.

"I am."

"Just like that?"

"Just like that."

Helms grimaced. "Well, can't say as I won't miss you, but I see you've made up your mind."

"Been good working for you." Morgan shook Helms's hand then went past him at a brusque pace, headed for the boardinghouse.

"You sure are in a hurry," Helms said.

A train whistle sounded at the end of the street, and a wisp of black smoke from its engine drifted up over the depot.

"Train's rolling in," Morgan said without looking back or stopping. "I might catch a ride if I hurry."

"You going across the river to the territory to work for the railroad again?"

Morgan didn't answer and kept on walking.

"Good luck, Clyde," Helms called after him. "Maybe the territory is the place for you. Lord knows, you're too damned mean for Texas."

CHAPTER TWO

Eufaula (formerly known as Ironhead Station),
Indian Territory

The young black man in the wide-brimmed hat was prettier than any man Red Molly had ever seen. Tall enough to almost completely fill the doorway in the false front of the tent that held her place of business, and with a square, dimpled chin, and skin the color of dark honey. He had a white-toothed smile that lit up his face, even in the shadows of the room.

"I hear this is the place a man ought to pay a visit," the young man said, still smiling.

On second thought, Red Molly thought he was too quick with that smile. It spoke of a man whose confidence bordered on arrogance, or one who counted on charming his way to anything.

"It depends on what you're after. I admit that Noodles there has learned to give a decent haircut." Molly gestured at the barber's chair on one side of the room, and the skinny Italian standing beside it.

Noodles picked a sheet up off the barber's chair, gave it a

brisk snap before folding it over one forearm, and gestured for the new arrival to take a seat. "At your service, *signor*."

The young black cowboy—that's what he looked like with his silk bandanna tied loosely around his neck and his tall-topped boots and rattling spurs—doffed his hat and ran his fingers through his unruly mop of curly black hair.

"Guess I could use a shearing," he said. "But I ain't so sure what you just called me."

"Take a seat," Molly said. "Noodles's English is touch and go, but he'll shorten your ears for you just fine."

"Your hat and *pistola* over there," Noodles gestured to the hat rack inside the front door. "I got rule. You don't shoot me if I no give you good haircut."

The young cowboy hung his hat on an open hook and came back to the chair. "I'll keep my pistol."

Noodles nodded like it wasn't the first time one of his customers insisted on keeping their weapon on, and he offered his hand with comical formality to the cowboy for a handshake. "Salvatore Finocchiaro. I am Sicilian."

"Say that again."

"Salvatore Finocchiaro. I am Sicilian." Noodles put prideful emphasis on those last words.

The black cowboy rubbed the palm of his right hand on the leg of his pants while his forehead furrowed in thought. "Now that's a mouthful. I speak both my mama's tongue and my daddy's, and a bit of Mex in a pinch, but I don't savvy you at all."

"Salvatore Finocchiaro. I am . . ." Noodles started again.

The black cowboy cut him off. "I know. I know. You're a Sicilian, whatever that is. I reckon you're a foreigner for sure. Nobody but a foreigner offers to shake a darky's hand like there ain't nothing to it. Not anywhere I ever been."

Noodles gave him a confused look somewhere between a smile and a perplexed frown.

The black cowboy shook hands with the barber. "Cumsey Bowlegs is my name. Glad to meet you, Sicilian."

Noodles gestured to the chair for Cumsey to have a seat.

"Never had my hair cut in a white man's shop. Never had it cut in any kind of barbershop, for that matter."

"*Signora Testa Rosa,* she say we don't turn nobody down," Noodles said.

"Who? What?" Cumsey asked with a wrinkled brow.

"He means me," Red Molly said from across the room. "And my business takes all comers as long as they behave themselves."

"You mean there's too many of us darkies and half-breeds in the territory for you to pass up a chance at our money, don't you? I like a woman with a business bent to her mind." Young Cumsey Bowlegs said those last words like they had another meaning, and it wasn't hard for Molly to guess what he was getting at.

"I mean I treat everyone fairly as long as they act like they deserve it. Why don't you sit down and quit making Noodles wait?"

Cumsey gave the barber's chair a glance and then looked back at Noodles with a grin. "Fancy, ain't it?"

"Cost me a hundred dollars," Molly said. "I had it shipped in all the way from St. Louis."

Cumsey looked over the ornate cast-iron armrests, the nickel-plated pedestal, and ran a hand over the red leather upholstery of the seat and backrest. He spun the chair once before he sat down in it, propped his boots on the footrest, and let Noodles fasten the cloth over him. He gave a startled jerk when Noodles worked the handle on the side of the chair and raised it up a few inches.

"Startled me is all," Cumsey said with a sheepish grin. "Fanciest chair I ever saw, but don't you put my head up in the ceiling, I'm scared of heights and I don't mind saying it."

Noodles limped to the table below the mirror behind the chair and took up a pair of scissors. He hobbled back to the chair and immediately began to snip away at Cumsey's hair.

"Hey!" Cumsey ducked away from the scissors. "Ain't you going to ask me how I like it cut?"

Noodles shrugged his narrow shoulders.

Red Molly had disappeared behind the canvas curtain that divided the front half of the big wall tent from the back, but her throaty laughter came through loud and clear. "Noodles doesn't know but one way to cut hair, and that's short. Real short."

The cowboy leaned back. "Hack away."

Noodles returned to his snipping, pausing between cuts in a most meticulous way with a comical expression of consternation and study.

"How'd you get that limp?" Cumsey asked.

Noodles gave another shrug and looked down at his game leg as if noticing it for the first time. "This leg don't bend no more. I work for the railroad, and the bastard rails they drop on me. Fix it so my knee stiff like board."

"Yeah, well I ain't got a gimp, but there's damned sure been a time or two when I zigged when I should have zagged."

Young Cumsey gave the room a more careful look while Noodles snipped at his hair, what little there was of it to see. Molly O'Flanagan's Barbershop was nothing more than a large canvas wall tent with a false front made of painted pine lumber and a couple of glass windows to make it appear as something more than a tent when viewed from the street. Those two windows lay to either side of the front door, creating the only light other than the kerosene lamps mounted on the tent posts and a few lanterns hanging from the ridge beam that ran down the middle of the sagging roof. A couple of battered chairs and a table mounded with old newspapers opposite from the barber's chair served as a sitting area for customers waiting their turn at a haircut.

But Cumsey's attention kept going back to the canvas wagon sheet hung up to divide the tent into two halves. "What's that I keep hearing back there?"

Red Molly reentered the front room through a slit in the tarp with a bland look on her face. "What?"

That devilish smile spread across his mouth again and he looked her up and down from head to toe, and from the thick mane of dark red hair crowning her head and down along every buxom curve of her.

"You do realize you're staring, don't you?" Molly said.

"Ain't no dress ever made could hide what you're packing." He flashed that smile again.

"Think you're a charmer, don't you?"

He glanced at the tarp wall again. "Didn't this place used to be the Bullhorn Palace Saloon when the railroad boys were still camped here and they were still calling it Ironhead Station?"

"You talk a lot."

"I hear tell that a haircut ain't all you sell."

His smile this time was more mischievous than lewd, and it helped Molly tolerate his insinuation. Besides, it wasn't like word of her former occupation wasn't well known along the Katy line. And she was more than a little sure that he was only doing it to try and make her squirm. A damned fool kid stunt, either way. For more than half her years some man or another had been sizing her up, though she had to admit that it didn't bother her at all that she could still draw a man's eyes, even if she wasn't having any of it. Age had a way of knocking the pretty off things, and maybe she had a few more years left before there was nothing worth looking at.

"I'm retired," she said.

"Must be a lot of money in haircuts to make you do that."

"It's a living."

Noodles finished cutting Cumsey's hair and spun him around so that he could look at himself in the mirror. The cowboy rubbed his hands over the paler skin revealed on the sides of his head where Noodles had cut him down to a stubble.

"Damned if you haven't found the only two white streaks on me," Cumsey said. "My old mama must have been lying about who my real daddy was. I'm thinking there's a white man in the woodpile instead of that old Seminole chief she claimed sired me."

Noodles spun the chair back to where it had been. He took up a brush and a bowl of shaving cream, and looked a question at Cumsey.

Cumsey shook his head and chuckled. "No, sir. Never have had enough whiskers to fool with. Guess it's the Injun half of me. And besides, I make it a rule not to let anybody get a blade anywhere near my throat."

"A real careful man," Molly observed while she took up a broom and began to sweep up the hair from the puncheon floor made of small half-logs laid on bare earth with their flat side up and sanded smooth.

"I'm still thinking on what I heard about you and this place," he said with his brown eyes twinkling.

"I told you I'm retired," Molly said with no humor in the words this time.

"It ain't those kind of pleasures I was referring to." He pointed to the tarp wall. "I heard that a man could find a drink here."

"And who told you that?"

"A little old birdy down the trail sung it to me."

At that moment a glass rattled from the back room, followed by the creak of a chair and a pair of men's hushed voices.

"I'd swear that was a whiskey bottle I heard clinking back there," Cumsey said.

"Don't you know selling whiskey in the Nations is against the law, boyo?" Molly threw back at him.

"Do I look like the law?"

"You look like nine kinds of devil."

"I thought I looked thirsty."

Molly thought about it for a moment and then held back the tarp for him. "I run a quiet place. Best you remember that."

"I'll be as quiet as a fox sneakin' in the henhouse."

Noodles took off the barber's cloth, and when he did both he and Molly saw the pistol lying in Cumsey's lap instead of in his holster where it had been when he sat down.

"Like you said, I'm real careful." Cumsey shoved the pistol back in its holster as he got up out of the chair.

Molly held up a hand to stop him from going into the back room. "Pay for your haircut first. Two bits. I don't want you drinking up your spending money and shorting poor Noodles for his work."

He fished a dollar out of his vest pocket and pitched it to the barber. "Keep the change."

"Big spender," Molly said with a sarcastic grunt.

Cumsey went past her through the door slit and gave a low whistle as she followed him into the back room. "This is more like it."

On one side of the room ran a short countertop of a kind that might be seen in any store, with the wall behind it covered in cubbyholes and cabinets. Two round tables and accompanying chairs took up the rest of the space, and at one of those tables sat four men engaged in a game of poker. All of them stopped their play and studied the newcomer.

Molly went behind the counter and opened one of the cabinet doors, revealing several bottles of liquor.

"The whole barbershop bit is a nice touch," Cumsey said. "One of the few businesses that a white can legally run in the territory, that is if she doesn't get caught selling spirits to us poor heathens."

Molly placed both hands on the countertop. "I run a quiet place here. If I give you the word that the law's coming, you hightail it out the back door."

"Got it. You ask anybody in the territory and they'll tell you Cumsey Bowlegs is like greased lighting when it comes to fast."

"What are you having?" She waved a hand in front of the wares displayed in the open cabinet.

"Pour us both a double of your favorite."

"How old are you, kid?"

"Old enough."

"Well, apparently you aren't old enough to know a thing about women. I told you I was retired, and even if I wasn't, I prefer my men older and not so full of blarney." She poured him four fingers of Old Forester, corked the bottle, and put it away.

The poker players hadn't resumed their game, and all four of them were looking at the newcomer to the room with no love. Molly tried to guess which one of them would be the first to make some crack about her letting a black man in her bar. It was an old complaint against her, and one that never ceased. But they usually took it with no more than a snide remark or two, as hers was the only bar in town, even if it had to hide under the cover of a barbershop.

She decided she would head it off before one of them could say what she knew they were going to say. "Boys, this is Cumsey Bowlegs. He's new to Eufaula, and wants to make some friends. Offered to buy the lot of you a round."

"Hey, I never . . ." Cumsey started to say.

"You're the big spender," Molly said with a smart-aleck smile of her own.

The offer of a free round didn't spark the enthusiasm she had hoped for amongst the bar's other patrons. Either they were too prejudiced to let Cumsey buy them a drink or they were trying to show her what they thought about her letting him in the bar. They continued to stare at Cumsey, and two of them whispered something between themselves.

Cumsey took up his whiskey glass and turned to face them with his lower back resting against the countertop. "Guess I'm lucky they ain't thirsty."

He lifted his glass in toast to the poker players, and to a man they took up their cards and made a show of resuming their play.

"No need for trouble, Cumsey," one the players muttered.

Molly looked from the young half-breed to the man who had muttered it, and wondered what that was about. She decided to let it ride, and went to the back door flap of the tent, leaving Cumsey alone with his drink. She liked the feel of the sun on her face, even if it was a hot, sultry summer afternoon. The pain in her chest was better today, even if it tended to get worse the hotter and more humid the weather got. But what had her departed papa used to say? Never look a gift horse in the mouth?

But what did he know? He was an old piker, anyway, who never had a dollar to his name right up to the day the whiskey and the fever put him under the Irish peat. But there were times when she missed him dearly.

From where she stood, she could see around the corner of the tent towards the railroad tracks, and the maroon-painted MK & T depot house and the two-story monster that was the Vanderwagen Hotel were both visible. It didn't seem like so long ago that there had been only a tent construction camp where the new town now stood. She had called the place home for almost two years, seen it grow, and given more than her fair share of blood, sweat, and tears to what was still nothing more than a two-bit spot on some railroad map.

She took in what she could see of the town, if it could be called such yet, and wondered for the thousandth time why she had chosen it to make her stand there, after all the different places she had temporarily resided in over the years chasing a living.

She turned back to her saloon. The mud-and-mold-stained canvas had once been snow white when new. And that was all she had to show for her trouble, a worn-out tent with a leaky roof and a false front intended to make it look like something close to a real saloon. Fake and shallow and not at all what it was supposed to be, the tent sometimes felt like the story of her life.

She fought off a cough and cleared her throat. Fifteen years of selling her flesh and her soul, and committing about every known sin, got her a hundred-dollar tent, another hundred in green pine lumber and paint, a barber's chair, and a cabinet full of whiskey and home-brewed beer.

"Damn it, Molly girl," she said to herself, "buckle up your corset like a big lass and put on your war face."

She stiffened her spine and the tense set of her jaw somehow matched the red of her hair where the sunlight landed on it. It was a start to something. Maybe a last chance. Who said it was going to be easy?

She mopped the sweat from her temples with her fingers and checked them to see if she had rubbed off her rice powder makeup before she went back inside. Never let them see you weak. She was Red Molly O'Flanagan, belle of the Katy line, queen of the Indian Territory from the Kansas border to Texas, and the toughest bitch ever to set foot in a saloon. As long as they thought that, she had a fighting chance to beat them at their own game.

No sooner had she stepped into the back room than Noodles hobbled his way through the tarp wall from the front.

"Poliziotti!" he said.

Noodles's English skills hadn't improved much over time, but Molly's interpretation of his native language had. *Poliziotti* meant the coppers were coming.

"Come on, get out of here, you manky blokes!" she said shooing the poker players out the back door, and then running behind the counter to make sure her cabinet doors were closed and nothing she didn't want showing was revealed. "The damned coppers are coming, you hear me?"

Cumsey Bowlegs remained at the bar. He seemed nonplussed.

"Get out that door, you fool. The marshals have hit town."

Molly went to the tarp wall to peer into the front room as she spoke.

"Ain't finished my drink, yet," Cumsey replied.

Before Molly could chastise him more, U.S. Deputy Marshal Lot Ingram stepped through the front door into the barber room. Molly stood frozen for a moment, with her face poking through the tarp, the barbershop in front of her and the saloon behind her, half in and half out of the two parts of her life, the fake and the real, and with a million frantic thoughts running through her mind. Behind Lot Ingram, she could see two more marshals and their horses through one of the front windows.

Marshal Ingram glanced at Noodles sitting in the barber's chair, and then his gaze landed on Molly's face peering out of the tarp. "Why so shy, Red? You're making me feel unwelcome."

"Hello, Lot. Where'd you come from?" Molly let go of the tarp and smoothed her dress, gathering herself.

He was a tall, thin man, and he made it to her in two strides. Molly barely had time to turn and catch a glimpse of Cumsey slipping out the back door before the marshal was past her and into the bar room.

"Rode down from Muskogee. Who was that going out the door?"

"I don't know. Some cowboy."

Lot looked down at her with his pale blue eyes, and the way his long mustache covered his thin-lipped mouth gave him a grim, threatening look. "Don't start this off by lying to me."

"He said his name was Cumsey Bowlegs, or something like that. I didn't pay much attention to him."

The marshal went tense, seeming to gain an inch or two in height. He yelled back into the front room and to his marshals in front of the barbershop, "Take a look around! Cumsey Bowlegs just went out the back door!"

The marshal drew his right-hand pistol from the pair that rode in holsters on either hip. The long barrel of the Colt Army was somehow in matching with his tall frame, and the boniness of his features. He went quickly to the back of the room and leaned out the door flap.

"Son of a bitch won't get away this time," he said under his breath, but loud enough for Molly to hear.

Cumsey must have already been out of sight of the marshal, for Lot holstered his pistol. "You harboring the likes of Cumsey Bowlegs and not telling me? After all the slack I've cut you?"

"I don't know what you mean." Molly tried to keep some temper in her voice. Lot Ingram was the kind that would push a little more if he saw you cringe. "I always tell them to run out the door so that you don't see them and they don't see enough to figure out our arrangement."

"You really don't know who he is, do you? The queen bee gossip of the territory doesn't have a clue." His voice was crackly and dry as the wind in the burnt summer grass.

"Never saw him before he came in here a bit ago."

"That half-breed bastard is trouble, that's what he is. I've had a set of handcuffs and good heavy shackles ready for him for a long spell now," Lot said, still towering over her. "He's one of that bunch of owl hoots from down at Sand Town. Worst horse thief of the bunch of them, and just smart enough to stay one step ahead of me until now."

"Oh." Molly said it like she was surprised, but she wasn't, really. The things men did had ceased to surprise her long before Cumsey Bowlegs walked into her saloon.

Lot took a glance out the back door one more time and scowled before he focused his attention back on her. "Speaking of our arrangement, where's my money? Come out with it. I don't have time to dawdle, as much as I'd like to. I'm going to catch that boy before sundown."

Molly stepped away and went behind the counter, glad to put more space between them. She produced a yellow manila envelope from one of the cabinets. Lot took it impatiently and tore it open, regardless of the fact that the flap wasn't sealed. He thumbed the greenbacks and sifted the coins, doing the math silently to himself.

"You're ten dollars short." A little more meanness crept into his voice.

"There's twenty dollars there," Molly replied. "I counted it twice to make sure."

"It's thirty dollars now."

Molly reminded herself to stay calm. It wasn't the first time Lot Ingram and his deputies had shaken her down, and it wouldn't be the last. Bill Tuck, the former owner of the saloon, had been a noted tough, but that didn't stop the federals from taking their cut from him. Keeping on the good side of the law had a dollar figure in the territory, but she had gotten through it pretty much unscathed each time so

far. Pay them a little and keep them off your back, and try
not to think on the unfairness of it. That was the way, like it
or not.

"Twenty dollars a month. That was our agreement." She
tried to keep her voice even, and thought she did a fair job
of it.

"Well, the price of selling liquor in the Indian Nations has
just gone up." He strode closer and stooped lower so that his
face was near to hers over the countertop. "Let's say my expenses are on the upswing and I'm passing a bit of them on
to you."

"You rotten bastard. That's half what I'll clear this week
if I'm lucky."

He clucked his tongue and shook his head in mock em-
pathy. "You always did have a nasty mouth on you for such
a pretty thing. 'Course, you ain't as pretty as you once were."

"I won't pay."

"You'll pay, or I'll burn this place to the ground and haul
your wide ass to Judge Story at Fort Smith. How would you
like that? Still want to play like you're tough?"

Molly took out her cashbox and paid him another ten
dollars. "There'll come a day . . ."

He clucked his tongue again and jerked the little cashbox
from her hand. He made a show of weighing it, then shook it
and listened to the few coins inside it rattling against the metal
sides. "Sounds pretty light. Best you hustle hard before I
come back next month so that you don't come up short again."

Molly said nothing, her lungs not working like they
should with the temper rising in her, and her hands trembling
beneath the countertop. Worse, she felt like she was about
to have a coughing spell, and be damned if she would let

Lot Ingram see her that way. She had already provided him too much pleasure today.

And then she glanced down at the pearl-handled .32 Smith & Wesson pistol under the countertop. Its grip was only a few inches from her hand.

"I don't like what I see you thinking on, Red," Lot said. "If I had to guess I'd say your pride is about to get the best of you. You keep that up and I'll quit being so lenient with you. Quit looking the other way when I shouldn't."

Why was it that his kind always turned things around and tried to make what they did your fault? She felt her eyes growing wet, and tried not to blink. It always shamed her that she was prone to tears when she was mad.

Lot saw how upset she was and clearly enjoyed it. "I'd love to stay and chat with you, Red. But I've got that Bowlegs boy to run down."

He set the cashbox down and went to the tarp wall, but stopped and looked back. The bastard couldn't resist sticking the knife in her one more time. Molly didn't know what he was about to say, but knew it would be nasty. The most dependable thing about Lot Ingram was that he was always nasty.

He lifted his hat and ran one palm over his balding head and made a show of looking her up and down, same as Cumsey Bowlegs had earlier, but with no fun in it. Mean, and leering to the point that she felt her flesh crawl.

"On second thought, old age hasn't made you plumb homely yet," he said. "Might be some that ain't real picky that would pay you for a hump if you didn't charge them too much. Help you earn that extra ten dollars."

She would have grabbed for the gun if she hadn't been

holding her breath to fight off the urge to cough. He disappeared in the front room in a clank of spurs and a thump of boot heels.

The coughing spell was worse than some, and better than others, as they usually went. When she looked at the handkerchief she always carried there was only a faint pink stain of blood. She took a raspy breath, fought down another cough, and reached into one of the cabinets and pulled out two bottles and a glass. One of the bottles held a quart of Old Tom Gin and the other was a tiny, square one with a wooden stopper and half full of a clear liquid. She poured the glass full of gin and added a small dribble of the clear liquid to top it off. She downed half the glass while she listened to the sound of the marshals' horses leaving her barbershop at a run.

"This can't last," she said aloud in a ragged, breathless whisper while she stared at the half-finished, opium-laced glass of whiskey like she was talking to it. "I won't let it."

The sound of the running horses' hooves faded as she downed the last of her drink.

CHAPTER THREE

Morgan Clyde, freshly unemployed and freshly out of Texas, had the train crew unload his horse and gear at the MK & T stock pens at Muskogee, one hundred and sixty miles northward into the Indian Territory. He had slept through most of the long train ride and woke to find himself looking out the passenger car window and wondering where he was until his groggy mind slowly recognized the place.

He left his horse in one of the corrals, stashed his saddle on the top rail of the fence, and walked along the street that paralleled the tracks on the east side. There were still more than a few tents and log shanties like there had been the last time he paid a visit, but the place had grown considerably since then. Two rows of buildings framed and sided with rough-sawn lumber faced each other from either side of the railroad right-of-way, one on each side of the tracks, with every one of those businesses wanting to be as close to arriving train passengers as possible. The massive, spinning windmill that powered a stone-towered gristmill rose up behind those structures on the east side. That windmill reminded Morgan of a Dutch painting he had once seen in Knoedler's art gallery in New York, but he had never expected to see such in the Indian Nations. It was like something out of a very strange dream.

A couple of the businesses on the east side of the tracks had a boardwalk of sorts fronting them. It was nothing more than a crude walkway built of scrap sawmill slabs running underneath the rusty sheet metal and moldy shake porch roofs, but it was a boardwalk, nonetheless, and would keep a man's boots reasonably dry when the spring rains turned the street to mud.

Four loafers were hanging out under the shade of that covered walkway. Three of the men were black, and the other was an Indian. The way they slouched and the insolent, sullen way they looked at him from under their hat brims made him sure that they were either getting over a bad drunk or working on their next one. He'd seen their type before—men without jobs, men who didn't want jobs, and men who could be counted on to be as troublesome as they were shiftless. And all three of them were wearing a pistol of one kind or another on their belts.

"Good day to find a bit of shade," Morgan said only to make sure that they didn't get the pleasure of thinking their antics intimidated him.

"Who the hell are you, and what business is it of yours?" the Indian said with his thumbs hooked in the galluses of his raggedy overalls.

The man's sidekicks were either too lethargic or too intent on appearing tough to snicker at his bold talk, but two of them did manage a grunt of amusement, and the other one shifted his pistol around to his lap and leaned his wicker-bottomed chair back on two legs against the wall behind him before he spat a stream of tobacco juice the color of tar into the dust off the edge of the boardwalk. He stared at

Morgan with a look that implied his spitting was meant as some kind of emphasis on one unsaid point or another.

Morgan only paused his stride for an instant—a slight hitch that they probably didn't notice—and kept walking while he reminded himself that it wasn't his town, nor were they his trouble. He shifted his cigar to the other cheek, and moved his attention elsewhere.

Everywhere he looked there was a surprising number of people moving along the street on one errand or another, some on foot, and others in wagons or on their saddle horses. Although Muskogee rightly lay inside the boundaries of land allotted to the Creek tribe, there were nearly as many white people that he could see as there were Indians. And there were as many black people as there were whites. No doubt most of them were former slaves, once owned by the slave-holding factions of the Choctaw, Chickasaw, Cherokee, Creek, and Seminole tribes, and freed during the war and since. It was a hard fact, but he didn't envy their predicament—trying to find their way in a new world with nothing to their names but the shirts on their backs and a newfound sense of freedom.

Other than the Katy stock pens and the gristmill, and maybe a little business with the nearby Fort Gibson or the Indian agency at Fern Mountain, he couldn't guess what was supporting the number of people he saw. And the more he looked, the more loafers like the ones on the porch were to be seen lounging about with no obvious intentions of doing anything. Another cluster of them stood in front of the blacksmith shop at the far end of the street. Young men, all, but with a reckless, defiant air about them.

He passed in front of a general store, breathed in the smell of fried pork wafting out the open windows and doors of what he took to be a restaurant, and moved slightly aside to let a group of soldiers pass before stopping in front of the Mitchell Hotel. It was a new two-story building of fine construction with a shiny coat of fresh paint, and it stood out amidst the other crude structures of the frontier railroad stop almost as much as the windmill did. He listened to the ring of the blacksmith's hammer while he looked at the front door.

After a long moment, he stepped up onto the hotel veranda and passed inside. A clerk stood behind a short counter to his left, and he was about to go to the man to check the register when he saw the two men seated at a table at the far end of the lobby in front of a large window that overlooked the street. Both men were nattily dressed in clean suit coats and neckties, despite the heat. One of the men nursed a cup of coffee while he watched Morgan cross the room to them, and the other lowered the newspaper he was reading enough to do the same.

"Hello, Huffman," Morgan said when he reached their table.

"You're a day late," the man with the coffee cup held before his chin said. He was a medium-sized, middle-aged man with distinctly large eyes, and an intense way of looking at you, as if he was fighting to keep those eyes focused. Despite the spit-and-polish look of him, his curly hair defied the hair tonic he had tried to slick it down with, and a few wild strands of it sprung out to either side of his head.

"I didn't get your letter until yesterday," Morgan replied.

The other man at the table lowered his newspaper, and set it neatly aside and straightened the lapels of his coat. He was a thin man, with hollow eyes and a long, cadaverous face, made longer by the mustache and goatee he wore from lips to chin.

"I take it you must be Mr. Clyde," he said with one eyebrow arched as if doubting his own assumption.

Morgan looked a question at the other man.

The one Morgan had called Huffman nodded at the man with the goatee. "Clyde, meet Hiram Whitley. He's come a long way to see you."

"I have, indeed," Whitley said.

Huffman pushed an empty chair away from the table with his foot. "Have a seat."

Morgan took the proffered chair while he gave Huffman a closer look. He had only encountered the MK & T's newest superintendent on two occasions. The first time both of them had been laid out in a hospital tent with bullet wounds in the aftermath of a gunfight with a group of Missouri bushwhackers intent on robbing the railroad payroll. The second time had only been a chance encounter in the very same town in which they now found themselves a year later. At that second meeting, Huffman, having just replaced the infamously corrupt superintendent that preceded him, had tried to get Morgan to take back his old job as chief of the railroad police. Considering that Morgan had flatly refused that offer, it came as some surprise to him when he received the letter from Huffman requesting a meeting in Muskogee.

"I see you're still carrying the pistol I gave you." Huffman gestured at Morgan's belt.

Morgan glanced down at the Colt in its holster on his left hip. It was a gaudy thing with its steel covered in scroll engraving and little stars engraved into the cylinder, and he still felt almost silly carrying it. In fact, he had kept it inside its fancy presentation case tucked in the bottom of his war bag until recently, choosing instead the familiar feel of his old cartridge conversion Remington Army, a weapon that had served him true for a number of years. But the greater power of Colt's newest model and the advantages of a close-topped .45-caliber revolver made truly for self-contained, center-fire cartridges finally caused him to hang up his old sidearm.

"It's a fine weapon," Morgan said.

Huffman nodded. "I understand that the Colt won the army contract, and that the production model of the prototype you carry is being issued to our soldiers in great numbers. I also have it that the pistol is already available to the civilian market via their catalogue."

"Like I said, it's a fine pistol," Morgan replied, already growing impatient with the small talk. "I have no doubt it will be a popular model."

"May I see it?" Whitley held out an open palm over the table.

"I got your name, but I don't believe I know you," Morgan said.

Whitley passed a glance to Huffman.

Huffman cleared his throat and then looked around the room to make sure they were alone, and as if gauging whether or not the hotel clerk could hear them from his post at the counter.

"Mr. Whitley is the director of our government's newest law enforcement agency," Huffman spoke in a quiet voice intended to avoid any eavesdropping. That seemed a little silly to Morgan when half the population of the territory could pick a lawman out of a crowd with ease and didn't need to eavesdrop. "And like I said, he's come all the way from the capital to meet with you."

"I take it you mean the Secret Service," Morgan said.

"So you've heard of us?" Whitley said.

Morgan shifted his attention to Whitley and drew the Colt and handed it to the man. "Only what I've read in the newspapers, and not much at that."

"Newspapers, yes. Unfortunately, we don't always succeed in keeping as low a profile as we wish." Whitley nodded as if whatever Morgan knew about the Secret Service was enough to satisfy him.

He leaned forward, holding the pistol before him and squinting slightly. He read the words on the engraved silver plate in the shape of a tiny badge set into one side of the ivory grips. "Morgan Clyde, MK & T Railroad Police."

"That's what it says."

"Fine weapon you have." Whitley handed the pistol back to Morgan. "Mr. Huffman here tells me that you earned every bit of it, and that the Secretary of the Interior himself contributed his personal finances to its procurement."

Morgan took his hat off and sat the black felt gently down on the table before him. He nodded at Huffman. "Did he tell you how many times his damned railroad almost got me killed?"

Huffman didn't look a bit squeamish and merely looked back at Morgan with that same intense gaze.

"And yet, here you sit," Whitley said.

"And here I sit," Morgan repeated.

Whitley leaned back slightly in his chair while Morgan holstered his pistol, and Huffman took another slurp of hot coffee from his mug. Morgan could tell that both men were weighing how to say what it was they wanted with him.

"I understand that you did some very good work for the

MK & T and the former superintendent, Willis Duvall," Whitley said after a time.

"Willis Duvall was a crook. I don't count my time with him as well spent."

Whitley waved a hand in the air as if brushing something aside. "I'm not here to question you about your time with Mr. Duvall. Mr. Huffman and others say that you almost single-handedly cleaned up that trouble in Ironhead Station and got his railroad across the river. Not to mention that you put an end to that bunch of Missouri border trash. President Grant is most pleased that the Secretary of the Interior survived, as no doubt is the secretary, thanks in large parts to your efforts."

"They weren't after the secretary. He just happened to be in the wrong place at the wrong time," Morgan said. "It was the Katy payroll they wanted, and looks like there were other factions at play that might have wished to keep the railroad stalled out or to see it fail as a business venture."

"No matter, your résumé is impressive. I understand you also have an admirable war record. First U.S. Sharpshooters, was it? And then there was some time as a New York City policeman before that, as well?"

"Well, pardon the impoliteness, but what have you brought me here for?" Morgan asked. "We've all come a long way."

"You have a reputation as a dependable man who can handle . . ." Whitley waved his hand in the air again, "let's say . . . difficult tasks. What do you know about my agency from the newspapers?"

"Not much other than I believe you specialize in counterfeiting cases and other fraud and currency crimes."

Whitley leaned back slightly in his chair and laced his fingers together over the belly of his vest. "Did you know that there are some in the Treasury Department that claim that half the currency being exchanged in the whole United States is counterfeit?"

"We've had our share of that out here," Morgan replied. "Although I wouldn't have guessed the problem was as bad as you say."

"Whatever the numbers truly are, it's safe to say that the issue is a problem of some magnitude, but that's not why I requested a meeting with you. What interests me is that you once worked for Judge William Story out of the federal court at Fort Smith before you took employ with the MK & T Railroad."

Morgan nodded. "The court was across the river in Van Buren then, but yes."

"And what was your opinion of the judge?"

It was Morgan's turn to lean back from the table a little, and his face tightened ever so slightly. "If you know I worked for him, then you know he fired me. Let's say we didn't get along too well."

"And what if I told you Judge Story's district is rife with corruption and fraud?"

"That's the rumor."

Whitley reached inside his coat front and pulled something from the slit pocket of his vest. He laid a shiny tin badge on the table and left it there. "I want to hire you to help me clean up Judge Story's court."

Morgan twisted the corner of his mustache and studied the five-pointed star lying on the table before him while he considered what the Secret Service chief had said. "There's no way Story would ever hire me back, and working close to him is the only way I'd be effective."

"You misunderstand me," Whitley added. "I already have

people in place in Fort Smith to investigate the judge. What I need is someone out here to handle this side of things."

"Go on."

"Judge Story is very adept at his accounting, if you know what I mean."

"You mean he's embezzling."

"A man in his position has a lot of ways to make a dishonest dollar if he so wishes and if he's creative enough with a pencil. And Judge Story appears to be a very creative man. We have mounting evidence that he has been withholding expense money from those witnesses he subpoenas to his court and then entering those expenses as fully paid, along with other exaggerations and falsifications of his court debits that he can write into his ledgers and then pocket the funds."

"Sounds like you need a bookkeeper with a badge to sort the numbers out."

Whitley's tone grew more serious. "I have plenty of bookkeepers, Mr. Clyde, but the fraudulent ledger work is not why I want to hire you. Among the judge's other transgressions is his tendency to foster and accept bribes. We have already removed the court's district attorney and the marshal through political means, rather than criminal proceedings, but we suspect the corruption extends much further into the employees of the court."

"And where do I come in?" Morgan asked, half suspecting the answer he was going to get before he got it.

"If there are federal deputy marshals taking bribes or running protection rackets in this territory, I want to know it. If some of them are as corrupt, as I suspect they are, then I want them brought to justice."

"Witnesses will be hard to come by. Most out here don't

trust any kind of court nor the government. And none of them will believe that we can protect them, even if they were of a mind to testify."

"Catch the scoundrels in the act if you have to."

Morgan pointed at the badge on the table. "Will I work up front or undercover?"

"Undercover."

"If it's like it was when I worked for Judge Story, some of his marshals aren't much different than the outlaws that they're supposed to be arresting. They won't come in easy."

"Get the goods on them, and then I'll get you all the help you need to arrest them."

Morgan stared at the badge while he tried to think things through. "How much does this Secret Service work pay? My experience with government employment is that they expect a man to risk his neck on the cheap."

Chief Whitley glanced at Huffman, and the two of them shared grins.

"Mr. Huffman told me that you were as much mercenary as you were peace officer."

Whitley held up a hand to cut off whatever Morgan had been about to say. "No matter, Mr. Clyde. I think I have a way to make all three of us happy."

"What's your stake in this?" Morgan asked Huffman.

"Certain of the judge's deputies have pulled their tricks on some of my employees, and I have long had a suspicion that those same deputies are turning a blind eye to certain outlaws who have caused me no end of trouble. A change of the territory's law enforcement could be good for railroad business."

Whitley pushed the badge towards Morgan. "You keep this hidden, and only show it if you need to."

Huffman produced another badge, this time one that was very familiar to Morgan. The shield-shaped badge was as shiny as polished silver, but actually only made of cheap tin. *RAILROAD POLICE, MK & T,* and a little pendant hanging under the shield was marked *CHIEF.*

"You wear this one out in the open," Huffman said.

"You will be carrying dual authority," Whitley added. "To the public you'll once more be in charge of security for the railroad, and at the same time you'll be working for me."

"You've put a lot of thought into this, haven't you?" Morgan said.

"Well, what do you say? Are you game to tackle this?" Whitley asked.

"You're taking way too long to think this over," Huffman said.

"It's my fat that will be in the fire, not yours," Morgan replied.

"Oh, let's quit the quibbling. I know it's money you're holding out for," Huffman said with a sigh. "The MK & T will pay you your old salary as chief. One hundred and fifty a month, and first month's wages in advance."

"I don't know . . ."

"That's on top of your government wages," Whitley said. "Seventy dollars per month and expenses. I add that up with what Mr. Huffman is willing to pay you, and I wonder if I'm not hiring a holdup artist."

Morgan nodded and reached out and took the railroad badge and pinned it to his vest. He then tucked the Secret Service badge into a little pocket inside the lining of his coat breast and looked at Whitley. "How do I contact you?"

"Send a wire to Mr. Huffman. He'll see to it that I get your message," Whitley replied.

"I'll do that." Morgan offered his hand around, and the three of them shook hands.

"One more thing, Mr. Clyde," Whitley said before Morgan could leave.

"What's that?"

"Hold up your right hand and repeat after me."

Whitley recited a short oath about duty and honesty and God and country, and Morgan repeated each line. Whitley stopped him one more time as Morgan was going out the door. "I wouldn't be surprised if you held a grudge against Judge Story, considering the claims he made against you," Whitley said. "But I expect you to act professionally and within the law, no matter how bad you may want to see his court brought down."

Morgan gave a grunt. "Are you telling me to go easy? If so, you'll be the second man to tell me that lately."

"I said professionally and within the law, if you call that easy."

Morgan grunted again. "That's always the challenge of peace officer work, isn't it?"

"What's that?"

"Playing by rules to catch men that don't recognize any rules." With that, Morgan left them alone in the hotel lobby.

"You know, speaking of rules, I don't think he ever said he agreed with yours," Huffman observed after Morgan was gone. Whitley opened his newspaper again, but hesitated over it in thought. "No, I think Mr. Clyde is a man that insists on doing things his own way."

Huffman took a sip of coffee and grimaced when he found that it had gone cold. "From what I know of Mr. Clyde, I'd say you best focus on results and not worry about methods. He's honest, but he's bloody."

"It's a hard task we've set him to," Whitley said as he looked out the window.

"He's a hard man."

Whitley looked over the top of his newspaper. "You act more impressed with him than I first thought."

"He's a difficult, mercenary bastard is what he is. But I've seen him in action, and I'd come closer to pitying the poor devils you've set him after than I would to doubt him."

"God have mercy on their souls," Whitley said with a slight smirk.

Huffman lifted his coffee mug in toast. "God have mercy on their rotten souls."

CHAPTER FOUR

Morgan rode south from Muskogee the next morning with a destination in mind for reasons he didn't care to admit, even to himself. And he kept telling himself that one place or another was as good a place to start his work as any, for Judge Story's deputies were scattered throughout the territory and his chances of encountering them or witnesses to help him build a case were as good anywhere he went.

The good zebra dun gelding he rode with the peculiar lightning bolt brand on its hip seemed as anxious to travel as its master. He let the gelding choose its own pace, and the hardy little Texas horse clipped along the trail at a ground-eating walk with its foxlike ears pricked forward and its head slightly swinging from side to side with each step. All there was to interrupt Morgan's solitude was the creaking of his saddle leather and the clop of the dun's hooves.

He thought some about Judge Story while he rode, and those were bitter memories. Those days when he had ridden as a U.S. deputy marshal had been when he first came west after the war—after everything else in his life had fallen apart and his only option was a fresh start. There had only been a handful of deputy marshals back then, and thousands of square miles of country to cover. The war had been hard on the territory, with the Five Civilized Tribes split along lines of the Blue or the Gray and fighting and killing each other just like their white counterparts, and both armies and irregular partisan forces raiding over the land until half the population had either moved elsewhere or had learned to be good at hiding. And then after the war some of the same trouble hung on. Outlaws of one kind or another flocked to the territory, where the Indians' tribal law didn't apply to them, the terrain gave them plenty of hideouts, and the deputy marshals out of the federal court in Van Buren were too few to roust them.

In his opinion, he had done his job as well as could be expected, but there had been hints by his supervisors that there was extra money to be made if he weren't so ethical. Nothing concrete, but hints that could be taken no other way. And then he heard a rumor that Judge Story himself wished him fired. He intended to quit as soon as he tended to a few things, but Judge Story didn't want to wait that long.

Returning from a patrol of the southeastern corner of the territory, he found that the district attorney was going to press charges against him, claiming that he had shot and wounded an unarmed and shackled prisoner during a raid on an illegal whiskey still in the Choctaw Nation. Nothing had been further from the truth. The man he had shot had nearly choked him to death with the shackles, but the truth wasn't any part of what the judge and his crooked court wanted.

In the end, they had settled for his resignation and his fall from grace didn't make much news, but the event remained a raw sore he carried, even after all the time that had passed.

But what was it that they said about things coming around full circle? Although he hadn't admitted it to Huffman and Whitley, they were right. He was going to take a great deal of pleasure getting even with Judge Story and his minions if he could manage it.

By late morning he had reached Checotah Station. Unlike the burgeoning town he had recently left, there was nothing but a small community of Indian cabins, a few plowed farm fields and hog pens, and a track siding and a little depot house to put Checotah on the map. Morgan did stop long enough to question one of the Creek farmers he caught tending his garden, but the Indian was leery of any white man's questions, and had nothing, good or bad, to report about the deputy marshals or their whereabouts.

Morgan moved on, paralleling the Katy tracks and following the old Texas Road that ran almost on top of the newer railroad right-of-way. The country he rode through held stretches of prairie with lush grass as high as his saddle stirrups and was dotted with hills clad with short, fat oak trees. Deer and other wildlife fled at the sight of him, but mostly what he saw was cattle—Texas cattle by the look of them, and likely belonging to some white rancher who, legal or not, was paying the local Indians a few cents per head to graze them on tribal land. Some of the cattle raised the wide span of their horns and calmly watched him pass, and others fled as wildly as the deer had.

Regardless of how the law read and how the land was supposedly set aside for the tribes, the white man was already pushing hard into the territory. There was too much space for the taking, too much timber, coal, grass, and other resources not to make some desirous of having a chunk of it for themselves. Some married into one tribe or the other to gain legal access, others took advantage of legal loopholes, and some simply proceeded by hook or crook, abiding by no boundaries or laws and pirating at will. And there were many that questioned why such good land was being given to the raggedy Indians when perfectly good Americans had no such land given to them, and justified their desire to have what was denied them by considering the Indians as inferior aboriginals. In Morgan's mind, a tide of his countrymen was waiting in the wings. First they would come in a trickle, and then a wave. It was all but inevitable. Time and time again the Indian tribes had been pushed off their land at the will of their conquerors and he could see no difference now. Just because it was unfair didn't make it not so. And the railroad had sped up the process, piercing right through the heart of the territory.

He stayed lost in such thoughts for several more miles, his body soaking up the hot sunshine, and enjoying the good feel of the dun's stride beneath him. He had been too long in town, and something about the wide-open sky and the wind on his face made him feel more whole.

The trail soon dropped down off the high prairie and cut its way through a denser stand of woodlands that marked the drainage of the North Canadian River. He quit his daydreaming and paid closer attention to what lay ahead and around him, both by natural caution and the lessons of experience. Such points were a natural place for someone to lay an ambush, and the territory was overrun by outlaws seeking refuge from the law and more than happy to take advantage of the unsuspecting and the foolish.

Such caution and attention to detail was how he heard the men's voices coming through the timber long before he spotted the dead horse lying in the road. It was still saddled and bridled, and a neat bullet hole showed on one side of its neck, so fresh that it was still slowly oozing blood.

Morgan shucked his '66 Winchester carbine from his saddle boot. He never had been especially fond of the weapon because its brass frame reflected too much sunlight and the rimfire .44 cartridges it shot were too underpowered. He had long intended to replace it with a repeater that better suited his tastes, but most of his recent time had been spent in town where a short gun was more than enough firepower and he had never gotten around to replacing it.

He levered the Winchester open a crack and confirmed there was a round chambered before closing it again and propping the carbine's buttstock on his thigh. He rode nearer to the voices he could hear coming from the timber, and finally dismounted and wrapped one of the dun's bridle reins over a low hanging cedar limb.

He made his way slowly through the thick growing vegetation beneath the tree canopy, stopping often to listen. For the first few yards, the sound of the talking ahead of him guided his course. But he had heard nothing for several minutes, and he paused behind the broad trunk of a giant water oak and peered through the brush ahead of him.

It took him a quarter of an hour to go perhaps fifty yards or less, and by that time he had decided that whoever he had heard had left. It was at that very moment he caught a flash of movement ahead. Without thinking, and more out of some involuntary instinct, he dropped to one knee with the Yellow Boy carbine tucked against his shoulder and half raised to shoot.

Again, he saw the same flash of movement. It was subtler and slower than he had first thought, and he became more curious than alarmed the more he watched whatever it was moving through the sunlight some fifty yards farther along.

He stood slowly and worked a wide arc, gradually closing the distance to whatever it was that he was seeing. Dead saddle horses with bullets in the neck meant trouble, and he was in no hurry to risk winding up like that horse or whoever had been riding it.

A gust of wind whipped through the river thicket, and the object ahead moved more than before. Morgan squinted down the barrel of the carbine and focused his front sight on a spot between two trees, waiting for whoever was out there to pass by into that opening again.

When the wind blew again a faint creaking sounded, and at the same time Morgan realized what he was looking at. He lowered the carbine and picked his way through the trees until he could plainly see the dead man swinging by his neck from a rope thrown over the high limb of a stark white sycamore tree.

The body of the young black man swinging by his neck was a gruesome sight to behold. A man hanged like that died slow, kicking and choking until the last life of him faded away.

Whoever had done the hanging had been in a hurry, or else they wanted the man on the end of the rope to suffer as much as possible. They had taken the time to tie their victim's hands behind his back, but their work was sloppy after that. They had used a smaller diameter manila hemp rope more like something a cowboy would use to rope a steer than the fatter-stranded selection a professional executioner would have chosen. Either that rope running from the dead man's neck up over the high tree limb had stretched under the weight of the body, or else they had failed to hoist their prisoner high enough to begin with. For the toes of the dead man's boots almost brushed the ground.

Morgan looked away and searched the area for sign of whoever had done the deed. He was no skilled tracker, but the best he could make out from the scrambled hoof marks in the leaf bed was that three, maybe four horsemen had ridden away from the scene.

He went back to cut down the body, pondering what had happened. The young black man suspended from the rope had his head tilted downward at an awkward angle, and Morgan stepped closer and stooped down in order to get a look at his face.

"Fellow, you're having a bad, bad day," Morgan said aloud to himself.

As if in answer, the body before him jerked convulsively, and the dead man's eyelids snapped open.

The rope was tied off to the trunk of a sapling nearby, and Morgan ran to it and cut through twisted strands with a quick slice of his sheath knife. The black fellow hit the ground with a thump and lay there twitching and jerking. Morgan ran back and attempted to loosen the constriction around the man's neck. The manila rope was pulled so tight into the flesh that he had a hard time getting his fingers under it. Once the noose was removed, Morgan cut the man's hands free.

The black man sucked in a ragged gasp and stared at Morgan once more out of those bloodshot eyes. The veins in his face and neck stood out like ridges, and his face was a sickly shade of blue.

Morgan hunkered there on his heels while the man he had cut down rolled onto his side and wheezed for air. There were lots of stories of men surviving hangings, but Morgan had always assumed that most of those stories were nothing more than wives' tales. Seeing a man he assumed to be dead come back to life was more than a little unsettling.

It was a long, long time before the black man sat up, and even longer before his breathing became more normal.

"You'd best take it easy," Morgan said.

"Hurts," the black man hissed, and immediately grabbed at his throat from the pain it caused him to utter those few words.

"I thought you were dead," Morgan said. "In fact, I've never seen a man who looked less alive."

The black man glanced at him out of the corner of his eyes and hissed, "I got . . . on my tiptoes when the rope sagged. That's . . . that's the onlyest thing that saved me."

"Maybe it's best that you don't talk. Your neck looks bad."

The black man felt gingerly at the raw rope burn below his swollen jawline. Already, the skin was discolored above and below that burn, and there was going to be some awful bruising.

"Water," he said in little more than a whisper.

Morgan left and soon came back leading the dun. He took down his canteen from where it hung off his saddle horn and handed it to the black man, who still sat on the ground.

"Who was it that hanged you?" Morgan asked.

The young man drank gingerly at first, grimacing with each swallow. When he spoke again his voice was still quiet, but less ragged. "Lot Ingram. He done it. Him and his Fort Smith deputies."

"You say they were peace officers and not some vigilantes?" The black man gave Morgan a cagey look, and Morgan realized that the badge on his own vest was visible and that the man before him had seen it.

"It's been my experience that, right or wrong, a man that

finds himself in this kind of trouble has usually done something to bring it on," Morgan added.

"I . . . I didn't do nothing," the black man's voice cracked worse than before with the increased volume. "You're law. What do you think about the kind of marshals that don't even give a man a chance at a fair trial?"

That was just the kind of peace officer Morgan had been sent to find, but he hadn't counted on stumbling onto their workings so quickly.

"What'd you do? Steal a horse? Kill a man? Bother some woman?" Morgan asked.

"Old Lot Ingram, once you cross him, he's going to make an example of you. Said he was going to leave me hanging until the buzzards picked my bones clean."

Morgan took back the canteen. "Think you can get on your feet?"

The black man took his trampled hat up off the ground, knocked the crown back out, and set it on his head. A little unsteady at first, but he stood. "You a federal?"

"Railroad police," Morgan answered. "Now that you're standing, do you think you can walk?" Morgan asked as he went to the dun.

The black man merely nodded.

Morgan brought the dun to him. The black man made as if to go to the horse, but Morgan laid the Winchester's barrel against his chest to stop him. He held the carbine one-handed while he gave the injured man a quick pat down. The black man wasn't wearing a visible sidearm, but that didn't mean he didn't have other weapons hidden on his person.

"No call for that," the black man sounded shocked and indignant.

"Get aboard. It isn't but a few miles into Ironhead."

"They don't call it that no more." The black man wobbled

to the horse, suddenly seeming weaker than he had been, and he staggered more than once. But he managed to climb aboard the dun easy enough, as if he might be faking the extent of his injuries. Morgan cocked the Winchester, and the metallic snap of its hammer caused the black man to look over his shoulder and find the weapon pointed at his back.

"I hope you don't have any fool notions about trying to escape," Morgan said. "Call me callous to your situation if you want to, but I'm naturally leery of a man somebody thought needed hanging."

"You keeping me prisoner?"

"Let's go to town and see if we can sort this out."

"Lot and them other deputies might be there."

"Then we'll talk about things. Hear their side of the story."

"Lot lies."

"Move along." Morgan gestured ahead.

"Lot's got it in for me, and he'd as soon kill me as eat his supper."

"There won't be another hanging. Maybe you deserve one, but if I find that you do, I'll see you to Fort Smith's jail and they can deal with you."

The black man kept the horse to a walk, and Morgan followed behind on foot. They soon found their way back to the Texas Road where the traveling was easier.

"I feel like I ought to know you," the black man said after a time.

"Morgan Clyde."

"Heard of you." The black man flexed his neck in a slow circle and winced. "You got a big reputation."

Morgan left that alone. "Got a name of your own, since we're being so friendly?"

Some of the painful distortion left the black man's haggard

face. And there was pride mixed in with something else when he spoke. "Cumsey Bowlegs. You heard of me?"

Morgan shook his head. "Don't believe I have."

"Cumsey, that's me. Folks here, they know me. Ask any of them." Even in his current condition, this Cumsey had a cocky air about him. Most men would have still been too shaken to act cocky, but not this one. No telling what kind of crime the fellow had committed to get drug out in the brush and strung up like that, but you couldn't deny he had sand.

"You keep that horse walking slow and don't make me shoot you out of that saddle, Mr. Cumsey Bowlegs, or else all anyone is going to talk about is how deep they dug to bury you."

"My neck hurts worse than it did," Cumsey said. "Can barely swallow and my head's swimming something fierce. Might be best if you let me rest a spell."

"Keep moving and save your air."

They came to the dead horse. Cumsey stopped the dun and looked down at his lifeless former mount. "I'll kill Lot Ingram the next chance I get."

"You're bound and determined to die of a hanging, aren't you?"

Cumsey looked down at Morgan from the saddle, and he swallowed twice and grimaced, as if trying to get his swollen throat to work. "You believe in fate, Clyde?"

"I believe in cause and effect. Consequences."

"I'm talking about what made you come along and find me hanging from that tree." Cumsey walked the dun ahead. It was a while before he spoke again. "Who is it that comes along and cuts me down but you?"

"What are you mumbling about?"

Cumsey kept the horse walking. "You remember a man you killed? Strawdaddy, they called him."

Morgan stopped, and Cumsey turned the dun broadside in the road and looked back at him. He was a big, strong young man, and there was a strange intensity burning in his dark eyes.

"You remember him, don't you?" he added with his voice cracking to the point that it was hard to understand him.

Morgan did remember. A man never forgot those kinds of things, and sometimes they came back all too vividly.

It had been his first day on the job as chief of the railroad police for the Katy when the track construction was stalled out on the north bank of the South Canadian and Ironhead Station was running wild with every kind of human trash that could find its way there to see if they could get in on the vice. And that first day there had been a young desperado about Cumsey's age, firing his pistol at an unarmed man who had given him offense. Morgan had called on him to throw down his gun, but Strawdaddy had made too many brags about how tough he was and chose instead to fire off his pistol and missed. And that was that. A man pulled on you and you had two choices, shoot back or die.

"I get the impression you and Strawdaddy were friends," Morgan said in a voice that was harder than before.

"He was my cousin."

"He was a two-bit outlaw who took a shot at me."

"True, Strawdaddy was a sorry one, but he was family."

"You live with it. I do," Morgan said. "Now get along."

Cumsey remained where he was. "Ain't no denying the fate of this, but I got to think on this some."

"Best thing you can do is to leave it be."

"Sounds easy enough, but ain't nothing easy, not in the Nations," Cumsey said. "Man sets out to do a thing, he ought to finish it."

"And what have you set out to do, Cumsey?"

Cumsey gave Morgan that odd smile again. "I swore to Strawdaddy's mama that if I ever ran across you, I was going to kill you."

Morgan shifted his hat to a more comfortable angle on his head, tilting the brim down to shield his eyes from the sun, and shoved the stub of a cigar butt into the corner of his mouth. "Like you said, there's nothing easy about the territory," Morgan said with clenched teeth while he fished for his matches. "And I guarantee you, I'm not any easier."

CHAPTER FIVE

Red Molly was sweeping off the walkway in front of her barbershop when she saw Morgan Clyde coming down the street. He was on foot and leading his mount, and Cumsey Bowlegs was up in the saddle. Morgan walked like he was tired, and the way Cumsey rode told that both men had experienced some difficulty. But Morgan Clyde was always in some kind of a scrap.

Molly leaned the broom against the wall and brushed down the front of her dress. Tired or not, Morgan had always been a handsome man, and as long as she had known him, she still couldn't help the way she felt when she saw him. Not exuberance or giddiness, but rather an aching somewhere down in the hollow inside her. There had been a time not too long before when she swore she didn't love him anymore, for what little good it had ever done her, but there he was again and the ache was like it had always been.

"Hello, Molly," Morgan said when he stopped in front of her. He said it so matter-of-factly, like it hadn't been more than a year since they had seen each other last.

"It's been a while," Molly tried to say with a nonchalance to match his own.

"It has at that."

Molly felt the ache inside her fading and being replaced with anger, and she never had been able to mind her tongue. It was as if her feelings had a direct line to her mouth.

"Is that all you have to say to me?" She did a better job sounding scorned than she had sounding like she didn't care. "Not a smile? Not a hug? Not even a damned handshake for an old friend?"

Morgan attempted a smile while he wrapped a bridle rein over the hitching rail. He put a hand on each of her shoulders. "You look good. I'd almost forgotten how pretty you are."

"You're a liar," she snapped, but let him hug her.

Instead of appeasing her, his words made her angrier, like she was some young fool to be bought off with a dose of flippant flattery. Knowing that he didn't mean them, and that words were all they were, hurt worse than him saying nothing at all.

He stepped back and looked down at her and shook his head. "And I'd almost forgotten that temper of yours."

"And you never were much good with the blarney." She pushed his hands away and pointed at the badge pinned to his vest. "I see you've taken your old job back."

Morgan pretended like he didn't hear her and looked down the street the way he had come. "It's grown a bit."

She looked where he looked and tried to see it with a fresh perspective, as if it were her first time in Eufaula. It couldn't even now truly be called a town, not yet; not by somebody from a real town. Some of the settlers and business owners from the settlement of North Fork Town to the east had torn down their establishments and moved them to be along the railroad. All those newer buildings paralleled the tracks, but her shop still lay on the old camp street running east to west on top of the old California Trail that had once carried miners and emigrants to the far coast during the gold rush of 1849 and the rush to Pikes Peak in the Colorado Territory a decade later. But there were no more gold rushes to bring droves of would-be miners tramping across the territory, and the trail was nothing but another seat of wagon ruts—a faded, wistful trail for a wistful town.

Most of the structures that made up the new town were built of nothing but weathered and rough-sawn lumber or dovetailed logs bearing ax and adze marks, but it was something, a start. And up by the tracks, at the end of her street— that's the way she had come to think of it, her street, her town—stood the rebuilt Katy depot house, painted maroon with yellow trim, and on the opposite side of the street was an enormous, two-story affair with fresh white paint on its siding. Even from a distance, Molly could make out the sign above its long front porch. VANDERWAGEN HOTEL.

Morgan turned and looked at the hotel. She couldn't tell if he squinted more from the sun hitting him in the face or the impact of those words painted on the sign. And then an ironic grunt escaped his chest.

"Fancy, isn't it?" Molly observed.

"Well, Helvina always did have expensive tastes and too high an opinion of herself," he replied.

As if on cue, a tall, slender, blond-haired woman in an expensive green dress walked out on the hotel veranda. She wrapped one arm around a roof column and used the other hand to shade her eyes as she looked down the street at them.

"I think she already knows you're here," Molly said, suddenly feeling more tired than angry. "Trust that bitch to put her nose into everything."

Morgan stared back at the woman on the hotel porch for a moment, then turned away. "Is there a city marshal here?"

"Don't have one." Molly gestured at Cumsey on the horse. "What's he done?"

Morgan looked back at him. "Now that's a good question. But the short of it is that somebody hanged him."

"Hello, Red." Cumsey tried a weak smile.

"You know him?" Morgan asked.

"Old lovers." Molly felt silly as soon as she said it, but her temper was still up.

Morgan looked back and forth between the two of them. "All right."

Cumsey seemed too tired to play along and didn't add anything or seem surprised at her games or the byplay between her and Morgan.

"He doesn't look too spry." Molly gestured again at Cumsey.

"He started out strong, but I'd say he's wilting. He even managed to quit talking the last mile or so on the way here."

Molly had already noticed that Cumsey didn't act so cocksure as he had earlier in the day, and it was obvious that he was injured. A closer look at him revealed his bruised and swollen neck, and she knew without being told that it was Lot Ingram that was responsible for the dirty deed. "They really did hang him, didn't they?"

"Do you know something about this?" Morgan asked.

Molly looked past Morgan and locked eyes with Cumsey. "No, you said he was hanged, and a man doesn't get a neck like that if you weren't telling the truth."

Morgan was about to question her further when three men rode around the corner of the depot house. The sun behind their backs threw long shadows on the street ahead of them.

"Who's that?" Morgan asked.

"It's them marshals," Cumsey answered. "That's Lot Ingram riding in the middle."

Noodles must have been watching out one of the windows, for he opened the front door and came out to stand with them. The little Sicilian nodded at Molly. "Signora Molly . . . Pork Chop, he already tell them in the back that the *poliziotti* come again."

A man in checkered pants and sweat stains at the armpits of his white, garter-sleeved shirt came out the front door behind Noodles. He was a man broad of girth with a bulbous red nose and potbelly that overhung his belt. His sagging jowls were shadowed in black whisker stubble, and long sideburns curled out like wild wings under his derby hat. He looked at Molly out of his hound dog eyes and nodded his head towards the marshals still a long stone's throw away but coming closer.

"Noodles gave us the word and I hustled the boys out the back door," the man in the checkered pants said.

"Thanks," Molly answered. "Best you go now. Maybe they won't stay long and you can get back to your game."

"I'll stay," he said.

She didn't argue, and for the thousandth time wondered why he hung around like some sad mascot. But she was glad that the old faro dealer was staying. Pork Chop was strangely loyal, even though he wasn't truly in her employ and never had been. She knew next to nothing about him, but he had once helped her out of a tight spot for no good reason that she could ever put a finger on. And then one day after that he had simply shown up at the barbershop and never left. She didn't pay him anything for the errands he ran for her, other than to let him use a table in her back room to set up his poker games and allowed him to sleep on a cot in the back room after closing time. His hands were too knotted with arthritis even if there had been a faro layout for him to deal, which there wasn't, but he was still good enough to win a little from her customers who felt like gambling. Sometimes she wondered if she had adopted Pork Chop, or if it was the other way around.

"I ain't liking this one bit," Cumsey said, glancing at the marshals. "Clyde, if they come any closer you're going to have to shoot me in the back, 'cause I'm putting the spurs to this horse."

Morgan handed his Winchester to Noodles, and the Sicilian barber was so surprised that he bobbled the weapon badly and almost dropped it.

"Take him inside and make sure he stays put," Morgan said.

Cumsey slid down out of the saddle and walked stiffly, but quickly into the saloon with Noodles coming behind with Morgan's carbine pointed at his back.

"Go with them," Molly said to Pork Chop, "and keep an eye on things."

Pork Chop went inside without comment or question. Only Morgan and Molly were left outside. They watched while the lawmen came on at a slow walk.

"You're acting mighty tense considering those are coppers like yourself," Molly said.

"It might be best if you go inside."

The trio of lawmen were upon them and Molly remained where she was without moving. The marshals on either side of Lot Ingram parked their horses a little wider apart than was necessary for a casual meeting, and Molly had seen enough trouble in her day to know that they were setting themselves up to put Morgan at a disadvantage.

Lot leaned over his saddle swells with both forearms resting on his saddle horn. His eyes were as flint hard as ever, and the crow's-feet wrinkles at the corners of them furrowed deeply. He ignored Molly as if she weren't even there and kept his attention on Morgan. The two men stared at each other for a long moment without saying anything, and with only the occasional blink of an eyelid or the twitch of Lot's bushy mustache to prove that they were real live men and not statues. The gray horse Lot rode switched its tail at a fly and stomped one hind hoof.

"I've got a warrant for that man you've got with you," Lot finally said.

"I have him under arrest," Morgan answered.

"Then you won't mind handing him over to me."

Morgan said nothing to that, and Lot took that silence as an answer he didn't like. He leaned a little farther over his saddle horn and squinted at the badge on Morgan's vest as if his eyes were having trouble focusing. "Railroad detective, is it?"

"Chief of Police for the Katy. Name's Morgan Clyde."

"I'd say my jurisdiction trumps yours. This is federal business."

"My commission from the MK & T includes an agreement from the U.S. Marshal granting my position deputation and authority in the Western District of Arkansas, including the Indian Territory," Morgan replied without a hint of any anger.

Lot straightened in his saddle and looked at the other deputy marshals. "You hear all them big words? What we've got here is some kind of lawyer with a badge."

Molly tensed, her mind racing to consider which way to break when the fight started, for that was surely what was about to happen. Morgan wasn't a man to tolerate insult. While usually cool and rational when it came to working his way out of a problem, he could be reckless when he felt he was cornered. She would never forget seeing them carry his body on a plank out of the old Bullhorn Palace, which was once housed in the very same tent where she now ran her own business. Shot multiple times, and bleeding all over, he had been, because he was fool enough and stubborn enough to take on the Kingman brothers and that Missouri snake, Deacon Fischer, at the same time.

Mad-dog mean with ice water in his veins, and a rod of spring steel down his spine, that's what the saloon talk all over the territory said about Morgan Clyde. Dressed and talked like a gentleman, but quick to shoot and not one to warn you more than once, they said. However, most of those that spread such tales about him had never met him and were only spreading gossip.

She had known Morgan off and on for better than eight years, since those early days in Sedalia, Missouri, and Baxter Springs, Kansas, when she was still working the dance halls and Morgan was wearing a cow-town marshal's badge. And their paths had crossed time and again when the Katy worked its way down into the Indian Territory, both of them following tracks to where the action was.

He was a man who kept his thoughts to himself and rarely talked of his past other than a sentence or two he dropped at random over the years, usually after he had been drinking. From those bits and pieces of that puzzle, she fathomed that he had once been a prosperous businessman back East before coming on to hard times and going off to war. She had often wondered what he was like when he was younger and before the wild country and the tent camps and the boomtowns. Maybe he used to smile more and laugh more and wasn't so brittle around the outer edges. For the man she knew now couldn't be the same, because the years and the miles worked their black magic on everyone until people became more the sum of a long chain of decisions and experiences, good and bad, than whatever they were in the beginning.

And there sat Lot Ingram on his horse and looking down at Morgan and talking to him like he was nothing more than some dude in a fancy frock coat. But Lot was maybe the only man that Molly had ever met who might be as hard as Morgan Clyde.

"You say that fellow in there is a fugitive," Morgan said without raising his voice, but with a crisp chop to his words. "Did he escape your custody?"

"No, but we've been hunting him for more than a month." Lot's eyes cut briefly to Molly, as if daring her to contradict his story. "And here we come across him."

"Peculiar," Morgan said.

"What's that?"

"I say it's peculiar that I found him out in the brush hanging by his neck," Morgan said.

Lot leaned back in his saddle and tried to appear surprised. "You don't say?"

"Cut him down myself. If he didn't have a neck like a bull he'd have been dead before I got to him."

"Doesn't surprise me," Lot said. "If you knew anything about him, then you'd know that he's the kind to bring a hanging on himself."

"Vigilantes," the deputy on Morgan's left said with a smirk. He was a short, pale-skinned man with what looked like a knife scar running down his cheek from the bottom of one eyelid. "Probably got caught stealing somebody's horse that had enough of those tricks."

"Did he say who hanged him?" Lot asked.

"He didn't know them, or else he isn't saying," Morgan replied.

It was the first lie Molly had ever heard Morgan tell, for she knew, and Morgan knew, that the men before them were the guilty culprits.

"I got papers on him. Best you let me take him and sort this out," Lot said.

Morgan shook his head. "I'll take him to Fort Smith and let the court decide what to do with him."

"Long ride to Fort Smith and back. Wouldn't want to keep you from your railroad work."

"Appreciate the offer, but I've got time. If there's vigilantes at work here, your party has the numbers to deal with it."

Lot worked a crick out of his neck and took a deep breath. "Are you trying to piss me off on purpose?"

"You're pretty quick with the insults your own self," Morgan replied.

Molly found that she was holding her breath without realizing it, and took a deep inhale. People up by the tracks had stopped what they were doing to watch what was going on. She doubted Lot would start a fight in front of those handful of onlookers, and the way Lot was talking in circles made it seem like he was going to stick to his innocent act. But Lot was as unpredictable as he was mean, and he was cagey smart.

"That railroad badge don't cut no wood with us," the deputy to the left said, the same one who had suggested Cumsey's hanging was the work of vigilantes. That livid red scar at the corner of his mouth puckered and flexed as he spoke.

"Mind your tongue, Brady," Lot said. "Think we got off on the wrong foot here."

Morgan shifted his attention slightly to the marshal on his far right, the one wearing a battered black cavalry hat with a brass pin of crossed sabers on the front of the crown. That deputy had his horse turned slightly so that his off side was hidden from view.

"I'd feel better if you had that man put up his rifle. He's a little fidgety there and making me nervous," Morgan said.

Lot glared at the man in the cavalry hat who shoved the Sharps rifle he had been hiding into the rifle boot hanging beneath his leg.

"Don't think anything of it. Cumsey and that Sand Town gang he rides with is a rough bunch. Didn't know when we rode up here if you weren't one of Cumsey's partners or not. Puts a man on the edge," Lot said. "How about we go inside and talk about this? Might be Red there can find us a cool glass of water or maybe something a little stiffer to cut the edge off our thirst."

"I'm not thirsty."

Lot tilted his head, either still working at the crick in his neck or willing himself to be more patient. "You will damned well show me a bit of professional courtesy, one lawman to another. You hear?"

"I've been nothing but courteous."

"Best thing you can do is to throw in with us and we'll all ride to Fort Smith together. That Cumsey is a sneaky little shit, and you'd be better off with us to make sure he doesn't try to get the drop on you."

Morgan sighed. "I understand there's a reward on Cumsey,

and to tell the truth, I don't intend to share it. Not with you, nor anybody else."

"There ain't no reward on him," said the scar-faced marshal whom Lot had called Brady. "Somebody done told you wrong."

Lot's voice lost some of its patience. "Or else you're in it with Cumsey. Maybe I ought to send a telegraph to check your credentials. Something isn't right here."

"Send your wire," Morgan said. "Superintendent Huffman was at Muskogee this morning, and he can vouch for me."

Lot looked up the street, as if counting the potential witnesses to what he really wanted to do. When he spoke again it was a quiet hiss. "You won't let me play nice, will you?"

Morgan reached out with his left hand and gently pushed Molly towards the front door. She looked from him to the deputies and then went inside. Morgan sidestepped until he was in the open doorway, still facing Lot and the other two.

"Clem, you ride around back and make sure that Cumsey doesn't slip off on us again," Lot said.

The marshal on Morgan's right, the one in the cavalry hat, kicked his horse to a trot and rode to the back of Molly's tent shop. That left Morgan facing Lot and the one with the scar.

"You're acting right suspicious, Clyde," Lot said louder than was necessary, wanting to make sure the gawkers up the street heard his act. "Or else you've got a cob up your ass about something I can't figure."

"Send your telegraph," Morgan said. "Send one to Fort Smith if you want. I'll go by whatever your boss says. I only want on the record for any reward there might be out for Cumsey."

Morgan ducked into the barbershop and closed the door. Molly was just inside waiting for him. The wall was thin, and she had been eavesdropping. She suspected Morgan lied again about the reward, and that he was only stalling for time.

"Who's watching the back door?" Morgan asked.

"I sent Pork Chop to keep watch," Molly answered.

Morgan glanced out one of the windows, and Molly went to his side and did the same. The scar-faced marshal was moving up the street like he intended to go to the depot to send a telegraph, but Lot remained where he was.

She turned back to the room behind her. Cumsey Bowlegs was reclined in the barber's chair with the back of one hand thrown across his forehead, as if the trials and tribulations of his day had finally and physically bested him. Noodles stood in the center of the room with Morgan's Winchester keeping watch on Cumsey.

"We have trouble, no?" Noodles asked.

"You don't know the half of it, you fool Italian," Molly threw at him.

"I tell you many times, I am Sicilian."

"They got us treed, sure enough," Cumsey said with his face still covered by his hand.

"Lot won't start a fight," Molly said. "Not in the broad daylight with witnesses watching him. Lot's mean, but he isn't stupid."

"These canvas walls aren't going to stop a bullet if they decide to open up," Morgan said. "Best we move up against the front wall. Those thin pine planks won't do much better, but it's something."

Molly went back to one of the windows and peered outside. "Lot's still sitting there like he's really going to wait for an answer to his telegraph."

"And what are you going to do when he finds out there

ain't no reward on me?" Cumsey asked. "What's your excuse going to be then, Clyde?"

"You could go with them," Molly said to Morgan. "Maybe they wouldn't try anything with you along."

Cumsey gave a painful chuckle from the barber's chair. "You haven't thought this through, have you? If he goes along they'd have to kill him, too. They get me by myself and then there are no witnesses to them hanging me. Even if they think I told Clyde they did it, it's just Clyde's word that some half-breed outlaw told him so. Either way, they intend on finishing what they started when they strung me up from that old tree."

Morgan nodded like what Cumsey said was true, and Molly knew that sometimes the truth was a bitter drink.

"I'll go to the depot. Send our own telegraph to wherever. Get you some help," she said. "Maybe the army at Fort Gibson will come."

"How do you know Lot won't bother you?" Cumsey asked. "And even if he doesn't, he ain't apt to let you send a tele-graph. Not until he's got his mind wrapped around this and thinks he's got all his loose ends sewed up."

"It's worth a try." Even as she said it, Molly didn't believe it would work, not really.

Morgan stood well to one side of a window and looked out at Lot Ingram sitting his gray horse in the middle of the street. "We'll see how it plays out. Sometimes the right answer is simply a matter of waiting."

There was the sound of a cocking pistol behind Morgan, and he turned to see Cumsey sitting up in the barber's chair with a little Remington derringer in his hand. The twin, .41-caliber, over-and-under barrels were aimed at Morgan's middle. Cumsey's other hand had hold of the barrel of the

Winchester Noodles had been entrusted with. He yanked the carbine away from the Sicilian.

"He act like hurt," Noodles said with an apologetic, nervous frown as he backed away from Cumsey. "Then he move fast."

"You should have patted me down better," Cumsey said to Morgan.

"Put that gun away and let's think our way through this," Morgan said.

"I'm not going to Fort Smith, with you or Lot Ingram." Cumsey rose from the chair and closed the distance between him and Morgan, lest Morgan decide to gamble against the short-barreled, inaccurate derringer and try to draw his own pistol.

"If you're innocent as you say, then what have you got to worry about?" Morgan asked. "I'd think you'd want to see the men that hanged you tried in court and get what's coming to them."

"Judge Story's court? He'll crook a white man for a dollar, much less a half-breed like me."

"I might have a way of handling that."

"Well, let's say I have reasons not to want to turn myself over to any court," Cumsey said with a weary, reckless smile that vanished as quickly as it had appeared. "Might be I have a few outstanding things on my record. I'm innocent of those, mind you, but they do present problems with me showing my face anywhere there's too many badges."

"There are good lawyers in Fort Smith."

"And what makes you think Lot Ingram is going to let me get to court? Like I said, I'm the only witness to my own hanging. He rubs me out, then poof, he has no more problems. He'd kill you too, if it came to that."

"So what now?"

Cumsey held the Winchester one-handed and pushed the barrel against Morgan's breastbone. The sound of the cocking hammer was like breaking glass in the quiet room. He raised one leg and tucked the little Remington into that boot top without taking his eyes off Morgan.

"What now? You tell me," Cumsey said. "I think this here is what my old teacher at the mission school used to call a 'predicament,' and if it ain't, I don't know what is."

Noodles shuffled his feet, perhaps because his game leg was bothering him to stand so long, or because he was nervous. Either way, Cumsey didn't like that. "You stay right where you are, Sicilian."

"You're digging the hole you're in deeper," Morgan said.

Cumsey snatched Morgan's Colt from its holster and tucked it behind his belt, all the while keeping the Winchester barrel pressed into Morgan's chest. "What have I got to lose?"

"Do you seriously think you're going to escape?" Molly asked. "There are three of them waiting out there."

"No, I doubt I'll get out of this one, but when I go, I intend to go down fighting."

"That's a fool thing to say," she threw back at him. "I'll make sure they put it on your tombstone."

"When this man here cut me down from that tree, the first thing that come to mind was that I wasn't ever going to let anyone make me feel that helpless again. That was the worst part, looking up through them old tree limbs with that feeling when there ain't nothing you can do but die." Cumsey clucked his tongue again and shook his head. "And you see, I swore I was going to kill Lot for what he did to me, and there he waits outside. Maybe I can get him before the other two get me, maybe not. But this time I get to call the turn."

"You do that, and they win," Morgan said.

"Old Lot out there ain't the only score I could settle." Cumsey shoved the Winchester's barrel a little harder into Morgan's chest. "Hell of a day. Woke up this morning like any other, and somewhere between hell and breakfast I swore I was going to kill two men. You ask anyone. I've been a lot of things that I ain't proud of, but I've never broken my word."

"What are you talking about?" Molly said, suddenly realizing that a bad situation had somehow gotten worse.

CHAPTER SIX

Morgan met Cumsey's gaze without speaking. Inwardly, he scolded himself for letting the young outlaw slip a hideout gun past him. At the same time, he was trying to figure out how he was going to regain the upper hand without taking a bullet in his chest. Cumsey was desperate, and people who felt they had nothing to lose were hard to deal with. This he knew, for he had been a desperate man himself more than once.

"I won't beg, if that's what you're waiting for," Morgan said.

"That cousin of yours pulled on me and I put him down. I'd do the same thing again if it came to that. Doesn't mean I took pleasure in it."

"He was family, about the last I had." Cumsey backed away with the .44 carbine still aimed at Morgan. "But you also cut me free of that rope. There's that to think on."

"If you shoot Morgan they'll hang you for sure," Molly said.

"Easy there, Red, I won't shoot your man. Not now. Like I said, I got to think on him some," Cumsey said. "How about you call your man in from the back?"

Molly did as he asked, and Pork Chop came through the tarp wall to find Cumsey waiting with the Winchester covering him. Pork Chop took a place in one corner of the front wall with the rest of them.

"Come here, Red." Cumsey moved to the front door cautiously, keeping out of the line of the windows.

"No call to bring her into this," Morgan said.

Cumsey ignored him and took Molly by the upper arm. "I want you to go up to the depot like you said before. Think you can do that?"

"You want me to try and send a telegraph?" she asked.

"Sure."

"Who should I send it to?"

"You send it wherever. Doesn't matter," Cumsey said. "All I care about is that those marshals pay attention to you, and not so much this way."

"That won't buy you enough time to get free," Morgan interjected, "and you'll be putting Molly right in the middle of a gunfight."

"I don't intend to go out the front door. Go ahead, Red. Just go down the street nice and easy like you don't have a care in the world."

Molly looked at Morgan for help.

"Go ahead," Morgan said to her. "They might stop you, but they won't harm you."

"That's right," Cumsey said as he opened the door a crack for her.

Molly hesitated.

"Scared?" Cumsey asked.

"I'm not looking forward to it."

"You got nerve. You'll do fine."

Molly frowned at him and took a deep breath.

"You ain't going to forgive me for this, are you?" Cumsey asked.

"Kid, I never liked you in the first place. Knew you were trouble the first time I laid eyes on you," she replied.

"That one out back will be waiting for you. You'll be right in his gun sights," Morgan said.

Cumsey ignored Morgan and kept staring at Molly. "I'll be out that door and to cover before that marshal back there even knows I'm moving. They'll play hell finding me once I hit the brush."

"That easy, huh?" Molly asked.

He gave her a playful wink of the eye. "I told you I'm shifty fast. Ask anybody. Cumsey Bowlegs, he's like greased lightning. Ain't a bullet that can touch him."

"You're full of sheep dung is what you are. Not even the good sense to be scared." But she smiled, too.

"I'd kiss you for luck if I thought you wouldn't slap me," he said. "I've always been a sucker for a redhead."

Everyone in the room saw that despite his determination, and despite the reckless act, he was scared right down to the raw quick of him. And he was hurting from his wounds. A funny look came across Molly's face and she bit her upper lip at the corner of her mouth as if considering something.

"What the hell?" she said as she put a hand to either side of her face and laid a long, wet kiss on his lips.

Cumsey was still standing there with a shocked look on his face when she went out the door and closed it behind her.

"She's something else, ain't she?" he said when he looked Morgan's way.

Morgan leaned over far enough to be able to see out one side of the window near him. He was barely in time to catch a glimpse of Molly as she went along the boardwalk and then out of sight.

The sound of Cumsey thumbing the cartridges out of his Colt and the rounds hitting the puncheon floor where they fell turned his attention back that way.

"I won't leave you unarmed." Cumsey laid the unloaded pistol on the tabletop. "Besides, I never was much good with a short gun."

"You won't make it," Morgan said.

"You'd best worry about yourself," Cumsey said. "The way I see it, we're even. The next time we meet, I'm not going to forget what you did to Strawdaddy. You see me, you had better cut your piece loose and go to banging."

Cumsey went through the tarp wall with the Winchester cocked and held at his hip. As soon as he was gone, Morgan strode across the room and took up the Colt. He went back to peer out the window while he snapped open the loading gate and thumbed fresh cartridges into the cylinder. Lot Ingram was riding his horse over to the edge of the street. He was looking back at Morgan in the window, but obviously intended to intercept Molly. The scar-faced marshal was there, also, with a Winchester rifle propped up on one thigh.

A rifle cracked at the back of the barbershop, and then there was another shot.

"Got any other guns in here?" Morgan asked.

Pork Chop went into the back room. Noodles remained where he was and slid an ivory-handled straight razor out of his waistband and folded it open. He gave Morgan a determined, but almost bashful, look.

Morgan nodded at him. "You'll do."

The gunfire had ceased, and then the marshal out back

shouted something to his companions that Morgan couldn't understand.

"Did you get him?" Lot shouted in return.

Pork Chop returned to the front room with a small, pearl-handled Smith & Wesson revolver in his hand. "Where's Molly?"

Morgan went out the front door with his Colt drawn. Molly stood on the edge of the street fifty yards away. Lot Ingram had his gray horse parked in between her and the depot house and was blocking her progress. Molly looked up at him and said something Morgan couldn't hear, and then Lot spurred around her and came towards Morgan at a lope. He pulled up in a cloud of dust practically right on top of Morgan.

Morgan kept the Colt hanging beside his leg with his thumb hooked over the hammer. Lot's horse fought the bit, and he glared down at Morgan while he held the animal in place.

"What the hell are you trying to pull?" Lot practically shouted.

"Cumsey had a hideout gun. Got the drop on me," Morgan answered.

He took a step to the right to put himself slightly on the opposite side of the gray horse and on the side away from the Winchester rifle Lot was holding in his right hand. In order to bring the rifle to bear, Lot would either have to rein the horse aside or lift the weapon over and across his saddle. It was a subtle little thing, but such things could make the difference. Morgan took another half sidestep, putting the sun more in Lot's eyes. Little things . . .

Another gunshot rang out from behind Morgan. The crack

of that gunfire startled Lot's horse and it scrambled sideways in a scattering of dust and gravel.

"I think I got him!" one of the other marshals shouted from somewhere in the timber behind the barbershop.

Lot gave Morgan a last, hateful glance, and then let his horse go. He went down the side of Molly's barbershop and disappeared from sight. Morgan walked quickly up the street and met Molly coming his way.

"Help him," she said when he reached her.

He took her by the arm and led her back to the front door. "Get inside and stay there."

Her face was flushed with the excitement, and she started to protest and pull away from him. But whatever she had been about to say was prevented by several hard coughs. Her body shook like it had suddenly gone weak, and she put a hand to her mouth and went inside.

Morgan reached the back of the barbershop in time to see the flashing tail of Lot's horse disappear into the timber. A pistol boomed somewhere farther ahead.

Morgan stayed where he was. He was afoot, and even if he retrieved his horse, there was no way to catch up with the pursuit. Whatever was going to happen was up to how fast and slippery Cumsey Bowlegs really was, if the marshals hadn't gotten him already.

No more gunshots came after that. He could hear the sound of the marshals' horses busting the brush as they searched for Cumsey, but that ceased after a while. The only sound was Molly's coughing coming from inside the tent. The dust the horses threw up on the street must have gotten to her.

Pork Chop came out the back tent flap to stand beside

him. The old faro dealer's sagging eyes were bloodshot and he breathed heavily through his mouth. "Did he make it?"

"Maybe."

Tree limbs shook not far away, and the head of a gray horse appeared out of the brush, followed by Lot Ingram's big hat above the horse. He rode straight to them.

"Did you catch him?" Morgan was afraid he knew the answer already.

Lot thumbed a .44 cartridge into the loading gate of his Henry rifle and didn't look up at Morgan until he was finished. He worked the lever and racked a round into the rifle's chamber. "Now that's the twenty-dollar question, ain't it?"

The angry deputy marshal spurred his horse past Morgan and went towards the train tracks. He soon returned and disappeared again into the timber, but not before Morgan noticed the can of coal oil he was carrying.

CHAPTER SEVEN

Morgan went to his horse and tightened his saddle cinch. He adjusted the knot in his latigo, ran his fingers under the cinch to check its tightness, and then put a boot in the stirrup and swung into the saddle.

A narrow strip of timber with dense undergrowth and heavy thicket in some places almost touched the southern edge of the settlement, and marked the course of a seasonal streambed like a crooked green finger pointing south. Eventually its course led it to empty into a little creek, and then the river farther along. If Cumsey had gone that way, he would be hard to find, but that coal oil Lot had retrieved made Morgan think they had run him to ground.

Morgan put the zebra dun to a long lope as soon as he reached the Katy tracks, and followed them south. By the time he reached the river about two miles away, there was already a dark cloud of smoke rising from the thicket closer to Eufaula. Apparently, his guess about the coal oil was right, and the marshals had set fire to a thicket, intending on smoking Cumsey out.

It had been a dry season so far, especially dry for the

earliest days of summer, and not a drop of rain since the spring. Lot was a fool to start a fire in such conditions.

There were no more gunshots while the billowing cloud of smoke grew larger. Morgan reached the high railroad trestle across the river, and turned east and went along the northern bank scanning for fresh tracks. The river flood channel was wide and sandy and dotted with clumps of willows and other scrub, and if Cumsey had tried to swim the river it would be all but impossible not to leave tracks.

The wind was out of the southwest, and that crosswind kept the worst of the smoke from him. Satisfied that it was less likely that Cumsey had made it to the river, he rode north into the timber, picking his way as best he could through the thickets and backtracking several times when the grapevines and greenbriars became too thick to allow the dun to pass. His progress was also slowed by knowing that the marshals were somewhere ahead of him. He wanted to see them first, if and when he came upon them.

The marshals might have intended to burn a small patch of especially dense brush where they thought Cumsey was hidden, but either the fire had gotten out of hand, or else they simply didn't give a damn if they burned down the whole world to get their man. A good portion of the river bottom between the trestle and Eufaula was burning, and the flickering red flames were visible for a great distance. From the way the fire was traveling with the wind, the old settlement at North Fork Town would be lucky if it didn't get burnt out.

Nearer the wall of flames on the south edge of the fire, it was almost impossible to see through the gray curtain of smoke. Glowing embers floated around him like fireflies, and the furnace wind caused by the heat swayed the treetops

not far ahead and above him. He judged the advance of
the fire by that line of swaying treetops, and several times he
looked behind him, gauging how far he had come from
the riverbank against the pace of the fire. If he went any farther
and the wind shifted, he might not have enough time to flee
to the natural firebreak of the river channel.

He took a silk neckerchief from inside his vest pocket and
folded it and tied it behind his head to cover his face and to
filter some of the smoke. Maybe the young half-breed had
gotten away. The kid was nervy enough to pull it off if he
was lucky. It galled Morgan to have lost a prisoner, and bad
man or not, it would gall him worse for the marshals to catch
Cumsey before he could recapture him.

The wind shifted slightly towards Morgan's face, and
that wasn't a good thing. The fire seemed to close half the
distance to him in a matter of seconds. One moment he
was thinking that he had better get out of the path of fire
and waste no time doing it, and the next moment there was
the roar of a gun and a bullet knocked a chunk of bark off
the tree next to him. He spun the dun on its hindquarters
in the direction he thought the shot had come from, and drew
his pistol.

He squinted into the thick smoke, and there was a split
second when he plainly saw the inky black silhouette of a
man in a big hat standing some fifty or sixty yards away with
his back to the flames and aiming a rifle at him. The Colt
bucked in Morgan's hand, and the man who had shot at him
disappeared. It was impossible to tell whether Morgan's
bullet had hit home or not. The wind was gusting stronger,
and it drove the fire to a frenzy. A treetop above him burst
into flames and a burning chunk of tree limb fell and almost

hit Morgan in the face. He threw up his gun arm to fend off the flaming bit of wood, and kept that arm up to shield his face from the heat as he spun the dun again and spurred it blindly towards the river.

It felt as if the fire were right at his back, and his nostrils filled with the smell of burning hair. Whether it was the dun on fire or his own hair singeing, he couldn't tell. The heat was so intense that his skin felt as if it had already caught fire, and he spurred the dun harder. Some limb or tangle of brush almost jerked him from the saddle as the frightened horse beneath him charged through the thicket ahead at a dead run.

With his arm still shielding his face and ducked low in the saddle, Morgan didn't realize that he had broken free of the thicket and out onto the open sandbar until the dun splashed into the river. He didn't stop the gelding until they were chest deep in the slow, brown current, and then he turned back coughing the smoke from his lungs and staring at the inferno he had so barely escaped.

He had no clue if he had hit the man who had shot at him, or who that man had been. It could have been one of the marshals, but the thought was there, too, that it could have been Cumsey Bowlegs.

The fire stalled at the South Canadian and along the railroad right-of-way to the west, and by the time Morgan reached the outskirts of Eufaula that evening, the flames had worked their way far to the east towards North Fork Town. The green of the timbered stretch of bottomland between the town and river had been transformed into a

brimstone world of smoldering black ashes. Thin tendrils
of the smoke lingered and twined amongst the charred
bones of the burned-over forest like dragon's breath, and
the smell of it was everywhere. The only color left in the
almost surreal, gray scale canvas before him was the occasional glow of a snag or a deadfall still burning amidst
the shadows, and the orange, soot-streaked orb of the sun
low on the western horizon.

Some of the townspeople were working with picks and
shovels and hoes to finish chopping a firebreak at the perime-
ter of the little clearing where the town stood when he arrived.
They had also hitched a team of mules to a moldboard plow
to help with the work, and another team was dragging a
green hardwood log wrapped in wet burlap to snuff out any
remaining embers along the line.

Morgan met Molly on the street. She was coming back
from the firebreak with a young, strikingly pretty black
woman. Both women had an arm thrown over each other's
shoulders as if they were exhausted, and from their sweaty,
sooty faces and clothes it was obvious that they had lent a
hand with the work. He pulled up his horse, and the black
woman said goodbye to Molly and peeled away.

Molly saw him watching the other woman. "Put your eyes
back in your head, Morgan Clyde."

"Who is she?"

"Do you remember Saul, the camp cook?"

"Of course, I remember him."

"That's his wife," Molly said. "Or was. Poor thing wasn't
married a few hours before she was made a widow."

Morgan nodded, knowing the story all too well. Saul had
been a good man, full of kind, simple wisdom, and he and
Morgan had whiled away many a slow hour back when the

Katy construction crew was camped there, although Morgan had quit the railroad before it moved on to Canadian Station where Saul was murdered.

"Saul was a good one," he said.

"Saul is past helping. It's Hannah there that ought to have your sympathy," Molly said. "She landed here after that trouble with nothing to her name but some bad memories and few prospects to make it better."

"How's she getting by?"

"I called in a few favors and had some of the men fix up that old powder shed down the tracks for her."

"Kind of you."

"I wanted to convince that skinny preacher to hire her to teach at the mission school. The girl's sharp as a tack, but Useless is too pious to give me the time of day. His church congregation might talk, and Moses himself might roll over in his grave if he were seen talking to me."

Morgan smiled grimly at her mention of the preacher's nickname. Euless Pickins, the Methodist missionary and Creek Indian agent, wasn't exactly a man that Morgan enjoyed remembering.

"Euless can be a pain, that's for sure," Morgan said.

"Oh, Useless doesn't bother me, not to my face, at least," she said. "But he doesn't miss a chance to spread it around that he can't understand how such a fine little town tolerates the likes of me. 'That dirty whore of Babylon,' I think are his exact words."

"What about Saul's widow?"

"She and Lottie Bickford have partnered up in Lottie's laundry business for now, although it isn't what it once was when the Katy crew was camped here."

"The Bickfords are still around?"

She gave him an impatient look. "Of course Hank's around."

"I saw the blacksmith shop, but didn't know if it was his."

"Hank's not a blacksmith anymore," Molly said. "At least not full-time. He's put in a funeral parlor."

"A funeral parlor?"

"A lot you know. Haven't you ever seen the woodwork that man makes? People saw the coffin he made for Saul, and it wasn't long before they were requesting him to make one for theirs that needed burying. So, he bought a book to learn about embalming and such, and set up shop. He's got his funeral parlor next door to his blacksmith shop."

"I never would have taken Hank for a mortician."

"He might be the only one in this town who's making money, and possibly the only undertaker in the territory right now. People are coming for miles and miles around to do business with him. That new embalming is all the rage now, you know."

Morgan couldn't help but chuckle at the thought of the town's blacksmith also being its undertaker. Where else but the territory could you get your horse reshod and a deceased loved one preserved in the same stop?

But Hank was one of the good ones, and another of the first ones to befriend Morgan back in the days when the railroad was still being constructed. And it didn't surprise Morgan that Hank was the one to find prosperity first, for he had always been industrious.

"Coffins, huh?" Morgan asked. "Well, if I was going in to the coffin business I couldn't think of a better place to do it."

"You're purposefully trying to keep me from asking any

questions about what happened today, aren't you?" she asked.

"Nothing to tell you."

"Did they catch Cumsey?"

"I don't know."

"That Lot Ingram, him and his damned coal oil," Molly said. "Everybody's always so scared of him, but I bet they'd tar and feather him and ride him out of town on a rail if he showed his face right now."

"Man like that will eventually get his due. It's only a matter of time."

"I know what you're thinking," she said.

"What's that?"

"That you're the one to make that happen," she said. "Don't do it, Morgan. Turn a blind eye for once. If you get Lot, then what? There will only be another come along just as crooked and just as mean. That's the way of the world."

"It's my job."

"You're a railroad detective. What's Lot Ingram got to do with the Katy?"

"Speaking of old acquaintances, you haven't seen Dixie Rayburn, have you?"

"Go ahead, try to act like you don't hear me. Put me off with small talk."

"Have you seen Dixie?"

"Don't drag him into this. Not this time."

Morgan rubbed at his face and his hand was black with soot when he pulled it away.

"Leave your horse at the livery and bring your gear to my cabin," she added with a bit of wistfulness in her voice.

"I'll fix us a bite to eat and we'll talk about the old days over a glass or two."

Morgan shook his head. "Don't want to impose on you."

"Impose on me?"

"All I want now is a hot bath and a soft bed." Morgan looked towards the Vanderwagen Hotel. "I'll buy you lunch tomorrow."

Molly brushed a strand of red hair back from her face and gave him a flirty and alluring smile. "There was a time when my bed was soft enough."

Morgan turned the dun and started towards the hotel.

"You go spend your money with that rich bitch," Molly called after him. "All you'll find there is a bed of nettles. Thought you would have learned that by now."

Morgan rode to the livery and left the dun and his tack there in the care of the liveryman. He walked to the hotel with a weary stride and his saddlebags slung over one shoulder. It was growing dark by then, and he paused on the porch with the lamplight spilling out from the windows and kissing his boot toes. He stood there for several minutes in the shadows before he took hold of the doorknob and went inside. Red Molly O'Flanagan could be difficult, especially when her temper was up, but Helvina Vanderwagen gave the word a whole new meaning.

CHAPTER EIGHT

Morgan had hoped she might have already retired for the evening and left the night's business to some clerk; however, there she stood in the middle of the lobby in that green dress smiling as if she were expecting him.

"Goodness, Morgan, you look positively awful," Helvina said. "If one didn't know you, they could easily mistake you for some street urchin."

Standing there like she was, most men would have called her beautiful—unusually and exceptionally beautiful with the kerosene lamplight playing softly on her perfectly arranged golden hair done up high, and the glisten of the green emerald necklace lying against the pale skin at her neckline, gems chosen, no doubt, because they matched her green eyes. But Helvina wore her beauty like a weapon with a sharp, cold edge.

"All I want is a room for the night."

She lifted her dimpled chin slightly and gave what anyone else would take as a playful smile. "And a hot bath, I hope."

"That, too."

Her dress rustled against the polished hardwood floor as

she strode across the room towards the register desk. There was a clerk there, a young man in a suit and necktie, despite the heat, but Helvina swept him aside.

"Make sure to have the tub in Room Ten filled with hot water," she said, and then gave Morgan a look from head to toe with her nose wrinkled up. "And make sure there is plenty of soap. Plenty of soap and a good stiff scrub brush."

The young clerk gave Morgan a glance that said he found Morgan as filthy and distasteful as his employer did, but he did as he was told, leaving Morgan alone with Helvina in the lobby.

"It seems you are back in the employment of the railroad." Helvina nodded at the badge Morgan was wearing. "I honestly don't understand how you find such distasteful work to your liking. But then again, your tastes and life choices have ever been a mystery to me."

"I don't want to fight," he said. "All I want is a room."

She dabbed a quill pen in a bottle of ink and made a show of scratching something onto the open register book before her. He took the time to look over the lobby. While probably not up to Helvina's luxurious standards, it was the nicest hotel lobby Morgan had encountered in the territory. The walls had been covered in floral wallpaper, and the kerosene lamps lining them were mounted in brass sconces. A huge wrought-iron chandelier bearing at least fifty lit candles hung down from the high ceiling, and a banister-edged stairway led up to the second floor and the balcony overlooking the lobby. Potted dogwood trees stood to either side of the glass front doors, and a wreath of twisted grapevines and dried floral arrangements decorated a scattering of tables that must have served as the hotel restaurant.

"Not quite as grand as the St. Nicholas Hotel on Broadway, but I think I've done quite well considering the place and the means I had at hand," she said. "Don't you think?"

Morgan couldn't guess how much it had cost Helvina to build the hotel, or where she had gotten the money and why she would want to spend it on such an establishment in such a backwater village as Eufaula. She handed him the pen and he signed the register.

"You always had a knack for decorating," Morgan said when he set down the pen.

"Such a nice thing to say. I thought you never noticed."

"Let's don't fight, Helvina. Not this time."

She arched one eyebrow at him while she retrieved his room key from a pegboard on the wall. The clerk started to take the key, but she pulled it away from him.

"I'll see Mr. Clyde to his room personally," she said. "We can't have the hero of the Katy Railroad receiving any less than my personal touch, now can we?"

Morgan followed her up the stairs, unable to avoid noticing the sway of her bustle as she preceded him. It was obvious that she was putting an extra sway to her hips with every step. No doubt, she was taunting him. That was her way.

They came to his room at the far end of the hallway on the second floor. She opened the door and stepped aside only far enough that he still had to brush against her to pass. More of her games. The smell of her perfume was strong enough to cut through the smoke in his nostrils and it brought with it old memories.

Morgan glanced at the iron bedstead with a feather mattress and a little woven rug on the floor alongside it and an empty porcelain bathtub set against the single window looking out over the street.

"Like I said, it's not exactly luxurious, but it's the nicest hotel between Kansas and Texas," she said from behind him.

He tossed his saddlebags on the bed and turned to find her leaning against the doorjamb.

"How's Ben?" he asked.

Her face tightened, and little frown lines formed at the corners of her mouth. She was in her midthirties, but had always looked younger than her age. However, the angry expression she showed him right then added a decade to her looks and showed what was there when you peeled back that pretty face. She was a shallow, selfish, conniving woman who spent all her waking hours trying to make sure she got her way. And then he smelled her perfume again and studied her standing in the door posed like some statue of a haughty Greek goddess. Though still tall and slim, she was fuller figured than she had once been, and the tightness of the corset she undoubtedly wore gave her a wasp waist and made her look bustier. Was the physical attraction all that he had once felt for her? He remembered her standing in the exact same way the first time he had seen her in a doorway at the edge of a New York party, like some talisman waved before him.

"I'm sure Benjamin would contact you if he wished you to know," she answered.

"He's our son."

"He was just a little boy when you decided to go off and play soldier." She straightened and practically spat those words at him. "A little boy, do you hear me? A little boy who needed a father and didn't have one. What right have you to any claim on him?"

"You took him from me. Poisoned him against me."

"And you left me with two children and barely a roof covering my head."

"You ran off and took them from me."

"I told you I would leave you. I told you I would if you joined up."

Morgan took a deep breath. They were only rehashing hurtful things, and neither of them was going to change the other's mind, nor undo what had been done. Talking of it was like peeling the scabs off old wounds.

"I would only like to know how he's doing. Is that so much to ask?"

"I think I've done plenty for you. I could have married anyone. Anyone. There were a dozen men courting me, but for some reason I chose you. I chose you though you didn't have a dollar to your name and nothing but big talk about the success you were going to be."

"It was always a business decision with you, wasn't it? You said you wanted it all, but I didn't know then what you meant."

"Don't play the poor, pitiful me, Morgan. It was you that took that policeman's job even though Father advised you that his lawyers could keep your debtors off your back," she snapped. "He showed you plainly how you could have avoided paying most of what you owed. If you had listened and been patient, you could have made a comeback, recouped what little fortune you had amassed and maybe improved it. Better men have recovered from setbacks and made their fortunes."

"I paid off every bit of what I owed, and I did it honestly. Not with crooked lawyer tricks, either. It took two years, one paycheck at a time, but I did it. Kept my obligations and made good on my word," he said, realizing that his own temper was rising. "And don't blame the war for why you left me. I felt you were preparing to go long before then. In fact, I don't know why I was so shocked when you quit answering my letters or when I mustered out and came home to find you gone."

It was her turn to take a deep breath, and she ran her hands down both hips as if drying the sweat from her palms, and then she patted at her coifed hair. "This is the very reason I hid from you. You couldn't take it that I didn't love you anymore."

"Oh, I can take that. Whatever spell you put me under wore off long ago."

"You would have made trouble for Benjamin and he was doing so well. I didn't want you coming back into his life and confusing him. And George would never have tolerated you being around. He was too jealous for that."

"Was that the mining man I heard about? Did you marry him, or was he only another of your boyfriends?"

"Don't you dare talk like that to me. George paid Benjamin's way through school, and saw to it that he got an appointment to West Point. I did what I had to do to take care of my children."

The look on both of their faces told that her second mention of another child reminded them both of something they would like to forget, but never would, the rawest of wounds.

"After I lost Rebecca to the fever, I swore that no matter what, I was going to see to Ben." Her lower lip and chin trembled, and there was a quaver to her voice. "You could fight all the wars you wanted and play the honorable man, but I was going to take care of me and him."

"And then you latched onto Willis Duvall and showed up here. Where did he come in? Did you use up all of poor George's money and have to find you another bankroll to keep you in style? How many men have you sucked dry over the years?" Morgan heard himself speaking almost as if he was listening to another man, and as if he had no control over what he said. It all simply poured out of him like a flood while he thought of the baby daughter he had lost while off to war. The last time he had seen her, she had been crawling on the living room floor, healthy and happy. And then came a letter a year later saying that she had died from the scarlet fever. The same letter informed him that Helvina was divorcing him.

Helvina strode forward and slapped him hard across the cheek. She reared back to hit him again and he caught her by the wrist. She fought savagely to jerk free from his hold, but he pushed her towards the door.

"I hate you," she snarled.

He thought of all the petty, spiteful things he had said to her and added that to his regret. Maybe Helvina had always brought out the worst in him. Truly, there was no in-between when it came to how he felt when around her. No calmness, and all passion to one extreme or the other. High or low, burning hot or frigid cold, sad or exuberant, but nothing lukewarm and just right. Nothing steady and solid and secure that you could hang on to, like it should be between a man and a woman.

"I hate you," she repeated and came at him with her hand raised again to strike him again.

And he hated her, also, as he had for more than ten years, as he had for all the time he had spent looking for her after the war, and as he had when he saw her again for the first time a little more than a year ago standing on the depot decking beside the train, the last person he had ever expected to see anywhere, much less the territory. And yet, when she fell against him the second time he couldn't help but feel the press of her breasts against his chest and the softness of her hair tickling his chin. Her perfume smelled like lilacs and sex.

She must have felt the change in him, or else she was spent, for she ceased struggling and tilted up her face to him with her lips pursed and her breath coming raggedly.

She had thrown herself at him once a year before after her newest fiancé and lover, the former superintendent of the railroad, had lost his job and was on the run from the law for his nefarious dealings. He had flatly and cruelly turned her down, not at all tempted and sure that she only wanted to remind him of the power she still held over him. Now, holding her, he reminded himself of all the reasons to shove her out the door and slam it behind her. Yet, the smell of that perfume filled his senses and the feel of her body against him left him reeling with a wash of emotions.

He kissed her softly, and then more firmly. She reared back and put distance between their faces, staring at him once again. Black soot from his own face was smeared on her chin.

"I hate you," she whispered.

"I hate you, too," he said as he kissed her again.

He cursed her and he cursed himself, calling her the vilest of names, both aloud and to himself. And she cursed him in the same way, and somehow, that added to the wrongness that was strangely right in the moment and excited them all the more. Their hands found familiar places and their bodies moved together in an old rhythm, not soft and loving, but urgent and almost frantic, as if the moment might pass them by. Need and longing mixed with vengeance and lust.

"Tell me I'm beautiful," she said as she pressed him into the mattress and looked down at him with her long hair undone and swaying wildly about her face and across her bare breasts. "Tell me like you used to."

Oh, how he hated her, and yet, he lifted her from him and rolled over atop her, pressing his face into her neck and tasting the sweet sweat of her and feeling the vibrations of her throat as she moaned softly and called his name.

And for a fleeting moment, as her body trembled beneath him, he saw his pistol belt lying on the rug beside the bed. And when he looked at her again, she had her face turned and was looking at the pistol, also. When she gazed back into his eyes her lips parted in a smoky smile, as if she knew what he was thinking and the knowing made the pleasure all the greater.

CHAPTER NINE

Morgan woke first and rolled away from the bright sunlight streaming through the window. The sheet and the quilt were gone from the bed and were crumpled on the floor, and Helvina lay nude beside him, deep in sleep. His gaze ran over the pale, smooth length of her and watched her little nostrils flaring in and out and the relaxed, contented set of her full lips above that dimpled, delicate chin.

Instead of reaching out and brushing a hand along the soft curve of her hip bone, he got out of the bed quietly, pulled on his pants, and stood at the window looking down on the street. He hated himself then. Hated himself as much for the woman who lay in the bed as he did for needing whatever it was he thought she had to give.

He rolled his shoulders and tried to knead some of the stiffness out of his hands. And he looked down at one of those hands, his right hand, and then he held it up before him with his fingers splayed. The middle joints of his pointer and the middle finger there were knotted, making both digits slightly crooked, and tiny scars marked the flesh where the Pinkerton detectives that Helvina had hired to scare him away and to keep him from finding her had smashed a pistol butt down on his hand.

He turned and glanced at her again and swore that he was a fool, and for the second time he looked at his pistol on the floor beside the bed and thought how easy it would be— pressing that gun barrel against her head and pulling the trigger. And what shamed him most was that murdering her was no greater sin than lying with her as he had, with the same emotions driving him to both things, and the same, sick, churning feeling inside him.

There was a washbasin half full of water on the dresser top, and he used it and a towel to scrub the worst of the soot and filth from him. He shaved with the same cold water, combed his hair, and dressed in a clean shirt taken from his saddlebags.

Helvina was still asleep by the time he had brushed his frock coat reasonably clean and donned his flat-brimmed black hat. Once more, he tossed his saddlebags over his shoulders and stood at the door, looking at her. The pistol still lay on the floor.

She murmured something and squirmed on the mattress until she found a more comfortable position, and she must have known he was up and about, for there was a sleepy smile half formed on her mouth.

He went to the bed and reached down and picked up the pistol. He stood there for a long time, looking down at her while she slept.

She was still sleeping when he slung the gun belt about his hips and buckled it, and she was still sleeping when he softly closed the door and went down the stairs to the lobby.

A young Indian woman in a plain dress met him at the

foot of the stairs. She was obviously a hotel maid, for she carried two buckets of steaming hot water. She gave him a sly glance. "I thought you might want your bathwater now."

He saw that she was barely suppressing a grin, and her eyes took a quick glance at the top of the stairs towards his room.

"I was going to pour your bath last night," the maid said, "but you sounded like you were busy." She couldn't hide her grin any longer and ducked her head and stared at the floor.

Morgan looked up the stairs himself. "I appreciate it, but maybe you ought to wait until I come back tonight."

A squeak of sound escaped the maid before she clamped her mouth tight and suppressed her giggle. She looked up and gave him that same sly look. "But Ms. Helvina said we were to pour you a bath. Think she'll mind?"

Morgan looked across the lobby and saw the hotel clerk glaring at him. He knew then that sound of he and Helvina's little ruckus must have carried through the thin plank walls and that he and Helvina seemed to be the scandal of the morning as far as the staff was concerned. He gave another glance at the clerk with that prim, sneering look on his face, and then at the maid standing before him with her head ducked so that he couldn't see her face. Scandalous? They didn't know the half of it, but they would learn if they kept working for Helvina.

"No, I don't think she'll mind if you wait until I return before you bring me my bathwater," he said and then went past the maid and out the front door. He heard the maid giggle again as he closed the door behind him.

Only when he saddled his horse at the livery and rode along the street, did he look up and see Helvina standing in the window wrapped in a sheet and looking down at him. Neither waved to the other as he passed.

He was almost out of town when he rode in front of Red Molly's cabin. It wasn't really a cabin, but the old tent she had lived in behind her barbershop back when that business had been the Bullhorn Palace. She had added pine siding to the tent's walls, along with a flower box and a rocking chair sitting in front of it, but it was still a tent.

He hadn't meant to pass so closely to her dwelling, and only the direction he wanted to travel had led him along that way. And he hadn't expected to see her that morning, for it was still early.

But she was sitting there in that rocking chair wearing the same soot-covered dress as she had worn before, and with her red hair in disarray and a bottle of whiskey in her lap.

"Good morning, Molly," he said because he could think of nothing else.

"To hell it is," she said without looking up at him.

"Thought I might take a ride," he said, letting the dun keep walking and not wanting it to come to a conversation.

She said nothing to that and kept staring at something beyond and behind him. He looked back at the hotel and saw that Helvina was still in the window, her pale bare shoulders and the white of the sheet she had wrapped about her naked body easily visible from Molly's front door.

"I tried, Morgan, truly I did," Molly slurred so quietly that he could barely hear her. It was plain that she was dead drunk and hadn't slept all night. "But I couldn't compete against her, could I? Too much history."

"Best you get some sleep, Molly," Morgan said, finally bringing the dun to a stop.

"History, that's the undoing of all of us, isn't it?" she asked when he dismounted and helped her up out of the rocking chair. "All of us got a history that we can't get away from. Shapes us and bends us to its will whether we want it to or not, and we don't even know what it's doing to us."

She was so drunk that he practically had to carry her inside the tent to her bed. He was surprised at how light she was. She had always been a tad on the heavy side, not fat, but what some called buxom. But now he could feel the bones where he touched her shoulders, and he noticed for the first time how her cheeks were sunk and hollow.

"You leave Dixie alone. You hear me? He isn't like us. He isn't a killer like you," she mumbled.

He unlaced her shoes and tossed them aside and covered her with a blanket and made sure her feather pillow was under her head. He looked around the tiny room and was surprised by its disarray. She had always been a fastidious housekeeper and was picky about how everything looked, from her clothes to her sleeping quarters. But the tent was a mess. Two empty whiskey bottles stood on her dresser amidst a pile of cast-off dirty laundry slung there. A stack of old newspapers had fallen over and lay scattered across the floor, and from the way some of them were shredded he guessed that the mice had been in them. Her bed was unmade with the bedding rumpled and sweat-stained and smelling musty and in need of a good washing and airing out.

Molly was a good one, hard talking and hard living on the outside, but with a kind spot and sense for right and wrong just under the surface that she kept hidden from most. He recalled the cholera outbreak in Baxter Springs, many years before. Some said that Molly was nothing but a foul-mouthed, loud-talking Irish whore, but it had been her that had nursed him back to health when the doctor said it was no use and that he was as good as gone.

"She'll break your heart again if you let her," Molly murmured with her eyes closed. "Break your heart as sure as day."

"Shh," he whispered. "You go to sleep now."

Molly coughed and he saw the blood in the spittle on her chin. He dabbed at her lips with the edge of the blanket covering her.

"You're coughing blood, Molly," he said.

She didn't answer him. From the sound of her breathing she had gone to sleep.

He pulled the whiskey bottle from her grasp and set it on the little table beside her bed. And it was on that table that he saw the little bottle of opium tincture sitting there. It was half empty. He went to her dresser and opened the drawers, one by one. In all, he found three more such bottles, two empty and one unopened and full.

He turned back to her, and wondered how long she had been using the opium. He was familiar with laudanum and had known more than one person to get hooked on the stuff. Half the snake oil sold in the territory contained one form of poppy or another, and the few doctors to be found were liberal with the prescription of such derivatives for a wide variety of ailments. He wouldn't have suspected Molly of being a dope fiend. True that many a soiled dove and crib girl relied on the dope, but he had always assumed Molly was too strong and too full of good sense to play with the dangerous stuff.

But that blood on her lips probably had something to do

with it. He knew that Molly had secrets, same as he did, the same as everyone, but he wondered what else she had kept hidden from the world.

He snuffed the lamp that she had left burning and went out to his horse. He rode east towards North Fork Town, heavy with memories and with a thousand thoughts running through his mind. When he passed out of the edge of town, Helvina was gone from the window.

Dixie Rayburn's farm lay on a flat stretch of bottomland north of the fork where the North and South Canadian Rivers split apart, and across the river ford from the old trading settlement of North Fork Town that had been all but abandoned when the Katy laid its rails and the merchants moved to the new town of Eufaula a few miles to the west. The fire that had burned eastward from Eufaula had either spent itself or been put out before it reached that far.

Morgan hailed the little log cabin, but no one came to the door or answered, even though there was smoke coming from the stone chimney. He called again when he had ridden almost to the front door, and someone answered him from the field some distance away. Morgan looked there and saw his former policeman standing behind a single sorrel mule hitched to a plow. Morgan rode across the plowed furrows of loamy earth, feeling the heat radiated up from the freshly turned earth. It was going to be a hot, sultry day.

Dixie was as whipcord skinny as ever, and looked to be making hard work of breaking the new field from the sweat on him and the stooped way he stood with the mule's bridle reins looped over his neck and his hands on the plow handles.

"You still don't look like a farmer," Morgan said as he pulled up the dun.

Dixie took his Confederate forage cap off and swiped at the sweat on his face with the back of his forearm. He slapped the gray wool cap against his thigh to knock some of the dust off it and sat it back atop his head. "I reckon I'm making a fair hand."

Morgan looked at the furrows Dixie had managed so far. They were as crooked as they were shallow, and Morgan couldn't begin to imagine how difficult it was to break up the hard ground with nothing but a single mule.

"If I didn't know better I'd swear a drunk had tried to plow that," Morgan said.

Dixie frowned at the crooked furrows as if noticing them for the first time. His Deep South, Alabama accent was stronger than ever. "And I don't suppose you're going to get down off that horse and help me."

Morgan gestured back to the cabin and the trees shading it. "Too hot to work. Thought we'd set in the shade and have us a talk."

"Can't make a crop sitting in the shade," Dixie said. "Sweat and hard work is the seed that makes things grow. That's what my old daddy used to say. 'Course he never could grow much of anything, but there's truth in the saying, no matter what, I guess. Something to think on at the least."

"Well, you have the sweating part down." Morgan looked at the cabin again. "Has that well of yours got any water in it, or are you boiling river water and filtering the sand through your teeth?"

"Sweet and cool like the Lord's own nectar. Best well in the territory, if I do say so myself. Took me three months to dig it." Dixie unhitched the mule and they started across the field with him leading the animal and Morgan riding beside him. Morgan noticed that one of Dixie's boot soles was flopping and the tears and patches in his clothes, but kept his thoughts to himself.

Dixie gestured to the small stand of corn in front of the cabin. There were maybe two acres of neatly spaced rows, but instead of being green, the cornstalks were a sickly yellow and the leaves drooping and wilted.

"Thought my first crop was going to be a wing-dinger, but I'm going to lose it all if it doesn't rain," Dixie said. "Thought about digging a ditch from the river to irrigate that field, but I wore out both my shovels finishing that well."

In Morgan's opinion, the whole homestead looked little better than the corn patch. The closer they got to the cabin and little barn beside it, and the more Morgan looked around, the more he saw the chinks missing between the logs and the way the roof on both buildings sagged and leaned.

"It's not much, I know," Dixie said, as if reading Morgan's mind.

"I didn't know a white man could legally purchase land in the Nations." Morgan dismounted and loosened the dun's saddle cinch. "Doesn't squatting on tribal land make you worry about putting in all this work only to get it taken away from you sometime?"

"I worry all the time, but I'm not a squatter," Dixie said as he drew a bucket of well water and poured it into a wooden trough for the mule to drink. "I lease it from a Creek fellow. Pay him a yearly fee and five percent of any crops I make. It's all legal-like and on the up-and-up."

Morgan looked again at the pitiful stand of corn. "How's that working out for you?"

"I guess packing a badge has made you rich and you've ridden all the way here to rub it in that I'm not."

"No, I came to see if you were sick of farming yet, and to ask you to come work with me again."

Dixie pulled up another bucket of water with the well rope and looked at Morgan's badge. "Gone back to work for the Katy, huh? Thought you had sworn off them."

"Huffman talked me into it."

"He's a far cry from what Superintendent Duvall was, but I don't know that I'd trust any railroad man. Remember what happened the last time you went to work for that outfit. We're both lucky to be alive."

"The tracks are laid, and this isn't about taming tent towns."

"Then what's it about? Have those Sand Town boys held up the train? Some drunk Indian cutting telegraph wires?"

"I need your help."

"I told you I was through with that kind of work. It doesn't suit me anymore."

"You once told me that you never were cut out to be a farmer. Swore you would rather do anything than work another field."

"I changed my mind." Dixie took a tin dipper and dunked it in the bucket. He put it to his lips and sipped at the water while he watched Morgan closely.

Morgan sat down on the upturned end of a section of log that Dixie had cut for a chair beside the firepit in front of his cabin. Morgan guessed that it got too hot inside the cabin in the summer to cook in the fireplace.

"You're the only man I trust," Morgan said.

"You won't take no for an answer, will you?"

Morgan waved a hand at Dixie's ragged clothing, and

then at the run-down cabin and the rest of the shoddy farm. "You're a good lawman, Dixie Rayburn. What are you doing out here playing like a farmer? Have you looked in a mirror lately? You are as skinny as a snake."

"I've always been skinny."

"When's the last time you had a good meal?"

"I ate this morning."

Morgan played with the dun's bridle rein he held and thought about what best to say. In the end, he decided to tell Dixie all of it, and how he was working for the Secret Service as well as the Katy. And he told him about what had happened with Cumsey Bowlegs and the marshals.

"Lot Ingram, huh?" Dixie said as he took a seat on another of the logs across the firepit from Morgan. "You don't ever tackle the easy ones, do ya?"

"What do you know about him?"

"I've seen him once or twice. Other than that, I only know what they say."

"And what's that?"

"He came up from Texas and supposedly was a lawman down there, but I don't know that for a fact. I guess he went to riding for that carpetbagger judge not long after you quit the railroad and rode off west to go buffalo hunting." Dixie gave special emphasis to the mention of Morgan's hunting trip. He looked at the zebra dun, and then at the lightning brand on its hip. "Still riding that horse, I see."

"He's a good horse."

"Better than his former owner, I hope," Dixie said with the same sarcasm.

"What about Lot Ingram?" Morgan asked.

"He was one of those marshals that snooped around trying

to investigate Molly for the killing of that railroad foreman, Tubbs."

"Do you think Molly was really the one that did that?"

"You and I both know she did it."

Morgan remembered how Tubbs, an all-around despicable human being and henchman for the serial rapist and former railroad superintendent, Willis Duvall, had been found shot to pieces in an outhouse on the edge of the old tent camp at Ironhead. Many then had believed that Molly had killed Tubbs for some part he had played in her own rape and beating, along with the same horror suffered by one of her prostitute friends.

"Nobody's saying much, but I take it that the general consensus is that Lot Ingram is crooked," Morgan said.

"As crooked as they come. Usually rides with Clem Anderson and a scar-faced fellow, Brady Watson," Dixie said. "You could ask the Indians around here, but they won't speak to a white man. Too afraid Lot and that pack of marshals will come around in the night and have a talk with them."

"What's his game?"

"Who knows? Like you said, there's not many that will talk," Dixie stated.

"Take your best guess."

"He confiscating whiskey and selling it himself. Old Josh Grubtree is a neighbor of mine, and he told me that. Lot and the marshals beat Grubtree pretty bad, chopped up his whiskey still, and carried off his makings. Swore that if he told anyone that they'd come back and finish what they started," Dixie said. "Two weeks later, Grubtree, he sees one of those marshals unloading a case of his whiskey jars behind a tavern in Muskogee."

"What else?"

"Nothing firsthand, just stories." Dixie dug in the cold ashes of the firepit with a stick he had picked up. "I hear that one of Lot's games is to hold up trail herds coming up from Texas and claim he and his marshals are collecting tolls for the Indians for crossing their land. And I also hear that a while back he went around with a certain riverboat captain that was buying sawmill lumber along the Arkansas. Rumor is that that boat captain was some kin to Judge Story, and that Lot was along to threaten anyone against selling to other buyers."

"Hard to believe somebody hasn't called his hand by now," Morgan said.

"Hard to do with Judge Story sitting on the bench, and Lot's enemies have a way of disappearing."

"Got any names?"

"If there are bodies, I'd guess he's sunk them too deep to find." Dixie jabbed at the ashes again. "And then there's the belief by most in the territory that he's letting certain whiskey peddlers and saloons operate as long as he gets a cut of the action."

"Is Molly paying him?"

"I'm pretty sure she is, though she does her best to keep it on the sly," Dixie said. "But don't you tell Molly I said that."

"Molly told you that she's paying off the marshals?"

"No, but every time Lot shows up in Eufaula she bustles her customers out the back door and locks up her liquor cabinet. There's no way he doesn't know what she's doing, and I'd guess that's all an act so that he can say he didn't see anything."

"Do you think he's supplying her with confiscated booze?"

"I don't know. Molly's too honest for that, but maybe she doesn't have any choice in the matter."

"What makes you think the judge is in it with Lot, besides the story about the boat captain?"

"Let's just say that the judge has some peculiar rulings, and any lawyer in Fort Smith worth his salt will tell you that you had better be ready to line Story's pockets if you want to win in his court," Dixie said. "I'd say you're bucking a stacked deck, for sure."

"There are others working on Judge Story. It's my job to handle things out here."

"If Lot gets wind of what you're really after, you won't have to go looking for him. He'll come after you."

"That's why I need someone to watch my back."

As was his habit when he was pondering a thing, Dixie rubbed at one of his ears where the lobe of it had been shot off in the war. Morgan had been on the opposite side of the same battle that very day, and at times he wondered at what a strange world it was that two men who might have once killed each other could have found friendship later.

"I feel for you, Morgan, I really do, but I'm not your man. Not anymore. Lost my nerve for the business."

"You've got more nerve and pluck than anyone I ever worked with."

"I ain't you, Morgan. You're made for this, as surely as a plow is made for plowing, or a roof is made to cover our heads."

Morgan thought about Molly calling him a killer that very morning, and he wondered if Dixie had also come to have such a low opinion of him. He stood and tightened the dun's cinch. "Come find me if you change your mind."

Dixie watched Morgan mount. "No, I think I'll stay here and wait for it to rain."

Morgan looked at the sky. There wasn't a cloud in sight.

"Keep a lookout for Cumsey Bowlegs, will you?" Morgan asked. "Send word to me in Eufaula if he comes around or you hear of him."

"I will," Dixie answered. "But you ride careful. Cumsey's a proud one, and all the young toughs walk easy and wide around him. They say he's hell on wheels with a rifle, and doesn't back up for anybody."

"I'll mind your advice."

"And you keep Molly out of this as best you can. Look out for her."

"Molly is my friend, same as yours."

"Yeah, but you ain't good to her like you ought to be."

"What are you saying?"

"Don't take this wrong," Dixie said. "The Lord knows the territory needs those that will stand for what's right, but you don't always notice the casualties around you."

"Don't hold back."

"You said you wanted to talk. I was happy with my plowing," Dixie said. "Reckon I'll get back to it."

"You do that."

Dixie stood and went back to his water bucket. "Cumsey ain't the only one to watch out for. Deacon Fischer is still around. Last I saw of him he was helping Useless build the new church house."

"Oh yeah?"

The mention of the deacon gave Morgan pause, and Dixie noticed that. "The deacon tells everyone how he's reformed and has found the Lord again, but I don't know how much I'd set store by that if I was you. That's the trouble with your kind of work, Morgan. Things get all tangled until there ain't no end to it."

"Like you said, somebody's got to stand."

"You've had a good long run wearing that badge, but your success is your problem. You've made too many enemies and you don't know when to quit. I'm afraid that will get you in the end."

"Well, don't dig the grave for me, yet."

Dixie smiled and took up another dipper of water. "I've done told you, I wore out all my shovels digging this here well."

CHAPTER TEN

Lot Ingram sat his horse in the brush atop a hill overlooking North Fork Town and the river crossing beyond it. Like the other marshals with him, he and his horse were sweat-caked with soot and road dust from spending a night and a morning searching the burned-over river bottom for Cumsey Bowlegs's body, or any sign that he might have survived. Lot was a man who disliked camping, and spending a restless night with nothing but a thin blanket between him and the hard ground had put him in a foul mood, not to mention that they had failed to find any sign of Cumsey, dead or alive.

"What's that railroad detective up to?" The scar-faced marshal beside him, the one called Brady, pointed down the hill at the rider splashing across the rocky river shoal.

Lot squinted into the morning sun and tried to get a clearer look at Morgan Clyde, but the railroad detective was too far away to make out anything more than it was him. Lot had climbed the hill simply to get a better lay of the land while he thought about his next move, and he had stumbled across Clyde merely by chance. However, the sight of the man brought with it certain issues, and more than a bit of irritation.

"Now where has he been?" The question was only Lot thinking to himself, but he said it out loud.

"I bet he went over to Fisher Town to ask around about whether anyone saw Cumsey passing that way." Clem adjusted the set of his cavalry hat on his head and wallowed his tobacco chaw around in his cheek.

Fisher Town was what the locals called the little Creek settlement on the far bank of the North Canadian and directly across from North Fork Town. There had once been a store there, but that had closed up at the start of the war and never reopened. All that was left was a handful of poor homesteads clustered together along the side of the road.

Lot looked across the river again towards Fisher Town. "That skinny Rebel has got himself a farm over there."

"I remember seeing him," Brady said.

Clem nodded. "Wears himself a Johnny Reb cap."

Lot frowned at his partners. "That farmer used to be railroad police, same as Clyde."

"How do you know that?"

"I make it my business to know things."

Clem leaned from his saddle and splattered a nearby leaf with a stream of brown tobacco juice. "Do you still figure Cumsey told Clyde that it was us that hanged him?"

"It's likely," Lot said. "He was playing it cagey with us, but that's the only way he could play it with us having the numbers on him. I imagine he thought to sneak Cumsey past us when it came nightfall, and take him to Fort Smith like he said."

"What's it matter what Cumsey claims? It's his word against ours, and nobody is going to believe a horse thief. Not without witnesses," Clem said. "And besides, the judge ain't going to allow that kind of trouble for us, no ways."

"No witnesses?" Lot asked. "Haven't you listened to a thing I've said? Who's to say Clyde wasn't watching us from the brush and waited until we were gone before he came and cut Cumsey down?"

The mere mention of Cumsey Bowlegs brought Lot's temper to a slow, rolling boil. Perhaps hanging the half-breed had been a rash decision, but the only thing he truly regretted was not sticking around to make sure Cumsey was dead. He had warned the smart-ass whelp more than once to toe the line, but you just couldn't get through to some people.

Cumsey wasn't your average horse thief. The boy could steal your horse with you sitting in the saddle and never knowing he did it until he was already gone. He and the rest of that Sand Town bunch were moving lots of horseflesh, holding the stolen ponies in a series of brush corrals and out-of-the-way homesteads scattered over a wide swath of country, and driving them to market after brands had been altered or when the time was simply right. Stolen horses from Kansas might go to Texas, and stolen Texas horses might go to Missouri, Arkansas, or any of the other states bordering the territory, as long as the horses went somewhere where the odds of somebody recognizing them were slim. The territory was a virtual crossroads for such traffic in horseflesh.

Cumsey was brazen enough and quick enough to make it work, but the problem with him had always been that he was unwilling to play by any rules. And if there was one rule Lot insisted on, it was that any business that went on in the eastern third of the territory was his business, and he demanded a certain amount of respect in the form of a healthy cut of the profits. Not only did Cumsey refuse to pay up, but he spread the word among his outlaw friends that it would be a cold day in hell before he would kiss Lot Ingram's ass.

And then Cumsey had gone even further with his flagrant defiance and stole Lot's favorite horse from in front of a roadside tavern down in the Choctaw Nation while Lot was inside gathering a "donation to support local law enforcement" from the tavern's owner. The horse was an especially distinct-looking animal, being coal black and with a blaze face and white stockings on its hind legs. Lot heard later how Cumsey had ridden that horse straight to Boggy Depot and paraded it up and down the street so that all there could recognize whose horse he was riding, and then he had sold the animal for a third of what it was worth and spent the money buying drinks and telling everyone who would listen that Lot Ingram wasn't anything but an old fool and was going to have to walk himself back to Fort Smith and beg Judge Story to let him have another horse.

No, Lot didn't regret stringing up that sass-mouthed pecker-head, not one damned bit. You couldn't let that kind of thing slide, not if you wanted to keep your thumb on things. You let one get away with that, and before long nobody was paying you any mind. It was a matter of respect. Hanging Cumsey had been intended to show the territory what happened when you crossed Lot Ingram. Cumsey Bowlegs would have made a fine example if it hadn't been for that uppity-talking, Yankee railroad detective.

"Shit, I'll show you how to handle this." Brady shucked his rifle from his saddle boot. It was Winchester's latest production, Model 1873, chambered in .44-40, and it had once belonged to Cumsey. The three marshals had cut cards to see who got to keep the gun while Cumsey hanged from that sycamore tree choking and kicking.

"What do you think you're doing?" Lot asked.

Sweat was trickling down Brady's scar, and flushed with

heat, the jagged line of it had turned a brighter shade of red. He flipped up the rear tang sight, made some adjustment to the elevation settings, and hefted the rifle to his shoulder, squinting down the long octagonal barrel and aiming at Clyde.

"That's too damned far to hit anything," Lot said.

Morgan was caught on a wide-open stretch of ground where the road passed through a little prairie with no cover to either side of him except for a long ride to either the river or a course that would bring him straight up the hill toward them.

"You watch me." The long Winchester rifle bobbled and swayed as the marshal tried to find his aim. It was better than a two-hundred-yard shot, and offhand at that—a chancy proposition under any circumstances.

"You already missed him once," Lot said. He was still mad at Brady for taking a shot at Morgan the day before without his blessing. Brady was handy to have around when you needed the rough stuff, but he never was one to think things through.

"I done told you, I'd have plugged him then if that fire hadn't been crawling up my back and I couldn't see my sights good for the smoke," Brady said, still tinkering with his gun.

Lot watched Clyde coming nearer, with his horse at a walk and riding like he hadn't a care in the world. Not only did Clyde present a risk, Lot simply didn't like the man. It was a dislike he felt the instant they had met on the street in Eufaula. According to half the territory, Clyde was ten feet tall and bulletproof. Despite all the talk of the men Clyde had supposedly killed in the line of duty, and the claim by some that he had all but single-handedly saved the Katy's railroad trestle over the South Canadian and fought off the gang of Missouri bushwhackers who tried to rob the Katy payroll, Lot guessed that it was nothing more than just that—talk and exaggeration. What he saw of Clyde hadn't impressed him. There was an arrogance about the man, and Lot realized that was part of what bothered him so badly about Clyde. The stubborn, straitlaced act he could tolerate, but it was that arrogance that grated on him. Clyde was a lot like Cumsey Bowlegs. Neither of them understood respect.

Lot was of half a mind to let Brady pop Clyde. It would serve the bastard right for sticking his nose in somebody else's business. With him gone, Cumsey would be the only loose end left, and Cumsey wouldn't dare show his face to any kind of court or lawman to make an issue of a little rough treatment. There would be plenty of time to deal with the half-breed.

But nothing was ever as easy as it ought to be. Killing another lawman was risky business, and Clyde was railroad. The railroad had deep pockets and political clout, and there could be too many questions if one of them went missing. The judge stayed out of Lot's business, as long as he kept things quiet and careful and backed the judge when he needed it, but making trouble with the railroad wasn't exactly playing it careful.

Clem slid his own rifle from his saddle scabbard. "Ten dollars says I get him first."

"Like hell." Brady's scar puckered into a grin where he pressed his face to his rifle stock.

"Let him be," Lot said.

Both marshals took too long lowering their rifles to suit him, but they did it.

"We might not get a better chance." Clem worked the

tobacco plug and pointed down the hill at Clyde. "We roll his body in a hole and no more problem."

"Let him be for now." Lot started through the brush, angling down the hill to strike the wagon road far behind where Clyde had passed.

"Where the hell are you going?" they called after him.

"Thought we might ride over to Fisher Town and have a talk with that Rebel farmer," Lot said. "If there's another one working for the railroad, I want to know it."

CHAPTER ELEVEN

Dixie ate his last piece of bacon and sopped the grease from the skillet he had cooked it in with a stale chunk of corn bread. He looked at his mule standing under the shade tree and felt as tired as the mule looked. He walked to the well and drank another dipper of water, hoping to fill his stomach and stave off the hunger where his meager lunch hadn't quite managed. The unplowed field was still waiting for him to finish it, but the sun was already high overhead and the day was getting nothing but hotter.

He was still debating whether to go back to work or to take a nap in the shade when he saw the two riders coming around the end of his cornfield. He recognized Lot Ingram, and guessed the man with him was another of the marshals. They were a good hundred yards away and coming in no hurry, and Dixie went to the cabin and took down his pistol from its peg on the wall inside the front door. He untucked his shirt and stuffed the brass-framed Schneider and Glassick Navy revolver inside his waistband and covered it with his shirttail. He went back to his firepit and took a seat on one of the stump chairs and waited.

"Hello, there," Lot said when he and the other man pulled up their horses a few yards away.

The man with him had a scar down one side of his face, and Dixie presumed he was Brady Watson. His neighbor, Grubtree, claimed that Brady had gotten fired from a job hunting meat for the Union Pacific Railroad because he was taking potshots at any Indian he saw instead of buffalo, deer, and such. A man like him probably found the territory better to his liking and where he could take all the potshots he wanted and nobody to fire him.

Dixie's mule twisted around the post it was tied to and brayed loudly.

"Jimmy John, you be quiet now. Act like you've had company before," Dixie said to the mule.

"Must get lonely out this far," Lot said as he trickled tobacco into a cigarette paper. "Get many visitors?"

"Not so many, but I like it quiet."

"In my opinion, a man that's taken to talking to his mule is spending too much time alone." Lot finished the cigarette and struck a match on the cap of his saddle horn.

"How come you give that mule two names?" Brady asked. "You called him Jimmy John."

"Used to have a Jimmy and a John, but Jimmy took the colic and died on me," Dixie said. "Guess I was in such a habit of fussing at them I kept calling old John there by both their names."

"Speaking of company, you had any visitors today or yesterday evening?" Lot squinted through his cigarette smoke.

"No," Dixie lied. "I see folks passing on the road from time to time, but they rarely stop to talk."

"What about Cumsey Bowlegs? You know him?"

"Don't know him, but I've heard of him."

"You haven't seen him passing on the road, have you?"

"No, I ain't."

"How would you recognize him if you saw him on the road?" Brady asked. "You said you don't know him."

"Here now, Brady," Lot interrupted, "I'm sure this man is an honest citizen, and wants nothing more than to help us out."

"That's me, law and order every time," Dixie said.

"Thought that all along," Lot replied. "A smart man like you with a going farm wouldn't be likely to lie to the law, would he? I'd go hard on a man that I thought was being dishonest on purpose. Might suspect him of working with the other side. Lot of that around, folks giving shelter to miscreants and felons."

"Aiding and abetting," Brady chimed in with a smirk.

Dixie shrugged. "Like I said, law and order."

"Then you're sure nobody's been by here to see you this morning?" Lot asked. "'Cause I would have sworn I saw somebody crossing the river not a half hour ago. Would've sworn he had to have come right by your place."

Dixie had been on the other side of such questioning enough to know that Lot was asking questions he already had answers for. "Oh, you mean that fellow."

"Yeah, that fellow," Lot said. "You'd best do your plowing in the cool of the morning. I think the sun's messing with your memory."

"He only stopped by to water his horse."

"Water his horse? Odd that a man would go out of his way when that river is full of water."

"That well there is good sweet mineral water. Get you a dipper full if you don't believe me."

"I'm having trouble believing you, and that's a bothersome thing." Lot leaned over on his right forearm, resting it on his saddle horn, and held his cigarette out to one side of his face between his thumb and pointer finger. "How about we start all over and you tell me what that Katy detective wanted with you? Are you an informant for the railroad?"

Dixie couldn't see Lot's right hand the way it was hidden in his lap, but he didn't have to see it to know that Lot had hold of the pistol riding on his left hip. "I quit the railroad a long time ago. Come out here to mind my own business and to grow a little corn."

Lot glanced at the withered corn patch. "Man that doesn't farm any better than you do might could use a little extra money for watching who goes up and down the road and telling the right people."

"I'd tell the same to you for nothing, or any lawman for that matter."

"There you go lying again," Lot said. "You ain't the man I thought you to be. Not at all."

"I don't appreciate being called a liar." Dixie stood carefully, keeping watch on both marshals.

"My guess is that Clyde came by here asking about Cumsey Bowlegs."

"He asked, but I told him the same as I'm telling you. If Cumsey came by here, I didn't see him."

Lot jabbed the cigarette into the air to give emphasis. "There now. We're getting somewhere. What else did Clyde have to say?"

"Nothing much. He was scouting for any sign of Cumsey, just like you said. We palavered a little, you know, small talk and such."

"He knows," Brady said. "I don't see why we're fooling around with him. Clyde told him everything."

"I know what?" Dixie asked.

He turned half away from them and bent over like he was going to pick up his skillet or maybe put out his fire. Bent at his waist like he was with his shirttails flopping out gave him the cover to slip a hand inside his waistband and find the butt of his Confederate Navy.

"I wouldn't do that if I was you," a voice said from behind him.

Dixie cursed himself for not recognizing that his mule had been braying because it had seen somebody riding up from behind the cabin. Grubtree had said that where you found one of the trio of marshals the other two weren't far away.

Dixie let go of the pistol and turned to look behind him. A man in a cavalry hat was standing at the corner of his cabin with a Sharps carbine pointed at him. He guessed that one might be Clem Anderson.

"He's right unfriendly," Clem said.

"Not at all sociable," Lot answered.

When Dixie turned back to the other two he found one of Lot's pistols aimed at him. Brady Watson didn't even bother with pulling a gun. He only smirked like it was all fun and games.

"You better hope you've got the itch and not a pistol in your waistband," Lot said.

Dixie heard footsteps right before Clem jabbed the Sharps into his back.

"I think he was about to take a shot at you," Clem said behind him.

"A man that was law and order wouldn't be worried when peace officers come to visit. He wouldn't stash a hideout gun in his britches in case he needed it," Lot said. "The question is, what do you know that you think I ain't going to like?"

"I can make him talk." Brady slid a sheath knife from his belt. It was a long, wicked blade.

"I'd suggest you start talking before old Brady gets down from his horse and starts cutting," Lot said. "It might be that Clyde is saying things about us that we might want to know about."

Dixie knew that they would kill him if he told what he knew, the same as they would kill him if he didn't talk. "Go to hell."

The butt stock of Clem's Sharps carbine struck Dixie in the back of the head and knocked him into the firepit. He rolled from the hot ashes and coals and tried to scramble to his feet.

Brady got down from his horse and kicked Dixie to the ground before he could get his legs under him again.

"You better talk while you've got the tongue left to do it," Lot said. "What vile rumors has Clyde been spreading around about me?"

Dixie caught Brady's boot the second time the scar-faced marshal tried to kick him. He gave the leg a shove and Brady fell on his shoulder blades with the knife in his hand slashing wildly. Dixie avoided the blade and staggered upright. His vision was blurred and his head throbbed, but he recognized the blade coming at him again and caught Brady's wrist with one hand and drove a straight, hard punch into Brady's face with the other. He felt the marshal's nose crunch against his fist.

Dixie lunged at Clem on the other side of the firepit, reaching for the pistol in his waistband at the same time. Something slammed him in the belly. For an instant, his dazed mind thought that somehow Jimmy John had kicked him, but the mule was way over on the other side of the yard.

He lay on the ground with both hands clutched to his

belly, and he felt the hot, sticky blood oozing out between his fingers—his blood. He intended to get up, but somebody kicked him in the head.

"Scrappy bastard," Clem said as he worked the breech on his Sharps and pulled free an empty cartridge case.

Lot looked down at Dixie from his horse. "I would have appreciated you letting me finish talking to him before you shot him."

"He come at me," Clem said. "Besides, Clyde told him about what we did to Cumsey. It was as plain as day."

Brady was walking a circle, cursing and holding both hands to his bloody nose.

"You all right, Brady?" Lot asked.

To answer him, Brady went over and kicked Dixie in the ribs. Dixie didn't stir, even when Brady kicked him again.

"No telling who else Clyde is telling his stories to," Clem said. "You should have let Brady shoot him when we had the chance."

"Yeah?" Lot snarled.

"People are going to ask questions about this." Clem nodded at Dixie's body. "You and the judge are always saying to keep things simple. I'd say this is getting complicated. Are you intending for us to follow Clyde around killing everybody he talks to?" Lot studied Dixie and noted the amount of blood soaking into the ground. It appeared that the heavy, .50-70 round had made a mess of Dixie's belly.

"Cut his throat and throw him in the well," Lot said.

"Come on, Brady. Quit your cussing and give me a hand," Clem said as he strode over and took hold of one of Dixie's legs.

Brady lent a hand and they drug Dixie by his heels to the well while Lot untied the mule, unharnessed it, and shooed it off with a wave of his hat. He took a little notebook and pencil from his vest pocket and scrawled a quick note on it. He tore the page free and wedged it in a crack between the cabin's door planks.

The other two marshals had reached the well, and they let Dixie's legs thump against the ground while they caught their breath.

"What did you write?" Clem asked.

"Gone fishing," Lot said.

"Now that's a nice touch," Clem said, and then looked at Brady. "What are you waiting for? Cut his damned throat and be done with it."

Brady touched gently at his broken nose and looked back at his knife lying on the ground where Dixie had knocked him down. His eyes were already starting to swell as badly as his wounded nose. "You do it."

"To hell with it. Bastard's already half dead." Clem took hold of one of Dixie's arms and pulled him to a sitting position.

Brady let go of his nose long enough to help heave Dixie's body over the little rock wall surrounding the lip of the well. They heard the body splash and stood looking down into the black hole for a moment. The well was too deep and dark to make out its bottom.

"That ought to do him," Clem said.

Brady was already heading for his horse. He only stopped long enough to pick up his knife.

Clem took one last look down the well, then went to his own horse and mounted. Lot rode over from the cabin.

"What next?" Clem asked.

"I'm thinking we ought to ride up to Elk Creek," Lot said. "Cumsey has got an aunt up there in that darky settlement old Rentie has started."

"What about Clyde?"

Lot pulled up his horse and gave his partners a hard look. "Plenty of wells in the territory. I suspect we can find one to fit Clyde."

CHAPTER TWELVE

Morgan pulled the dun up and stared at the Vanderwagen Hotel. He had ridden a circle of better than forty miles, crossing the Katy tracks following the South Canadian's northern bank all the way to Choate Prairie and then back to Eufaula. He had questioned everyone he came across, mainly Choctaw and Creek farmers and stockmen, but like Dixie had warned him, most of the Indians seemed reluctant to talk to a white lawman and wouldn't admit to having seen Cumsey Bowlegs, even if they had.

The thought of a good hotel bed and a hot bath sounded better than ever, but he remained where he was. Helvina would be there, and he didn't know how to handle that.

He was thinking on the matter when the same young black woman that he had seen earlier with Molly walked across the dusty street a few yards in front of him. She was carrying some kind of bundle under one arm. Morgan watched her cut down the alley between the depot house and the general store next to it. He recalled Molly saying something about them fixing up the old powder shed where the Katy construction crew had once stored their explosives, and he assumed that's where the black woman was heading.

It was already growing dark, and he rode forward in the dusky gray light of evening until he reached the livery. He unsaddled and brushed down the dun, while the liveryman poured the horse a bucket of corn and saw to it that there was hay and fresh water in the stall.

Morgan stood in the open door of the livery barn watching the hotel. He could see the candles burning in that monstrous chandelier through the glass front doors. The only other lights showing in the town other than someone's home was the soft glow of lamplight visible through the canvas side of Molly's barbershop.

He crossed the street to the barbershop. The front room was dark with nobody about, but he could hear someone moving around in the back and that's where the light was coming from. When he pushed through the tarp wall that divided the two rooms he saw that Pork Chop was dealing a hand of poker at one table, and another group of men were telling stories and drinking beer at the other table. Molly stood behind the little countertop that served as her bar and gave him a look that he couldn't quite read other than she was mad at him.

Once offended, Molly could dwell on a thing for days or even weeks. He dreaded having to talk to her almost as much as he dreaded going to his hotel room, but he wanted a drink badly, and he wanted time to think. He doubted Molly would give him peace and quiet, but he was sure she would sell him a glass of whiskey.

She didn't ask him what he wanted, and took a bottle of Old Reserve out of the cabinet behind her and poured him two fingers in a glass and set it on the bar. He took a healthy drink of the bourbon, and the warm bite of it going down his throat was a pleasant distraction from the way Molly stared at him.

"I suppose you went and saw Dixie," she finally said.

"I did." He turned up the glass a second time.

"And what did he say?"

"Nothing much."

"Did you talk him into helping you?"

"No, he seems pretty content to starve himself to death out on that farm of his."

"Don't you belittle him. He's making a start. Takes a while, and you damned well know it."

He finished the whiskey and held up a hand to her as a peace offering. "I swear, I'd think you two had been sparking each other if I didn't know better. I say one thing about either of you and the other jumps on me with both boots."

He saw Molly's expression change from anger to something resembling embarrassment. "Has Dixie been sparking you?"

She scoffed and waved him off. She left the bar for a while and made a show of pretending to watch Pork Chop's poker game and checking to see if anyone needed a refill. He chuckled to himself and couldn't help but grin when she came back.

"What are you grinning about?" she asked.

"How long has Dixie been sweet on you?"

She waved him off again and poured herself a drink.

"I imagine Dixie's lonely out there on that farm. A good wife might be just what he needs."

The almost bashful way she had been acting disappeared and she gave him another of her hard stares. "And what would Dixie want with a woman like me?"

"Don't talk like that. You're the one who convinced Dixie

to try this farming thing," he said. "Oh yes, he told me all about your speeches when he quit his policeman's job. Told me all about beating swords into plow shares and fresh starts. You could make one, too."

"And you wouldn't care at all?"

"Care? I think you would make a handsome couple."

He could always tell when Molly was getting really mad, and right then her face was flushing red. "You would, wouldn't you?"

"I would what?"

"Never mind."

"You could do worse than Dixie Rayburn. He's as good a man as I know."

"You don't have to tell me that. I can count the number of good men I've known on one hand."

Morgan nodded to appease her.

"And don't you stand there nodding your head and acting like you're one of them, 'cause you aren't."

"I wouldn't have brought up the matter if I had known you were so touchy about it."

"Dixie and I are friends, nothing more," she said. "He gets puppy dog eyes for any woman that will pay him a little attention."

"Uh-huh."

"I'm not the marrying kind, and I've never given him any reason to think otherwise." She downed her whiskey in a single swallow and started to pour them both another round.

He covered his glass with his hand. "I believe I'll pass, and you should, too."

"And now I suppose you're going to tell me I drink too much."

"You didn't used to."

"What would you know about what I used to do? I've been every kind of bad a girl can be from here to County Kerry and back again, and getting drunk is the least of them by far."

"You're still a young woman. You ought to take care of yourself."

"I got here on my back, and I'll go out the same. None of us can do any different in the end."

"I would have thought you would have given up that act long ago, Molly. You don't have to prove to me how tough you are. I know."

She poured herself another drink to spite him, and slopped a good bit of it down the sides of the glass and onto the bar. He didn't stay to watch her drink it and went out the back door into the night. He heard her coughing through the thin walls as he was leaving.

He went back to the livery and checked on the dun, and then he stood leaning against one of the corral posts outside the barn while he smoked half of a cigar. He finally rubbed out the cigar and went up the street to the hotel.

The hotel clerk and a drummer were the only ones in the lobby when he entered. He nodded to the clerk, who frowned back at him. Morgan looked around the lobby again.

The clerk cleared his throat and adjusted his necktie. The boy had a snooty way about him, no doubt why Helvina liked him enough to hire him.

"If you are looking for Ms. Vanderwagen, I'm afraid she's gone away to Kansas City on business," the clerk said.

"I thought the place had a more pleasant feel, but I couldn't put my finger on it until now." Morgan gave a tip of his hat brim and left the clerk frowning at his back as he went up the stairs to his room.

The maid, despite Morgan's instructions, had gone ahead and poured his bath during his absence. Morgan dipped a hand in the water and found it had long since gone cold. He shrugged, locked the door, closed the curtains, and hung his pistol belt on the bedstead before he stripped and settled into the tub.

The water felt good once his body adjusted to it, and he leaned back against the high porcelain backrest and closed his eyes. He considered relighting his cigar while he soaked, but the thought was short-lived and he soon fell asleep. As it was, he never heard the three horsemen passing by beneath his window on the way to Molly's barbershop.

CHAPTER THIRTEEN

It was well after midnight when the last of Molly's customers finally left. She had locked the front door and blown out almost all of the lights in the back room when she heard horses outside.

"I'm closed," she called out to whoever was outside.

She heard the clank of spurs and some rough laughter, and then Lot Ingram came through the back door followed by the other two marshals. The three of them took chairs at the nearest table.

"I said I'm closed." Molly was tired and half drunk, and she was scared. Noodles closed the barbershop down every day at five o'clock, and Pork Chop had gone off somewhere else when the cards weren't running his way.

"Well, you're open now," Lot said. "Bring us a bottle."

Molly went behind the bar and glanced down at her pearl-handled pistol the way she did every time Lot came around.

"Hurry up," Lot said.

She took a bottle of her cheapest whiskey from the liquor cabinet. It was from a case she had bought off a local peddler, and it was so bad she never bought another from him.

She took the bottle and three glasses and carried them to

the marshals. Lot jerked the bottle from her hand as soon as she came within reach. He gave the label a look, and she immediately regretted not getting him the best whiskey she had in her cabinet. But he simply gave a grunt and uncorked the bottle and poured his glass full. He grimaced when he took the first drink, but smacked his lips once when the taste had passed and took another swallow.

"That's got a bite to it," he said as he poured himself a second glass and then slid the bottle across the table to the other two.

Maybe it was a petty little victory watching Lot and his men drinking the awful whiskey, but it was a victory, nonetheless, and it was all she could do to keep from smiling. She started back to the bar, but Lot reached out and blocked her way with his arm.

"Sit with us a spell." He reached under the table with one leg and shoved a chair out for her.

Molly took a seat and folded her hands in her lap. The other two marshals were watching her, and her skin crawled under their gaze.

"Have a drink." Clem pushed the bottle her way.

"It's late." Molly tried to appear calm, and to give no offense with her tone or her bearing.

"Now that's no way to be when you've got company." Lot looked at her over his whiskey glass and his eyes were shining and his face was flushed. It wasn't an especially hot night, and she assumed that they had been drinking even before they arrived.

"She thinks she's too good for us," Clem said. He seemed the drunkest of the three of them.

Lot laughed at that, and so did Clem. Brady didn't laugh and only glared at her. He seemed in a bad mood, and it probably had a lot to do with his nose. It was swollen so badly that the swelling had gone to his face and left him nothing but slits to see out of. His chin was crusted with dried blood. She tried not to stare at his battered nose or his scar.

"One thing I hate is an uppity whore," Clem added.

"Drink," Lot said in a way that left her no doubt that she had any choice in the matter.

She started to go get another drinking glass from the bar, but Clem reached over and grabbed Brady's glass and slid it to her.

"Use his. He ain't drinking, no ways," he said.

Brady muttered something to him, but it was almost unintelligible with his nose swollen so badly and with the way he had to breathe through his mouth.

Molly poured a little whiskey in the glass, but Lot took hold of her wrist and forced her to fill it to the rim. He then let go of her and leaned back and made a show of waiting.

She sipped at the whiskey and had barely set the glass down when the raspy tickle in her chest overcame her and she gave a cough. Clem slapped the tabletop and gave a little hoot, and Lot smiled wickedly. They thought the cheap whiskey had been too strong for her, and she was willing to let them think that.

"There now, that's better," Lot said. "All friends here."

"What do you want, Lot?" Molly asked.

"Want? Why, nothing but to have a drink with my business partner." Lot looked around at the peanut hulls on the floor and the stack of empty beer bottles scattered on one of the other tables. "Looks like you had a busy night."

"Not too busy, just the usual crowd."

He took the bottle again and poured himself another glassful. "I think you could do better."

"How's that?"

"I don't know, maybe hire you some girls. Put in a few cribs out back at the edge of the woods. You know, rev the place up a little," he said.

"I told you I'm retired from that game."

"Oh, you wouldn't have to manage the ladies. Me and the boys here will do the collecting," he said. "You'd sell a few more drinks and make a few more dollars, and that means I make a few more dollars."

He wasn't asking her permission. She could tell by the way he gloated. Lot was big and he was tough, but he was petty.

"I don't recall this being a partnership," she said after she had time to gather her composure. "And I've paid my fees every month."

"True, true, but times are changing and I've decided to expand my operations."

"Why me?"

"'Cause you're my whore, and it so happens that you're the best-known slut between here and Texas. Word gets out that you're running sporting girls and it's bound to be profitable."

"And what if I say no?"

"Then I'd have to bring in somebody else to run this place, and you wouldn't like that much."

Clem chuckled and slopped whiskey on his shirt, but Brady only stared at her.

"Tell him to quit looking at me like that," she said.

"Tell him yourself," Lot replied.

She had already said too much and wasn't about to add to her troubles, but it was already too late. Brady reached across the table and grabbed her by the front of her dress. One hard yank, and he pulled her across the table until his face was only inches from hers and she could smell the stink of his breath.

"You uppity bitch." He whipped a knife from under the table and pressed the blade to her throat. "Go ahead, scream, and I'll cut you so that you don't ever so much as squeak again."

His grip was so tight on her dress that he was cutting off her air, but to struggle meant the sharp edge of the knife kissing her throat would cut her.

"Easy there, Brady," Lot said.

Brady didn't let go of her, but he did remove the knife from her throat. She tried to get her fingers inside her collar but he kept it twisted in his fist too tightly. Her legs kicked frantically and knocked over the whiskey bottle. Lot and Clem pushed back from the table, enjoying the show.

Brady gave another yank and pulled her the rest of the way across the table. Before she could strike at him he shoved her onto her back and shifted his hold to one of her ankles. The cold steel of the knife blade touched her inner thigh, and she went still again.

"I think she likes that," Clem said.

Lot went over to the bar to get another bottle of whiskey. She tilted her head back and saw him standing there with his back to her and the terror of what she thought that meant sent a shiver throughout her body.

Brady pushed up her dress and drug the blade farther up the inside of her leg. He did it in stops and starts, pushing her dress up until it was almost to her hips. She didn't look at him, but she could hear him breathing through his mouth.

"That's enough," Lot said.

Brady looked up at Lot and the knife lifted from her leg for an instant. She took that moment to kick out at him with her free leg, and struck him full in the chest. The blow wasn't a strong one, but it did break his hold and shove him back in his chair. She rolled to her belly, and the table tipped over and dumped her to the floor.

She scrambled across the floor on hands and knees, but stopped when Lot put a boot sole to her forehead and shoved her against the base of the bar. She pressed her back against it and looked frantically for anything she could lay hand to that might serve as a weapon, fully expecting them to try and finish whatever they had started.

However, Clem and Brady seemed content to remain on the far side of the room, and Lot was putting the stopper back in his whiskey bottle.

"You brought this on yourself, Molly," Lot said.

"You pox-ridden son of a bitch," she spat at him.

Lot continued like he hadn't heard her. "Bothers me that you won't be reasonable. Bothers me to see a woman abused."

Molly pushed to her feet and slung her mane of red hair back from her face. All she had to do was reach over the bar and under it. Her pistol was right there.

"We've got us a good business arrangement here," Lot said. "And it's going to get better. You play by the rules and me and the boys won't have to come back here and let Brady finish with his knife."

He pitched the bottle he held across the room to Clem, and then reached across the bar and took two more from the cabinet. "You find us some doves and have a crew get started on a few little cabins for them. I expect it shouldn't take you a month or two to be operational."

Molly's breath was coming too raggedly to answer him.

"Say it," Lot stepped closer to her. "Let me hear you say it."

"All right," was all she could manage in a whisper.

"All right what?"

"All right, I'll do as you say."

"That's better," Lot said. "There's only one more thing."

She didn't ask.

"I understand you know that railroad detective, Morgan Clyde," he said. "Might be that the next time I come back here I'll ask you to set me up a meeting with him. You know, make up some excuse to get him somewhere out of the way and private for me."

"He won't listen to me," she gasped.

"You'll do like I say. Nod your head so I know you'll do it.

Molly nodded and hated herself for it.

Lot went past her headed to the door with the other two marshals following him. She lurched over the bar and coughed until her eyes watered, groping for the pistol and fighting the weakness in her legs. She fell to the floor clutching the little nickel-plated revolver, and her head swam like the whole world was spinning too fast. She held the pistol tightly to her chest, afraid she would drop it. And she didn't let go of it until the sound of the marshals' horses was gone from her ears.

CHAPTER FOURTEEN

Dixie was vaguely aware of the marshals dragging him along the ground and hoisting him above the lip of the well, and then he felt the awful sensation of falling and tumbling helplessly down into the darkness. He groped wildly for something to lay hand to but found nothing to break his descent. The shock of the cold water startled him even more, and then he was floating weightless in the inky black. He tried to cry out, but only managed to suck water into his lungs. He kicked and waved his arms about trying to find the surface.

Amidst his panic, his feet found the bottom, and he launched himself upwards until his head broke free of the water and he sucked in a great gulp of air. The diameter of the well was narrow enough that he could hold himself up by bracing his feet and back against the muddy wall. He remained like that, clutching his wound, and listening to the marshals talking to each other above him. The little circle of sky above him seemed miles away.

He had no clue how long he waited. His body trembled under the strain, but he feared to drop back in the water. Either the blow to his head or the bullet wound to his gut had left him weak to the point that he couldn't be sure he wouldn't drown, and the thought of going back down into that black water almost made him beg for help.

The voices above him sounded no more, and yet he waited, watching that circle of blue sky above him and expecting to see one of the marshals suddenly peering down at him to find that he was still alive.

Eventually, he could hold his position no longer. First a foot slipped on the wall, and then he was sliding beneath the surface once more. He willed himself to remain calm, and was surprised at how quickly his feet touched bottom again. Usually the well held at least twelve feet of water, but he found he could stand on the bottom and keep his face out of the water if he tilted his face back and stood on his tiptoes. The unusually meager spring rains and summer drought had dropped the water table farther than he had realized, and it had only been his blind panic when first falling down the well that had made its depths seem endless.

When he was sure the marshals were gone, he wedged himself against the mud walls again, keeping his back pressed into the earth by the extension and force of his legs. The well was only twenty feet deep. He knew it to the last inch, for he had dug every bit of it by hand, measuring its depth at the end of each day's work to gauge his progress. But looking upwards, the distance seemed much greater. His efforts before had left him exhausted, and his wounds made it hard to concentrate.

He started working his way up the wall a little bit at a time. Even above the waterline where the mud ended, the wall was damp and slick with algae and slime, and where it wasn't slick, the dirt was apt to crumble and break away. It took the right amount of pressure to allow his back to slide up the wall and then to walk his feet up to gain another purchase. Twice he fell to the water and had to start again, and with each attempt he felt his strength waning.

He found a hump in the bottom that he could stand on and not have to tiptoe to keep his head above water. He leaned his head back against the wall and closed his eyes, hoping to rest before attempting the climb again.

The longer he stood there, the less important escaping seemed. His mind refused to focus where he wanted it to, and the urge to rest and relax all but overwhelmed him. When he began to shiver he knew that he must make it out of the well on the next try, or remain there forever.

Once more, he wedged his back against the wall and began crabbing his way upwards. He almost lost his purchase several times, but recovered. No more than a body length away from the rim, he stopped. His heart thudded in his chest and his legs trembled with fatigue. The wound to his abdomen felt as if it were tearing him in two each time he made the slightest movement.

He heaved again with his teeth gritted, and slid up ever closer to the rim. He walked his feet up to place himself closer to horizontal and heaved upwards until he could reach up and catch the lip of the stone wall. Another heave, and he had gone as far as he could go in that fashion, suspended over the well like a spider with all four limbs splayed about to keep him there.

Arching his belly upwards in a painful thrust, he pivoted to one side and grabbed with the opposite hand at the rock wall. At the same time, he threw a leg over the wall and rolled with a sudden lunge to the side. He sobbed with relief when he tumbled to the ground.

Wet and coated in slime and mud, and exhausted and

weak from his wounds, he lay with the hot sun hitting him in the face and the heat from the ground baking through his wet clothes. A furnace breeze blew through the corn patch and rustled the dry, brown leaves, and he closed his eyes and said a prayer of thanks that he hadn't said in a long, long time.

Whether from adrenaline or his last bit of energy, he managed to prop his back against the well in a sitting position and raised his shirt to examine his bullet wound. There was a knot the size of his fist over his belly button, and a ragged bloody gouge worked its way from the contusion and around his side, as if the bullet had bounced off him where it struck and skidded along his flesh like a flat stone thrown and skipped across a pool of water. And then what had happened dawned on him, and he said another prayer of thanks.

The pistol he had been wearing had slipped from his waistband during his initial struggles at the bottom of the well, but it was plain that the heavy, but soft lead bullet had struck the frame of the pistol and deflected to one side, leaving him an ugly gouge instead of blowing a hole through him. It was the only explanation, no matter how miraculous.

The rip in his side was bleeding, but only slowly, and he took off his shirt and wrapped it around his waist and tied it tight to form a makeshift pressure bandage. He rose and started across the yard in an unsteady stride towards his cabin. He crumbled the note left on his door in his fist before he stumbled inside. He still held the crumpled bit of paper long after he fell onto his bed and went to sleep.

CHAPTER FIFTEEN

Cumsey lay on his back in the dimly lit room with his hands laced behind his head, and liking the feel of the soft, corn-shuck mattress and the breeze coming through the open window and tickling his bare skin. The woman lying against his side squirmed in the tangled sheets and rolled over and flopped an arm and a leg across him. He had tried to wake her twice to talk, but each time she only grunted and tossed a little until he left her alone. Her skin was dark and beautiful, a rich, deep shade of brown shining with the sweat of their recent lovemaking. Tendrils of tight curls had come unbound from her braided hair and were soft against his chin.

"Don't you ever sleep?" she murmured into his chest.

"Too much on my mind to sleep," he replied.

"At least be still. Some of us have to work today."

He ran a palm down the smooth skin above her hip bone and readjusted his shoulders against the mattress until he was more comfortable. He looked around the tiny room, and the walls felt like they were closer than ever. Somebody had added two glass windows and a coat of paint to the plank walls, but it was still a shack barely big enough to sleep in.

Two nights and a day of hiding out there had left him restless and talkative.

"I can't take it anymore," he said.

She gave another little grunt and rolled over on her belly to look at him with her weight resting on her elbows. "You can, and you will. I saw Clyde yesterday evening when I was coming home from work."

"What about Lot Ingram?"

"I haven't seen him, but he wants you bad. Best thing you can do is lay low until he gives up on finding you."

"I bet that Lot is madder than a rutting bull, ain't he?"

"Lucky they didn't burn down the town looking for you."

He liked how even and white her teeth were when she smiled, and he liked the sharp cut of her cheekbones and that pointy little chin. But it was her eyes he liked most, big and full and brown with thick, dark lashes that batted like a moth's wings every time she blinked. He liked women of all kinds, but she was no doubt the prettiest woman he had ever seen. He had known it the first time he saw her doing laundry down at the creek.

"I fooled them, didn't I?" he said.

"You fooled them? All by yourself?" She gave a huff and sat up in the bed, still looking at him.

"Well, you might have helped some." He ran a lazy finger between her breasts, and she shoved his hand away.

"Some? Who's been bringing you food and keeping a lookout for you?"

He reached out for her, but she swung her legs off the bed and turned her back on him.

"Hannah, you come back here."

"You're a frustrating man. I should have known it when

you first started coming around, talking all that fool talk and strutting like a barnyard rooster."

He grabbed her around the waist and pulled her to him. "It worked, didn't it? You must have liked my fool talk."

She pretended like she was going to pull away, but he kept her close.

"You stay here," she said. "You stay here until I tell you it's safe to come out. You promise me."

He pressed his face to the nape of her neck, and liked the way she smelled, sweaty but feminine sweet—woman smell. "Promise you what?"

"That you won't leave here until I tell you it's safe."

"That's what I've been doing, ain't it?"

"You promise me you won't go after Lot Ingram for what he did to you."

"I won't go at it foolish like, but I'm going to get even with him first chance I get."

"You get even with him by staying alive." She twisted away from him and began to put on her dress. "You get even by leaving here and going some place where he and his kind can't find you."

He shoved himself back until he could use the wall for a backrest, and reached for his cigarette makings on the crate that served as a bedside table.

"You don't smoke in here," she said. "I've already told you that. When this is over, you can go outside and smoke, but until then you'll mind your manners and do without."

She was a real stickler for manners, a thing that tickled him. And she talked smart, used big words, and she had more book learning than he had gotten in his years going off and on to the missionary school. He liked a woman he could talk to, even if sometimes she was stubborn and apt to corner him with her wit.

"Lot Ingram and those other two, they strung me up by my neck. Do you know what that's like?" he said. "Ain't but one way to make that right."

She sat on the edge of the bed to lace her shoes, but stopped before she was finished. "There's more ways of vengeance than killing a man. You already struck Lot the worst blow when you got away from him. Everyone's talking about it."

He started to argue with her, but then what she said gave him pause.

She saw the look on his face, sensed some advantage, and continued. "You made Lot look silly, and that's the worst thing for a proud man. He's looked for you high and low, but here you are right under his nose."

Cumsey smiled. It had been a neat trick, maybe one of the best he had ever pulled. Instead of running, he had started working his way towards the old powder shack that Hannah lived in as soon as he had struck the brush at the edge of town. While Lot and the other marshals were searching the thickets for him, he had been crawling up a ditch leading to a drainage culvert that ran beneath the tracks. Not one of them had suspected him to be out in the wide open with nothing to hide him except that shallow ditch and a little tall grass. Lot and his bunch had ridden within a few feet of him several times while going to and fro in their hunt. He had lain under the tracks until it became dark enough for him to sneak to Hannah's shack, and he had been there ever since.

"Everyone's talking about how you got away," she repeated.

"What are they saying?"

"They're saying that maybe Lot's getting too old for the job and losing his edge, and how nobody's as slick and cunning as Cumsey Bowlegs."

He knew that she was intentionally flattering him to keep him in the shack, but he enjoyed it, anyway. "Reminds me of the time I stole Lot's horse down at Boggy Depot. Everyone laughed at him then, too."

"I bet they did," she said. "Like I said, you don't have to kill a man to get the best of him."

Cumsey gave her a lazy smile. "Maybe you're right, the more I think on it."

"First thing you should have learned is that I'm always right," she said as she finished tying her shoes. "I'll bring you some lunch if I can."

She stood and went to the little square of mirror she had tacked to the wall and brushed out her hair and braided it into a tight knot at the back of her head. He saw her glance at him several times while she worked at her hair, and he smiled back at her.

She turned to him again. "What are you smiling about?"

"I'm smiling at you, and I'm smiling about what I'm going to do to Lot."

She came to the edge of the bed and stood over him. "What are you going to do?"

"I'm going to steal his horse again. I'm going to steal it right out in the broad daylight, and then I'm going to follow him everywhere he goes and steal more horses from him. I'm going to steal from him until he's too ashamed to show his face anywhere in the territory. I'm going to break him hard like a stubborn old mule, until nobody's scared of him anymore."

"That's not what I meant, you fool."

"Maybe not, but you gave me the idea."

"That's the most foolish thing I've ever heard."

He took her by the hand and looked up at her with another sleepy smile. "Marry me, Hannah Cole. Say you'll marry me when this is over."

"Marry you?" she scoffed.

"Say yes."

"You're nothing but a silly-talking horse thief with every lawman in the territory looking for you, and probably not a single dollar to your name. What makes you think I'd marry you?"

"Marry me for love."

She pulled her hand away and went to the door before turning back to him. "I've already been widowed once, Cumsey. When and if I marry again, it won't be to a man that's as likely for a hanging as he is to make a good husband."

"You know I love you."

"You haven't even known me but a few weeks."

"And I figure you love me, too, or you wouldn't be hiding me and letting me sleep in your bed."

"You're a fool, Cumsey Bowlegs, a stupid crazy fool. Now you quit that talk, and let's start thinking about how we're going to get you out of here."

She went out and shut the door behind her, but not quickly enough for him not to see her wiping at the corners of her eyes and the little smile on her mouth.

He went to one of the windows and looked along the tracks at what he could see of the town. He couldn't see much from his narrow vantage point, and it bothered him that Lot might arrive in town without his knowing. Waiting was hard, but waiting was what he was going to have to do—

wait like an old panther cat up on a high limb for a plump little deer to come moseying under him. For the next time Lot Ingram showed up, he was going to find himself short of another horse.

He paced the room and reminded himself that patience was what it was going to take. But the more he thought about it, the more he decided that it was liable to be a while before Lot returned. It didn't make much sense being cooped up in the tiny shack for no good reason. And he had been thinking about a good sip of whiskey since he woke up, and a pal or two to talk to would help pass the time. It wouldn't hurt to slip out for a bit as long as he was careful. Hannah would be mad when she returned and found him gone, but he could likely get back in a day or two. There would be plenty of time to make it up to her, and there would be plenty of time to pull his trick on Lot.

He dressed and took up the Winchester he had taken from Morgan Clyde, and then slipped out the door. He pulled his hat brim down low over his face, and skirted the edge of town headed towards the train tracks. He was short of a horse to take him anywhere, but he could hear a train coming up from the south. He would have preferred a horse, and it had been his intention to steal the first one he came across, but a train would do fine. It wouldn't be much of a trick to sneak into one of the boxcars, but a man couldn't be exceptional all of the time.

CHAPTER SIXTEEN

Morgan went to the depot to check the next northbound train's arrival time. He was on his way back to the hotel to retrieve his saddlebags when he saw Molly going from her cabin to the back of the barbershop. He waved at her, but she seemed in too big of a hurry to notice him. While it wasn't unusual for Molly to be in a fizz, it was unusual to see her up and at it so early. It was less than an hour after sunrise, and the late hours a woman in her profession kept usually made her a late sleeper.

He was too busy watching Molly and almost ran into the black woman he had seen the evening before. She was going at nearly as quick of a pace as Molly had been, and seemed equally distracted.

"Pardon me," he said as they brushed shoulders and he caught her to help with her balance.

"Sorry, I must have been daydreaming," she said.

"Morgan Clyde." He gave a tip of his hat brim.

She gave him a look that seemed a little dazed but took his hand. "Glad to meet you, Mr. Clyde. I'm Hannah Cole."

"I hear you're a schoolteacher, Miss Hannah."

She looked behind her, and then to either side of him, as

if she felt he was keeping her where she didn't want to be, and he wondered what kind of stories she might have heard about him to make her nervous.

"I've never had a teaching job, not yet," she said. "But yes, I've been trained to teach. Three years at the Freedman School at Quindaro, Kansas."

"That's fine, fine indeed. The territory could use more teachers, and more schoolhouses for that matter. The Indians have some fine boarding schools, and there's a few more run as church missions, but they're scattered too thinly."

Hannah seemed to have regained her composure a little. "Molly tells me that you yourself are an educated man."

He stood a little straighter and lifted his chin to a snooty angle. "Yale, Class of '52."

She laughed. "Impressive."

"Not so much. Some of the most educated people I've met never set foot on a university campus, but they were well read and experienced, and they had the questioning kind of mind that wants to learn from everything."

She took a deep breath. "I want to thank you, Mr. Clyde."

"Thank me for what?"

"I understand you did for the one that killed my Saul," she said. "I never got a chance to offer my appreciation."

"I only wish I had caught that man sooner," he said. "I thought a lot of Saul, and it pained me greatly to learn of his passing."

During the manhunt that had followed Saul's murder, he and Dixie had been the ones to come across the Hilltopper, a giant of a man and a violent thug who had worked as a strong-arm and killer-for-hire for Molly's old saloon boss, Bill Tuck. Morgan had done things that haunted him but putting a load of buckshot in the Hilltopper's face wasn't one of them.

"Where are you off to so early in the morning?" she asked.

"As soon as the train gets here I'm taking it to Muskogee," he answered. "I saw a few stores there and thought I might replace a rifle I recently lost."

"Are you coming back?" she asked. "Here, I mean."

"I plan to catch the next train back after I've tended to my business there. Why do you ask?"

"Oh, no reason." She made a show of studying his frock coat. "Only, I was thinking that fancy coat of yours could use a good brushing and maybe a spot cleaning. I could do that for you. Mrs. Bickford and I have a laundry business."

"It could use a little attention." He shrugged out of the coat and handed it to her. "I'll pick it up when I get back."

He could hear the train coming up from the south.

"Are you still hunting that horse thief?" she asked before he could move on.

"Do you mean Cumsey Bowlegs?"

"That's him."

"Yes, I'm still hunting him. You haven't seen him, have you?"

"Me?" she exclaimed. "Goodness no, and I hope I don't. It's hard to sleep at night worrying about the likes of him around."

"I imagine he's long gone by now."

"I heard those marshals hanged him."

"Did Molly tell you that?"

She took a step back from him, and he noticed she had her lower lip clenched between her front teeth. "She wasn't supposed to tell me, was she?"

"It's all right, but I must ask you not to spread that around. Talk to Molly and she'll explain it all, but I can't stress how important it is. You hear me?"

"I won't tell a soul."

He tipped his hat to her and started for the hotel. Already, the finger of coal smoke from the locomotive was visible over the tree line south of town.

He went quickly to his hotel room. He didn't plan to be gone long, hopefully returning by the evening or the next morning at the latest, and he decided to leave his saddlebags and his bedroll in the room's closet. He made an overnight kit by wrapping a small towel around a bar of soap and his toothbrush and stuffed the small package into his vest pocket before he went back down the stairs to the lobby.

The clerk was waiting for him with the same snooty half-frown as always. "Will you be checking out, Mr. Clyde?"

"Keep my room for me. I should return tonight, or tomorrow at the latest."

"I take it so far that you've found your stay with us enjoyable?" the clerk said as he went behind his register. As with everything the clerk said, the question was loaded with blatant innuendo and sneering hints.

Morgan glanced up the stairs the way he had come, and his face wrinkled for a moment in reflection before he gave a wry smile. "You might call it entertaining."

The clerk gave a little grunt and made a show of checking his register book.

"How much do I owe you for my two nights' stay?" Morgan asked. "I'd be more than happy to pay my bill now if that's what's worrying you, but the train's here and I need to board soon."

"Your stay is on the house," said the clerk. "That's how they usually say it out here, isn't it?"

"I don't believe I caught your name."

The clerk stood a little straighter and tugged at his coat lapel as if he were presenting himself on a formal occasion. He couldn't be past his late teens, but was a stuffy sort for one so young.

"Charles Dunn," he said.

"Where are you from, Charlie?"

From the look on his face, young master Dunn didn't like being referred to as Charlie. "Chicago, Illinois. I worked for Ms. Vanderwagen as her valet and driver when she resided in that city."

"Lucky you. How much do I owe you? I told you I've got a train to catch."

"And I have relayed to you that you have no bill to pay," he replied. "Ms. Vanderwagen left concise instructions that your stay here was free for as long as you are with us."

Morgan flipped a five-dollar silver piece on the counter. "I'd guess that more than squares me."

"You don't seem to understand . . ." the clerk started.

"Call it a tip if you want to, I don't care," Morgan said. "But if you've worked for Helvina as long as you say you have, then you should have learned by now that nothing's free with her. It's only a matter of when she decides to collect."

The clerk was about to protest, but Morgan went out the door before he had the chance. The train was already parked at the station, and Morgan hustled across the street. Not only did he intend to procure a new rifle in Muskogee if a suitable one was available to replace the one Cumsey had taken, but he also intended to pay a visit to the tavern there that Dixie had told him about where his neighbor had observed his stolen whiskey. The odds of recapturing Cumsey Bowlegs were growing slimmer, and so far he had no case against the marshals without Cumsey as a witness. Evidence of selling stolen goods or other contraband would be a solid start to building a case that might stand up in court, and he might also begin to get a better feel for the extent of the marshals' crimes in the territory.

There was only a single passenger car, and the conductor glanced at his ticket and put him aboard as quickly as he stepped onto the depot decking. Two soldiers and an elderly woman were the only passengers, and he took a seat by himself at the back end of the car well behind them.

He watched the little town slide away before him through the window as the train rolled out of the station. The hotel clerk was standing on the porch watching the train leave with that same sour look on his face. He wondered if the boy slept with that expression, as it seemed a permanent part of him.

Morgan laughed to himself, and was about to snuggle down on his passenger bench and catch a catnap when he saw Molly again. She was going down the street at the same brisk pace as she had been earlier.

"Now there's a woman on a mission," he said quietly to himself.

He didn't know how right he was.

CHAPTER SEVENTEEN

What was to be the new Methodist church, and the first church in Eufaula, was still under construction. The timber framing of its steeple stood high on a small knoll overlooking the town, and nearby to the cemetery. The pale lumber stood out starkly against the skyline, and Molly used that landmark to guide her.

She was a fast walker, and always had been since her days as a young girl on the roads of County Kerry in the old country where there weren't so many who could afford a horse and your own two stout legs had to get you where you were going. Regardless, it wasn't only habit that added to her speed, but because she was afraid she would change her mind if she slowed her pace in the slightest.

The first person she saw when she reached the foot of the hill was Useless Pickins, known by his congregation and the few others who liked him as Reverend Euless. He was a tall, skinny man with a receding hairline and an equally receding chin, and an Adam's apple as sharp as a hand ax bobbing up and down on his throat.

Useless straightened from the floorboard he was nailing

down. Even standing upright, he was a knotty man of sharp angles, and always appeared stooped over to a degree.

"Come to lend a hand, Molly, or have you come to repent?" He looked at her over the glasses perched on his beak of a nose as she took the steps that led up to his church two at a time. "I would guess neither."

"Stow it, priest," she said as she went past him, crossing herself in the sign of the Trinity and in the Catholic way before she stepped inside the walls.

"Papist harlot," he half hissed in reply.

"Protty hypocrite," she gave him back under her breath.

She walked to the middle of the plank floor and looked up at the top of the back wall. Another man sat atop that wall driving a hardwood peg into place with a large mallet. He was every bit as thin as Useless, but the similarity ended there. He was neither a big man nor a small man, average in all appearance except for the fine, sharp bones of his face and the intensity of his gaze. He wore a plain white muslin work shirt tucked into a pair of brown canvas pants, but she remembered a time when he had favored black as his color of choice, from his hat to his frock coat and string tie.

The little flat-brimmed straw boater he now wore on his head with the red ribbon hatband did little to shade him from the sun, and he was a ghostly pale, fair-skinned man who would burn easily.

"Hello, Molly," he said.

"Hello, Deacon," she replied, resisting the urge to take a step back.

His eyes had that effect on her, always had. They were languid, burning things, those eyes of his. Unsettling, they were, and at times filled with the hint of madness.

"What can we do for you?" His voice was deep and

crackly, yet surprisingly gentle. His accent was Deep South, and despite his calm tone, there was a hint of some kind of fervor behind everything he said. "Like Reverend Pickins, I get the sense that you haven't come on the Lord's business."

She studied him sitting there atop the wall. If you didn't know him, it would have been hard to believe that he was such a dangerous man. There was nothing fearsome about him, other than those eyes and the cold bearing that hung about him like a cloak. But she knew him for the slim, pale killer he was, no matter how many church house walls he hammered on or how he claimed to have reformed.

Oh, there was always the pious, Bible-thumping act that had gotten him his name, but despite his preaching, he was the same man that had ridden as a Missouri bushwhacker during the war with the likes of William Quantrill, Bloody Bill, and the James boys. And it was the hands-down opinion of most of the territory that he was the deadliest man with a pistol that was ever born.

"I want to hire you," she blurted out, more quickly and loudly than she had intended. She had worked up half a dozen more subtle ways to bring the matter up, and practiced saying one or two to herself on her way to the church house. But there it was anyway, out in the open.

He jumped down from the wall, landing lightly on his feet, and she took a step backwards to put more space between them. From the agile way he moved, she guessed his wounds had finally healed, but she noticed that he still wore a silk handkerchief wrapped around his throat like a cravat to cover the ugly knife scar Morgan had given him during their fight in Bullhorn Palace. It was rumored that he was cut so badly that the doctor had to sew his windpipe back together, and that it had taken twenty stitches to close the slash in his skinny throat.

"I can't imagine what you would want to hire me for," he said.

"I want to hire your gun."

"I don't wear a gun anymore." He hefted the mallet and held it up for her to see. "The tools that a man bears should produce good works that honor the Lord."

She laughed out loud. Of the bad ones she had known, Deacon Fischer might well be the worst. Simply to be around him made her instantly want to be somewhere else. But that was exactly the kind of man she needed.

"Save the act for the congregation, Deacon. I didn't come to hear how you've got right with the Lord, or how you've repented from your sins. A man like you doesn't change."

"The Lord's grace can save the blackest heart, even a man like me," he said, not at all seeming bothered by her insults and insinuations. "My convalescence and time with Reverend Pickins at the Ashbury Mission have given me time to reflect on my sins and to realize how far I had strayed from the Good Book."

"It's your sinful side that I came to talk to."

"You filthy whore of Babylon!" Useless said behind her.

"Forgiveness, Brother Pickins, forgiveness." Deacon held up a hand to silence the preacher.

Useless had the good sense to shut up when Deacon asked him to. He went back to his hammering, mumbling to himself.

"What do you really want with me?" Deacon asked. He suddenly sounded tired.

"I want to hire you as my bodyguard," she replied, and it sounded crazy to her own ears, even though she had stayed up half the night thinking it through. The Deacon wasn't only a killer, he was also crazy. On his worst days, he was little short of stark, raving mad. But he was also known for his strange, twisted sense of honor. A dark-souled, complex man that would kill you without batting an eye, but one also known to keep his word. A weapon is what he was, and she wanted him as her weapon.

"You must feel you are in some danger," he said.

"Maybe, or maybe I'm sick and tired of losing," she said. "It seems like everybody in this territory has got the edge on me. They're either bigger and stronger, or better with a gun, or they've got the numbers to make what they want stick."

"And you think hiring me will make it any different?"

"I'm looking for an edge, and you're all I could think of."

"What about Clyde? It's no secret that he's back and wearing the badge."

She tried to detect any change in his voice when he said Morgan's name, but she missed it if it was there.

"Morgan plays by the rules, and that's no way to win," she said.

"How do you expect to win?"

"Any way I can."

"And you would trust me to help you?"

"I trust you could kill a man if I told you to, and I'm gambling that if I pay you enough you'll watch my back," she said.

"Maybe Reverend Pickins is right," he said.

"About what?"

"That you may have been sent here by the devil himself."

"The only devil I'm worried about is Lot Ingram."

That was the first time his icy demeanor and sanctimonious act seemed to crack a little. "You want me to kill Lot?"

"If it comes to that," she said. "But I'd be satisfied with some breathing room."

"I take it he's bothering you."

"Let's just say he's making it hard to do business."

"Lot's a dangerous man."

"I aim to be just as dangerous. How's two hundred dollars sound?"

He looked at the mallet again, and then at the steeple framing high above him. "I'm not that kind of man anymore. I've put my iniquity behind me."

"Three hundred dollars."

The Deacon turned his back on her and went to his knees. He knelt there with his head bowed, and she stood behind him not knowing what else to say, or what she would do next.

"What are you praying about?" she asked.

"I'm praying for you, Molly, and I'm praying for me," he answered with his head still bowed.

"Well, say a good one, 'cause I've got a feeling I'm going to need it."

She turned and went across the floor towards the steps, passing Useless again. "Careful there, Useless, that you don't smash your finger."

He looked up from the nail he was starting and scowled at her.

"Jezebel!" he said.

She blew a kiss at him and it startled him so badly that his hammer stroke missed the nail and struck his thumb. He was waving his wounded hand about him wildly and saying a few words no preacher should say when she went down the steps on her way back to the barbershop. And with every stride she was asking herself what she was going to do now that the Deacon had turned her down. Lot Ingram would come back exactly like he said he would, and she still didn't have an edge.

CHAPTER EIGHTEEN

Morgan unpinned his badge and slipped it inside his vest pocket as he was getting off the train. There was a chance he might run across someone who knew him, but it wouldn't do for him to advertise his affiliation with law enforcement while he snooped around Muskogee.

He had barely gotten off the train before he was recognized. Helvina came along the tracks in a brand-new buggy pulled by a pair of fine black geldings. She had the top down on the buggy and nothing but the fancy feather hat she wore to protect her from the sun, which was unusual for her, for she was ever conscious of keeping her complexion blemish-free. She spotted him and waved, and soon stopped the buggy alongside him.

"Hop in and I'll give you a ride," she said.

He took too long responding, and she laughed at him.

"For goodness sakes, quit standing there like some awkward teenaged boy," she said. "So we had some fun for old times' sake. What of it?"

"Yeah, old times," he answered without the same flippancy.

"I'm not going to want to hold your hand, if that's what's worrying you," she said.

He climbed into the buggy.

"You really should get you some new clothes made, you know, and a shave more often wouldn't hurt you a bit," she said as she waved her buggy whip over the blacks and started them forward at a good clip.

"Where are we going?" he asked.

"I want to show you something."

She was a reckless driver, and crossed the tracks at such a speed that he had to hang on to keep from being bounced from the seat. Soon, they were flying along the prairie west of town, and she had a smile on her face that he rarely recalled seeing.

"I've never known you to drive yourself," he said when the horses tired and she allowed them to slow to a walk.

"Oh, I know. It's unseemly, isn't it?" she said. "But I must say, it's quite exhilarating from time to time. In fact, this whole country is exhilarating, isn't it?"

"I guess you could call it that."

"Don't be such a boring ninny. You're ruining my good mood. And just when we were beginning to patch things up."

"Helvina . . . about what we did the other night. That was a mistake. A mistake for both of us."

"There they are." She pointed ahead of them.

All he saw was a large cloud of dust. It was exactly the kind of dust that a large herd of cattle or horses would make.

They came within sight of the herd after another mile. It was, indeed, a big one. A trail crew of cowboys was driving the cattle along at a leisurely pace. A chuck wagon and a remuda of saddle horses traveled off to one side of the herd.

"That's quite a sight," he said, trying to make a rough estimate of how many of the long-horned Texas cattle he was seeing.

"Two thousand and fifteen cows plus whatever calves they might have birthed since leaving Texas," she said proudly.

Helvina knew even less about livestock than she knew about driving buggies, and he gave her a sharp look.

"Oh, yes, they're mine," she said. "I contracted for them last winter."

"So you're going into the cattle business?"

"I am."

"I understand that it's beef steers that most drovers take to market."

"I'm not sending this herd to market. That's why I bought cows, not steers," she said. "Cows have babies, and more babies and more babies, and you sell that offspring as soon as they come of age. It's really quite simple."

"I don't think it's so simple as you make it sound."

She frowned at him. "I assure you I have made a diligent study of the matter. I have two more herds coming up from Texas, one another herd of cows, and the other consisting of yearling steers. I've purchased some good shorthorn bulls that are being hauled down on a railcar from Missouri as we speak. In another year I will have a packing house built to ship my own beef."

"When did you get so interested in business?"

"I've always had a mind for business, only you wouldn't or couldn't see it."

"You like the money, but you never did understand how hard it is to earn."

She gave him a cold look.

"Where are you going to run these cows of yours?" he said to avoid a fight.

She waved her hand across the horizon. "Why, here, of course."

"This is Indian land."

"For now," she said. "But that won't last, and you know it. It's only a matter of time."

"What about the here and now?"

She sighed as if explaining to him the childish details was taxing her energy. "My partners and I have arranged a grazing lease with the Creek tribal council to cover the legalities."

"Your partners?" He considered the hotel she had built and the ranching enterprise she was suggesting, and the capital required to start such ventures. It was a healthy sum.

She stopped the horses and turned on the buggy seat. "I wanted you to see this, Morgan. I wanted you to see what I'm doing, because this could have been you and me. I'm going to succeed, and I'm going to do it where you, and even my father, failed. This country is going to boom before long. All this land, there's no way the Indians will get to keep it, not with so many seeing the territory for what it is."

"And what is it?" he asked.

"Opportunity, if we're strong enough to take the necessary risks. Did you know that there are coal deposits south of Eufaula in the Choctaw Nation? Big coal deposits."

"I've heard."

"There are certain men already working to take advantage of those resources, and to gather mining rights."

"What you mention is stealing and plundering, not business."

"What else is business other than taking a dollar and making it into two? And besides, I won't be stealing. I'm simply putting myself in a position to take advantage when things change. Timber, land, coal, water, it's all here waiting for those strong enough and smart enough to bend things to their will."

"A nicer way of putting it doesn't make it better."

"Save your speeches. I've heard them all before. What have you got to show for your honor?"

"And what then? What's enough for you?"

"Come down off your high horse," she said. "Just because I let you bed me doesn't mean you get to lecture me. The only reason I brought you out here was because I thought you might like to see what I'm doing. You used to dream big, too."

"You wanted to show me this to rub it in. You wanted to remind me what a failure you think I am," he said. "You're gloating, Helvina."

She scoffed at him. "All the years sitting and listening to you men talk, smiling at your nasty little innuendos and crude come-ons, letting you paw at me, and flittering about and acting the silly woman without a brain in her head. I paid my dues and put up with you all. Sold my flesh like some cheap tramp. But I was listening, too, and I was learning. And I was thinking and planning how I could do it better than any of you if given half a chance."

Her voice had a tremble to it the way it did when she was mad, and she gripped the buggy whip so tightly in one fist that her hand was bright red. "I see how you're looking at me, you judgmental bastard. Yes, I've done things, things I loathed. But every time I gave a little piece of myself, I took a little back and set it aside, planning for this very day, should it ever come."

"And what now?" Surprisingly, he wasn't angry with her.

"I'm going to have it all."

"I feel sorry for you, Helvina," he said. "Surprises me as much as I see it surprises you, but truly, I do."

"You feel sorry for me?" Her eyes went big and she clutched the buggy whip even tighter.

"People like you never have it all. Always wanting and scratching and clawing, and never realizing that no matter how much you have, there's always something else to want," he said. "I'm ashamed I spent all these years hating you when I should have only pitied you."

She chopped down at his face with the whip, but he caught the stock in his hand. He didn't jerk it away from her, only held it, feeling as if he were seeing her for the first time for what she really was, just a petty, selfish, scared little woman trying to take care of herself because all she valued in the whole wide world was herself.

"I'm sorry," he said.

"Damn right you should be sorry." She tried to jerk the whip away, but he held tightly.

"I'm sorry that I left you and the children, and I'm sorry for the way I've hated you and put none of the blame on myself," he said. "And I'm sorry for the other things I would have done differently if I had it to do again."

She quit trying to pull the whip away from him, and a strange look formed on her face. She was silent and still for a long moment, and simply sat there looking up at him, as if at a loss for words.

"You don't know how long I've waited to hear you say those words," she said breathlessly and threw out her arms to wrap around him. "I never wanted to leave you. I only wanted you to see things the way I see them. I only wanted you to be the man I knew you could be."

He pushed her away. "Like I said, I'm sorry for many things, but most of all, I'm sorry that I ever loved you."

Her vanity and her pride were too great for his words to truly sink in, and he could tell that they had yet to strike home.

"There will be no more rolls in the hay. No more fun between old lovers, as you called it. That wouldn't be doing either of us right," he said while she stared at him with her prim little mouth hanging open. "No more bickering and tearing each other apart and digging at old wounds. We're done, because I'm finally done with you as you were done with me."

She reared back as if to slap him, but paused with her hand held there.

"Go ahead, if it makes you feel better," he said. "I'll take it this one time."

"You aren't worth it. Never were." She laid the whip to the black horses and wheeled the buggy around and pointed it for town. "I used to pray at night that you would be killed during the war to save me the trouble of divorcing you."

Her parasol blew out of the buggy, but she didn't stop. She laid the whip to the team again and urged them to a run. He held tight to his seat as the buggy bounced and skidded over the uneven ground. Not another word passed between them until they reached the train tracks at the edge of town.

She pulled up the winded team beside the depot house where she had picked him up. "Get out."

He stayed put for a moment longer. "I'm going to find Ben. I'm going to find him whether you tell me where he is or not."

"He wants nothing to do with you," she said.

"I'm going to find him and tell him I'm sorry."

He stepped down from the buggy, and she barely waited until his boots touched the ground before she lashed the horses again. He stood in the middle of the street and watched her go.

"I guess there went my free hotel room," he said to himself.

Free hotel rooms or not, he felt better than he had in a long time. The old ghosts that haunted him for so long were slowly fading.

CHAPTER NINETEEN

Morgan took lunch at a little café, then spent the rest of the afternoon loafing about town on the off chance that he might spot Cumsey Bowlegs or catch some bit of gossip pertaining to the outlaw's whereabouts. He also fished about for any pertinent information pertaining to Lot Ingram's operations, but he had no such luck on either score.

It was late in the day before he purchased a brand-new Winchester, Model 1873, from a hardware store along the tracks. The store's selection of firearms was small, and the weapon he chose cost him three times what he could have ordered it from the factory for, but he purchased it, regardless, rather than wait for a mail order to arrive.

He chose the rifle variation over the carbine version. The rifle had a case color-hardened receiver, a crescent butt-plate, and pair of deeply notched buckhorn rear sights mounted into the long octagonal barrel. The tubular magazine held fifteen rounds of .44-40 cartridges, and he could carry a sixteenth in the chamber.

"Load that thing on Sunday and shoot her all week without reloading," the storekeeper had said when Morgan had first taken the new rifle down off the rack to examine it.

It was already an old, overused saying, but funny, regardless. Confederate soldiers in the war had supposedly coined some similar variation of the saying after encountering the first fast-firing Henry lever-action repeaters in the hands of Union forces.

Morgan felt the .44-40 round was a bit too underpowered for a rifle cartridge, but it was the repeater's high cartridge capacity that led him to make the purchase. He added four fifty-round boxes of ammunition to the store counter, paid his bill, and had the storekeeper package the lot and promise to deliver his purchases to the depot house.

Morgan checked his pocket watch when he returned to the street, and found it was after five o'clock. He eyed the sun as if the watch might lie about the time, and then studied the wall of dark thunderclouds far to the west.

The storekeeper came out the door behind him carrying his purchases.

"Looks like it might finally rain," Morgan said.

"Don't count on it," the storekeeper said. "Summer rains around here are spotty at best, and don't usually last long."

"Any kind of rain would be nice."

"It would." The storekeeper was a talker, and seemed especially fond of discussing the weather.

"Speaking of dry," Morgan said. "You wouldn't know where a man could wet his tonsils, would you?"

The storekeeper gave him a suspicious look. "Intoxicating spirits are illegal in the Nations, fellow. Hasn't anyone told you that?"

Morgan leaned closer to him and gave him a conspiratorial wink. "Why, sure."

"Thought you might be some kind of lawman testing me," the storekeeper said with a chuckle. "I don't drink myself, but there are lots around that will sell you a bottle. If it's a tavern you're looking for you'll have to go out of town."

"Which direction?"

"You'll find Ma Moon's place up by the river," the storekeeper said. "Just follow the tracks north after you pass the Katy pond, and then take the footpath you see cutting off to the east when you hit the river."

"Sounds easy enough. Think I'll meander that way, then." Morgan started along the street.

"That's a three-mile hike," the storekeeper called after him. "And I'd mind my manners if I stayed after dark. Ma caters to a rough crowd, and it gets worse when the sun goes down."

Morgan debated on whether or not to try and rent a horse for the trip to the tavern, but decided not to. A good stretch of the legs and time to think was what he needed. Soon, he was out of town and passing along the edge of the large pond that supplied Muskogee with most of its water. A trail skirted the edge of a thick stand of cattails and then hugged closer to the Katy tracks going north.

He walked at a leisurely pace, and it was almost an hour before he reached the dense forest that marked the wide Arkansas River bottom. At the edge of the highest flood bench the trail forked, and a well-beaten footpath split off to the east, following the river. It was a narrow trail, overhung by tree limbs and other growth, and barely wide enough to allow a horse to pass.

The trail abruptly ended in a tiny clearing, and in the middle of that clearing stood a house with a high-peaked roof and a slanting porch running across the front of it. A stone chimney at one end of the house leaned as precariously and as out of plumb as the porch.

Several men stood both on the porch and in the yard in front of it, and they watched with caution, if not alarm. He nodded to them as he went past and received a few nods in return.

The house was held up by stacked stone piers, and the ground beneath it sloped off to the front, leaving the porch high off the ground. A set of weathered and warped walnut plank steps led up to that porch, and he mounted the steps and passed through an open door into what appeared to have once been a large dining room. A bar had been built across the back wall, and a heavy, scarred table was set against the front wall with a bench down either side of it. In the space between stood several more men, and three soldiers sat at the table.

No sooner had Morgan entered the room than a short, stout, elderly black woman in a faded blue gingham dress and smoking a corncob pipe entered the room from a side door carrying a black cast-iron skillet. She gave him a speculative glance before she set the skillet down on the table and began forking pork chops and fried potatoes onto the soldiers' plates. The food was dripping grease, and the skillet looked like it hadn't been cleaned in years, but apparently the soldiers didn't mind, for they dug into their meal with relish.

"Ma, I can't believe somebody that can cook as good as you hasn't been snatched up and married," one of the soldiers said after he washed down a mouthful of pork with a slug from a brown bottle of beer.

The black woman, who Morgan assumed was the Ma Moon the storekeeper had referred to as the owner of the backwoods tavern, gave a laugh. "Hush, you. I done swore off any more of you hairy-legged man chillen. Done been married three times, and every one of them was worse than the one before. Just wanna lay around all day eatin' my vittles and drinkin' corn liquor whilst I do all the work."

The soldiers laughed at that, and Ma started back for her kitchen with the empty skillet, using her ample bulk to brush aside anyone too slow to get out of the way.

"Out of the way, you fools," she said.

She disappeared into her kitchen for a moment, and when she returned to a position behind the bar she gave Morgan another frown. "You goin' to stand there all day, or have you got money to spend?"

Morgan went to the bar. "Give me a shot of your good stuff."

She snorted at that and reached under the bar and brought out a fruit jar full of clear liquor. "Ain't but one kind of stuff here, but I guarantee you it will do the trick."

Morgan looked down the bar at a railroad worker in overalls and a red bandanna. The man was slumped over a half-finished drink, appearing to have either gone to sleep or on the verge of passing out from the effects of too much whiskey.

Ma Moon looked at the same man and said to him, "You either get to drinkin', or you go out in the yard and sleep it off 'til you're fit to come back. You're takin' up space from my payin' customers."

The railroad hand gave her a bleary-eyed look and then started for the door, staggering badly.

"And mind you don't fall in the hog pen," she called after him. "That sow, she's got little ones and she won't tolerate no drunk fools around her litter."

Morgan took up the glass she had poured for him.

She stopped him before he could drink. "That'll be five cents. This here is a pay first, cash business."

Morgan produced a nickel from his coin purse and paid her. She tucked the coin into a pocket on her dress below her waist. The pocket also showed the butt of a small pistol sticking out of the top of it.

He took a sip of the whiskey. Surprisingly, it wasn't bad, nor was it unusually strong. He had no doubt that it was well watered down to make her stock go further and to increase her profits.

"Ah, now that's good," he said, making a show of enjoying the drink.

She tucked a curl of gray hair under the cloth she wore wrapped about her head. "Where you from?"

"New York."

"New York, hmm?"

He took another sip of the whiskey. "On my way to Texas. Got off the train at Muskogee and thought I'd see the sights."

"Well, you're seein' them. What do ya think? You ain't goin' to find no New York City down in the Arkansas River bottoms."

He held up the whiskey glass. "Make this yourself?"

She picked up the fruit jar and gestured at his glass. "You like it so much, why don't you finish that and I'll pour you another?"

He laid another nickel on the counter while he downed the last of his whiskey. She promptly poured him another one as soon as he set his glass down.

"Been here long?" he asked.

"You ask a lot of questions. You want sippin' liquor, I got plenty. If you're hungry, I set the best table in the Nations.

Answers that don't put money in my apron, I don't waste my time with."

"Didn't mean to offend. The reason I asked about your whiskey is because I represent a distiller back in New York."

"A dis what?"

"A manufacturer of spirits."

"Is that a fancy way of sayin' you're a whiskey peddler?" she asked. "I had two drummers in here yesterday tryin' to sell me silver-plated dining sets. Can you believe that? Most of these fellows eat with their hands if you don't slap 'em down and remind 'em of their manners."

"You misunderstand me. My intent was not to sell you an alternate product, but rather to inquire as to its origin in order to possibly obtain the brand for my company's line." Morgan did his best to imitate the form and pitch style of the many traveling salesmen he had met over the years.

"You don't look like any drummer I've ever seen. You're all pistol, far as I can tell." She looked down at the Colt on his hip as she spoke.

"A man needs to protect himself from time to time, though I'm not much good with this thing," he said. "I was robbed twice in one month while in Chicago last year. Both times in broad daylight."

"You don't say? There's plenty here on the scout that'll lighten your pockets for you if 'n you don't keep on the lookout."

"Thought the appearance of a firearm might give the rougher sort pause before they accosted me."

"You've got a fancy line of talk. I see why you're a drummer." She took a draw from her tobacco and then removed the stem from her mouth and gestured at Morgan's pistol with the pipe. "Best you try to talk your way out of any trouble and sell that shooter. Most of the fellows 'round these parts don't wear their pistol poppers for show, if ya know what I mean."

Morgan swirled the whiskey in his glass. "First drink I've had since I left Kansas City. Must be a terrible inconvenience for you, what with the laws against selling whiskey in the territory, and all."

She placed the corncob pipe back in the corner of her mouth and looked at him suspiciously. No matter his act, he knew he had gone too far. A woman like her didn't succeed in the kind of business she was running without an ample dose of cunning. She went down the bar and tended to one of her customers, a tough-looking young Indian in a big hat and with an Open Top Colt revolver threaded behind his belt buckle. Morgan couldn't hear what she was saying, for she kept her voice down, but it appeared that the Indian was a regular customer. Twice Morgan saw her look his way, and got the impression that she was talking about him.

It wasn't long before the Indian man came down to near where Morgan stood. He leaned against the bar nonchalantly on one elbow facing Morgan.

"Ma doesn't like the way you're nosing around. She suspects you might be a spy," the Indian said.

Morgan noted the way the Indian was making sure that the pistol behind that belt buckle was seen. Young and tough, and with a reckless air to him like most of the young men Morgan had seen on the streets of Muskogee, he was dressed like a cowboy. It seemed like most of the Indians in the Nations who didn't look like farmers wanted to look like cowboys, especially the young ones.

Ma Moon came back. "Quincy, you leave him be. I can handle my own affairs, I can."

Morgan noted how the other men in the room were watching him. Ma must have spread the word quickly that there was a possible lawman or informant in their midst.

"You've got me all wrong," Morgan said. "I was merely commenting about troublesome liquor laws you have here in the territory, and what an inconvenience it must be."

"Were you, now?" Ma asked.

"I must admit, we have our own troubles where I'm from," Morgan continued. "A man finds himself a cozy tavern like this one and wants to blow off a little steam, and the next thing he knows some copper is strong-arming him and complaining about loud and disorderly conduct or squeezing him for a little bribe. Or asking to see liquor licenses and such just to cause a hassle. This country has gotten so that a man can't enjoy himself."

A few of the men in the room nodded at that.

"Government's got no right to tell a man what he can or can't drink," someone muttered.

The young Indian with the pistol in his belt was still trying to look hard, but he had relaxed a little. "Mister, I don't know nothing about where you come from, but you don't know the half of it down here in the Nations."

"Shut your trap, Quincy," Ma said. "Don't you make trouble for me, or for you, neither."

"Trouble?" the Indian asked. "This here Yankee talking, fancy man ain't trouble. Are you, fancy man?"

Morgan passed him an innocent look, and lifted his glass and took another drink.

"Ma, I think you're getting scary in your old age," the Indian said.

"And you're half drunk and blind to boot," Ma said, and then she looked at the rest of the room. "You boys get back to your drinkin' and mind your own business. Nothin' to see here."

She moved closer to Morgan until she stood directly across the bar from him, still puffing on her pipe. When she spoke, her voice was quiet enough that only he and the Indian beside him could hear. "I don't know what your game is, but if you're a whiskey drummer, I'm the Queen of Sheba."

"I told you that I represent . . ."

She shook her head. "I've been put to the question by better than you, and I know when a man's snoopin' around my door like a hungry old pot hound after table scraps."

"You are mistaken."

She reached out and tapped his chest gently with her finger. "Got a fuzzy spot on your vest where you usually pin your badge. Took me a bit to notice it."

Morgan knew that his game was up, and there was no sense taking it any further. And he had also noticed two other men watching him from the open doorway leading out to the porch, both wearing sidearms. One was a black fellow who looked enough like Ma to be her son, and the other was a mean-looking white man with such a thatch of whiskers on his face to make it hard to tell who he might belong to. Neither man had been there before, and both had obviously somehow been signaled by Ma that there might be trouble.

"That drummer act might have fooled me," Ma said. "Only you ain't pesky enough to be a drummer, and I can tell you don't wear that gun for no child's play."

Morgan finished his whiskey and set the glass back down on the bar top. "Well, you do serve a decent glass of whiskey. That much is the truth."

"You're a federal, ain't ya? Did Lot send you here to spy on me?" she asked.

Morgan saw an opportunity and took it. "Just making my rounds. Lot likes us to keep an ear to the ground. Make sure things are like you say they are."

"Like I say they are?" she asked. "You tell Lot that he doesn't have to send you snoopin' around. I'll pay up like I always do."

"You've got a lot of nerve coming here by yourself, law dog," the Indian said. "There's more than a few of us that don't like how you Fort Smith boys are treating Ma."

Ma took a glance out the front window. "Are Lot and them others out there in the brush?"

Morgan was about to hint that he might not be alone, when he took his own look out the window and was startled to see Cumsey Bowlegs on the front porch and peering inside. He was gone from the window as soon as he recognized Morgan staring back at him, and his running footsteps sounded loud on the porch boards.

"You'll have to excuse me," Morgan said, starting for the door.

The Indian put a hand to his pistol and stepped in front of him. "Where do you think you're going? I ain't done talking to you."

Morgan heard Cumsey's boot heels thump on the ground when he leapt off the porch, and the horse thief was going to be long gone if Morgan was delayed any longer. He hit the Indian hard—not a full punch, but a short, tight stroke with his knuckles extended that struck the Indian full in the throat. The blow had barely landed when he yanked the pistol out of the Indian's belt and backhanded him across the temple with the weapon's heavy barrel. By the time the

Indian hit the floor choking and gagging, Morgan was already moving towards the front door with the pistol aiming at the two still blocking his way.

"Out of the way, boys," Morgan said as he cocked the pistol hammer.

Neither of the two seemed to want any part of what their friend at the bar had gotten, and they both got out of his way. There was a big barn with a second-story hayloft at the top of it twenty yards to one side of the tavern, and the first thing Morgan saw when he hit the porch was Cumsey disappear into that barn. Morgan glanced at the two men he had run out of the doorway. They were standing at the other end of the porch watching him.

"Stay out of this," Morgan said.

"You go right ahead. Old Cumsey won't have any problem taking care of you by his lonesome," the one with the whiskers said.

Morgan bailed off the porch and ran towards the barn.

CHAPTER TWENTY

A wide hallway ran down the length of the barn, and Morgan paused to one side of the open doorway at the end of it and took a quick glance inside. He half expected to be fired upon, but no gunshot came. He quickly ducked through the doorway and moved into the corner to his right to break up his silhouette where the sunlight splashed into that end of the barn.

Beyond that pool of sunlight, there was nothing but shadows. He adjusted his position again, putting a parked wagon in front of him. The rest of the barn floor was littered with other junk and equipment put there out of the weather, and a corn-crib shed lined one long wall. What appeared to be two horse stalls occupied the opposite corner at the far end, catty-cornered from where he stood.

Something thumped on the other side of the hallway, and he knew that Cumsey was still in the barn. He thought the sound had come from the horse stalls.

"Throw down your gun and show yourself, Cumsey," Morgan called out. "No need for more trouble than you're already in."

"Not a chance, Clyde," Cumsey answered.

Morgan had been right. Cumsey's voice came from some-where near the horse stalls.

"I'll promise you safe travels to Fort Smith and you can tell your story to the court," Morgan said.

Morgan couldn't spot where Cumsey was hidden, and the outlaw's voice seemed to come from a slightly different loca-tion each time, as if he were moving. Morgan kept watch on the far end of the hallway in case Cumsey made a run for it.

"Best thing you can do is to leave me alone," Cumsey said. "No sense in it coming to shooting. I thought on it some and decided to let what you did to Strawdaddy slide. I never did like him, no ways, and his mama was always mean to me except when she wanted me to get him out of trouble or loan him a dollar or two. I reckon you and me are a clean slate."

"I can't let you go, Cumsey, you know that." Morgan ducked lower behind the wagon, not at all sure Cumsey wasn't baiting him into talking so that he could locate him to take a shot.

"What do you care how many horses I steal?" Cumsey's voice seemed to come from somewhere close. "I never stole any railroad horses, at least not in a long while."

Morgan glanced out the door nearest to him to make sure nobody at the tavern was going to get involved. From where he crouched, he couldn't make out the porch, but nobody was in sight between the house and the barn that he could see.

"You're coming with me," Morgan said. "I'll do what I can to get you a plea bargain if you'll testify as witness against the marshals that hanged you."

"You're a little too late in the game if you think that's how things go in the territory," Cumsey said. "And I'd as soon die here as be hanged in Fort Smith."

A board creaked above Morgan, and he knew where Cumsey was. He had all but forgotten the hayloft, and understood then how Cumsey was moving around without being seen. He aimed the Open Top Colt at where he thought the board had creaked.

"Last chance, Cumsey. I would rather see you to Fort Smith than tend to your burying."

"Run for it, Cumsey!" somebody shouted behind Morgan.

Morgan twisted on his heels in time to see the man with the whiskers holding a double-barreled shotgun aimed at him. He dove under the wagon, and a load of buckshot knocked splinters from the side of the wagon where he had been crouched only a split second before.

His head was still full of the shotgun's boom when he landed on his belly and thrust the pistol out in front of him. There was no time for aiming, as the man with the shotgun already had another bead on him and was about to fire his second barrel. Morgan simply pointed and squeezed the trigger. His bullet struck the man above one knee, dropping him to the ground, and causing the shotgun blast to go high and pelt the wagon above him again.

The man he had put down scrambled on his back towards the horse, clawing at the pistol he wore as he went. Morgan thumbed the Colt's hammer and put a second and a third shot through the bib of the downed man's overalls. He kept his aim and waited to make sure that the man was out of the fight.

Boards creaked again above Morgan, and he knew that Cumsey was running for the hayloft door. He rolled from under the wagon in time to see Cumsey ride the haymow rope down to the ground and land heavily at the end of the hallway right outside the door. He was clutching Morgan's Yellow Boy Winchester, and somehow managed to hang on to it after his fall.

"Throw it down!" Morgan yelled, shifting his aim to Cumsey's back.

Cumsey threw a wild look over his shoulder at Morgan and took off running. Morgan cursed and lunged to his feet. Before he could get out the door a bullet whipped through the plank barn wall and knocked over a milk pail at his feet. He skidded to a stop in the patch of sunlit doorway in time to see Ma Moon's son aiming a rifle at him. The other men in the yard were running in all directions at once, and Morgan was afraid to return fire because of those by-standers. The damned fools had stood around to gawk and now found themselves in the middle of a gunfight.

Morgan dove back into the barn, rolling on his shoulder until he was clear of the door. A bullet spanked the straw-strewn earth of the hallway, and then a second bullet. The first shot sounded like it had come from a rifle, and the other a lighter weapon.

He peered through a crack between the wall slats. Ma Moon's son wasn't in sight, but the old woman herself was hanging out of a house window with the little pistol he had seen in her dress pocket aimed his way.

"You damned fools," she cried. "Look what you started."

Another bullet whipped along the barn hallway and hit the far end wall.

"You shoot straight, Elijah!" she called out. "You finish what you started, or we're in trouble, sure."

Both Ma Moon's little pocket pistol and her son's rifle fired at the same time. And they kept firing. Bullets whipped through the barn siding all around Morgan, and he couldn't tell if others had joined in. Like most such places in the territory, most of Ma's customers were a shady bunch, and more than a few of them might jump at the chance to get rid of a lawman foolish enough to ride alone into their midst.

"Ten dollars to the man that tacks his hide to my barn wall!" Ma yelled.

Another volley of bullets riddled the barn walls. Morgan drew his own Colt and waited with a pistol in each hand. The gunfire ceased as quickly as it had begun, either because they thought they might have already killed him, or because they were simply reloading for another go at him. He took a quick glance through the crack in the planks and saw Cumsey leap on the back of a horse and spur it out of the yard at a run. Morgan could do nothing to stop him.

"One of ya'll git around back and make sure that law dog doesn't put the sneak on us!" Ma called out again. "You boys fetch him and I'll feed him to my hogs!"

Morgan had had his fill of mean hogs back in Texas, and wasn't about to wait around for someone to block his only means of escape. He jumped to his feet and ran for the other end of the barn, snapping blind shots behind him with the Open Top Colt as he ran.

The ground outside that far door dropped off steeply and down to a little dry creek bed. Going at such a pace, Morgan tripped and tumbled all the way to the bottom of the slope, coming upright on his knees in the deep leaf bed covering the streambed. He lost hold of the Colt he had taken off the Indian, but managed to hang on to his own pistol. A hat showed itself above the lip of the creek bank, and he snapped a hurried shot at it. Whoever was wearing the hat stopped their charge and ducked out of sight.

Morgan thumbed another blind shot that way, and ran down the creek bed, using its high banks as cover. Somebody must have heard him crunching through the dead leaves and fired at the sound, but the shot came nowhere close to him, merely rattling through the treetops behind and above him.

The timber was dense and the undergrowth heavy where he ran, and an occasional glance above him or behind him revealed nothing. He halfway expected one of his pursuers to drop into the stream channel before him, or to fire down on him from the high banks. But nothing hindered his flight other than the few times he tripped and fell in his haste.

Heaving for air, and unable to run any farther, he crawled on hands and knees up a narrow cow trail beaten into the creek bank and sat down when he reached the top. The river bottom around him was relatively flat and more open than before, and he could see a good ways in all directions through the trees. There was no sign of his pursuers, and he tried to slow his breathing so that he could hear better. To his surprise, there came no sound of horses or men busting the brush in search of him.

He holstered his Colt and shoved to his feet. It took him a while to get his bearings, and even then, he wasn't sure he was heading in the right direction when he finally struck out through the woods. Maybe Ma and her minions had given up on catching him, but he wouldn't be happy until he had put a little more distance between himself and Ma's tavern. The thought of having his hide tacked to a barn wall and his flesh fed to the hogs wasn't a pleasant one. And she had seemed to be such a pleasant woman at first.

The sun was getting low on the western horizon when he traveled far enough to see it shining through the trees where the dense woodland ended at the edge of a small prairie of tall grass. He stopped at the edge of the prairie, scanning the open ground for any sign of horsemen. The train tracks lay in sight and the footpath along the tracks he had taken on his way to the tavern was right before him.

It was dusk by the time he passed the Katy pond again, and almost full dark before he reached the depot house. The telegraph operator was about to close up shop, but Morgan blocked the door as the man was about to go out.

"I need to send a telegram," Morgan said and pulled his badge from his vest pocket and pinned it in place on his breast.

The telegraph man took one look at Morgan and nodded his head as if he understood. "You look like you're having a bad day."

"You don't know the half of it."

"Who do you want to address your message to?" the man asked as he lit a lamp and sat down behind his telegraph keys with a pencil and notepad to jot down Morgan's message.

"Send it to Bert Huffman, Superintendent of the MK & T Railroad."

"Yes, yes, I know who he is."

"Copy this exactly," Morgan said. "Exactly."

"Yes, indeed."

Morgan flexed his neck from side to side to work some of the stiffness from it and to give him time to think. "Case progressing. Help needed. Send at least four good men to Muskogee, I.T. Signed, Morgan Clyde," Morgan dictated.

"Got it," the telegraph operator replied.

"I'm not finished yet. Add this," Morgan said. "Will contact tribal police for assistance from my end. Talk to Chief Whitley and advise if necessary. Send correspondence to Eufaula, I.T."

"Has that got it?" The telegraph operator asked.

"That's it."

Morgan stood over the desk while the man typed the message with one machine's keys and then took a strip of punched paper it produced and fed it into the transmitter. The transmitter began to click away as it read the punch paper's message and transmitted it down the line in Morse code.

"One more thing," Morgan said. "Do you know where I can find Sergeant Harjo with the Creek Lighthorse? I'm not even sure if he's still around."

"He's still riding for the Lighthorse. Don't know where you can find him, but I understand their tribal court is in session. I would imagine he might be at their council house at Okmulgee for the proceedings."

"Can you send a telegraph there?"

"There's no line going there."

"How far is it to this council house?"

"It's a day's ride west."

"Is there anyone you know who could deliver a message for me?"

"My boy could, if you pay him fairly."

Morgan laid two dollars on the desk. "If he finds Harjo, have him relay that I need the sergeant and a few men to meet me here as soon as possible."

"And if he doesn't find Harjo?"

"Have the boy tell whoever's in charge of the Lighthorse that I need their help raiding a whiskey operation."

The telegraph operator raised his eyebrows at that mention. "If it's Ma Moon and her boys you're talking about, I suggest you request more men to help you."

"You keep quiet about this and send your boy to find Harjo," Morgan said. "If word leaks out I'll know it was you that did the telling."

The telegraph operator looked at Morgan's badge and shrugged. "No worries about me blabbing my mouth. I like my job, and besides I never did care for Ma's cooking, nor her whiskey, either."

Morgan went down off the depot platform and started along the street, walking slowly and thinking. So lost in thought was he that he didn't see the woman cross the tracks behind him.

Ma Moon was a quick walker, despite her age, but she was afraid the telegraph office would be closed before she made it there. It was near full dark with a sliver of moon already shining overhead by the time she reached the depot. She was more than a little surprised to see lamplight shining through the office window.

The telegraph operator was sitting at his desk and about to blow his lamp out when she went across the platform and looked in his window.

"Is that you, Clyde?" he asked. "I told you I'll send my boy in the morning after those Lighthorsemen, just like you said."

Ma stepped through the door. "Who's this Clyde you're squawkin' about?"

"Oh, a fellow I know."

"Tall, black-haired man with a mustache and a big pistol on his hip?" Ma had heard Cumsey saying Clyde's name in the barn, although Cumsey hadn't stuck around long enough to tell her any more than that. That fool, horse-crazy boy never did stay anywhere long enough to be any account.

The telegraph operator was doing a poor job of hiding his nervousness. "Maybe that was him."

"You damn well know it was him," Ma said. "You say this Clyde fellow wants you to send your boy after the Lighthorse?"

"I already said too much."

"You'll say plenty more, or I'll tell your wife how often you've been comin' around my tavern. I hear she's a good Christian woman and don't hold with the whiskey drinkin' and gamblin'."

"I sent a telegraph for him, but I can't remember everything it said."

"How's a good bottle of busthead and a sugar-cured ham the next time I come to town sound?"

"Clyde's with the railroad," the telegraph operator said. "I could lose my job if he finds out I told you."

"Told me what? Speak up."

"I can't."

She pulled the small, nickel-plated Colt House revolver with a birds-head grip from her dress pocket and pointed it at his face across the desk. "You can, and you will."

He told her everything.

"Sent for help, did he?"

"I'd be getting gone if I was you," he said. "Sounds like he's bringing a posse after you."

"No, I'm not goin' anywheres. Not yet. What you're going to do is to send a telegram for me."

"All right. What should it say, and who do you want to send it to?"

"You send it to Deputy Marshal Lot Ingram."

"I don't know where he's at."

"You send the damned thing up and down the line to every stop on the Katy. Send it to Fort Smith if you have to. Somebody will get word to him."

"And what should it say?"

"You tell that old highbinder that one of his marshals, this Clyde galoot, shot up my tavern and killed one of my boys."

He grabbed up a notepad and began taking notes, but

paused over something. "Clyde isn't a marshal. The badge he was wearing said railroad police."

Ma took a heavy puff on her pipe and nodded at that information. "Is that so?"

"Want me to change your message?"

"No, but you add Clyde's name and you add this. Tell Lot that I'll be damned if I'll pay him if he can't hold up his end of the bargain."

The telegraph operator scribbled on his notepad, trying to keep pace with the flow of her thoughts.

"No, scratch that last part," Ma said. "You just tell him that first part I said. I don't want him down on me. All I want is for him to take care of that Clyde."

He finished writing the message as she wanted it and typed it into his machine. He fed the punch paper into the transmitter and listened to it clicking away as the message went up and down the line.

"Is that it?" Ma asked.

"It's sent."

"You don't send that boy after the Lighthorse, and you don't tell nobody about this. You hear me? If you do, I'll send Elijah down here to pin your ears."

"I won't tell a soul, Ma. I'm no blabbermouth."

"You talked easy enough when I poked my pistol in your face."

"That was to you, Ma. That's different."

"You'd best mind what I said. I'll send you that whiskey and a ham first chance I get." She shoved the pistol back in her pocket and left the office.

"I'm looking forward to it," the telegraph operator said. "Hard to tell which I like best, your whiskey or your cooking."

CHAPTER TWENTY-ONE

Lot Ingram had spent another night camped in a thicket, and it put him in a foul mood long before he rode back into Eufaula the next day. Cumsey Bowlegs be damned, he was going to get a good hotel bed and a decent night's rest before he did any more chasing around after that half-breed Seminole.

He and the other two marshals had spent the previous day busting the brush along the river bottom and hills from the mouth of Gaines Creek to Hoyt's Ferry ten miles downriver to the east. They visited several possible hideouts, including Sand Town, the old outlaw camp that Cumsey and some of his kind had once used in the sandy bottoms not far from Canadian Station. They found nobody at that camp, and nothing much was left of the place but a few abandoned cabins littered with trash, and what remained of a brush corral. Drought or no drought, Lot insisted that they burn every structure. They killed the rest of the evening watching the flames. They didn't want to start another forest fire, for the local opinion about the fire they had caused several days earlier was a harsh one. That delay to burn Sand Town was the main reason they had to make camp in the brush rather than overnight in town, but Lot only blamed Cumsey and the misfortune that had made him unable to catch the boy.

Saddle sore and cranky, Lot and the marshals tied their horses in front of the Vanderwagen Hotel and went inside for lunch and to inquire about rooms for the night. Lot was sitting at the dining table in the lobby waiting for his meal to be served when a young boy brought him the telegram from Ma Moon. He read the message and then flung it on the table for the other two to read while he stormed over to the hotel register.

"Is that damned Clyde still staying here?" he asked the clerk behind the counter.

"Yes, but he took the northbound train yesterday morning," the clerk said.

"That figures," Lot said, not at all liking the boy's smug tone, but too irritated with the day in general to do anything but to chalk it up as one more tiny needle pricking him.

"Mr. Clyde is set to return sometime today, I believe," the clerk said. "I took his coat he had cleaned up to his room right before lunch, and he was not there. But perhaps he has returned since then without my knowing it."

"What room is he staying in?"

"Room Ten. Take a right at the top of the stairs, and it's the last door at the end of the hallway," the clerk said not only with his smug air, but also with a bit of enjoyment that he hid poorly.

Lot didn't know what that was about, and he didn't care. He started up the stairs, and the two other marshals followed on his heels. They stopped short of Morgan's door.

"How do you want to play this?" Brady asked in a quiet voice. "Are we just talking, or are we here for business?"

"I'm done talking." Lot drew one of his cartridge conversion Army Colts and cocked the .44 while he gently tested the doorknob.

The door was locked, and Lot passed a look to the other two marshals. Brady and Clem stepped quietly to the other side of the door. Clem pulled his own pistol, a rusty Smith & Wesson American with a strip of rawhide wrapped around the grip frame to cover where the grip panels had been broken sometime in the past. Brady grinned at them both and slid his big knife from its sheath.

Lot found the doorknob was locked, and he gently rapped on the door with his knuckles. No answer came from within, and he knocked on the door a second time, staying well back from in front of it. Again, there was no answer.

"Go get a key from that clerk," Lot said to Clem.

"Here's your key." Brady stepped in front of the door and gave it a kick beside the doorknob.

The door latch broke loose under the force of that blow, and the door swung inward in a wild crash. Brady was the first one to charge inside, and Lot thought what a fool the scar-faced marshal was to charge into Clyde's room with nothing but a knife in his hands.

Lot and Clem were close on his heels and found Brady standing in the middle of an empty room. There was no sign of Clyde.

Lot looked around the room, and went to the closet and opened its door. A pair of saddlebags and a bedroll lay at the bottom of the closet, and a freshly cleaned black frock coat hung above them from a rod. He slapped the coat out of nothing more than frustration, and was about to shut the closet when he heard the metallic sound of something falling to the floor. He saw the glint of some bit of silver-colored metal and picked it up.

"What's that?" Clem asked.

The three marshals gathered together, and then Lot opened his hand to reveal the badge he held.

"U.S. Secret Service?" Brady asked after he had squinted at the words engraved on the badge for a moment. "What the hell is that?"

"Treasury Department," Clem said. "Ain't that so?"

Lot bounced the badge up and down on his palm. "Secret Service, same as that fellow that came down from Washington a while back and snooped around Fort Smith asking about the judge. What was his name? Whitley?"

"I remember him," Clem said. "That was over that whiskey peddler claiming he had paid off the judge to keep from getting indicted."

"You figure Clyde is working the same case?"

Lot pocketed the badge. "What I figure is whatever he's doing means bad news for us."

"You think he's gathering evidence on us?" Clem asked.

Lot went to the window and stared down at the street. He stood there for a long time while the other two marshals waited.

"I asked if you think he's after us?" Clem repeated.

"Whatever he's after, it's about over, because I'm going to kill the son of a bitch."

"Now you're talking," Brady said.

Lot turned back to them. "Brady, I want you to go send a wire to Ma Moon."

"What do you want with her?" Brady asked.

Lot acted as if he was about to strike Brady for interrupting him. "You tell her to bring her boys and anybody else she can round up."

"Going whole hog, aren't you?" Clem asked.

"I'll deputize every man she can bring," Lot said. "Clem, you go around town and talk to folks. I want it spread around real subtle-like that Clyde got drunk in Muskogee and killed a man for no other reason than he could. Make it sound bad. Muddy the waters."

"Want me to wire Fort Smith?" Brady asked.

"No, you damned fool. The last thing we want is any other marshals here," Lot said. "We'll stomp on this problem ourselves, and with Clyde gone our version of the story will be all that's left."

Clem started out the door but stopped, blocking Brady's way.

"What are you going to do while you've got us running errands?" Clem asked.

"I'm going to be waiting right here," Lot said.

He went to the window to pull the curtains closed to keep anybody on the street from seeing him pacing back and forth in the room. The hotel veranda was directly below the window, and before he closed the curtains he looked down where their horses were tied.

"And make sure our horses are taken care of," he called after the other two marshals going out the door.

And then he heard someone shout and saw a storekeeper across the street waving his arms at someone as if trying to stop them. At the same time, it dawned on Lot that there were only two horses where there should have been three. His gray horse was gone.

He ran out of the room and down the stairs.

CHAPTER TWENTY-TWO

The little red roan gelding Cumsey had stolen at Ma Moon's tavern was a slow and rough-traveling beast, and its stamina was so lacking that it was all but exhausted by the time Cumsey reached the North Canadian, no matter the easy pace he had set for the horse. The roan almost quit him in an especially boggy stretch of sand while crossing the river, but floundered and scrambled its way up the far bank with a little encouragement from Cumsey's spurs. He regretted that Morgan hadn't given him the proper time needed to steal a better mount, and he hated the thought that someone might see him riding such an inferior animal. However, his mood improved when he finally reached the edge of Eufaula and came into sight of Hannah's little shack.

He was already practicing the required apologies that he was going to have to make to her and thinking how good her bed was going to feel after a long ride, when he spied Lot Ingram's big gray gelding tied in front of the Vanderwagen Hotel. His plans changed at that very moment.

While it was the middle of the afternoon, the traffic on the streets was so light as to be nonexistent, decreasing the odds of someone stopping him in the act of stealing Lot's horse. Furthermore, the degree of difficulty and audacity required to steal a marshal's horse in broad daylight sounded much more impressive and would make a far better story after the fact. Taking that gray out from under Lot's nose while he sat inside the hotel would be sure to make Lot all the madder and increase his embarrassment tenfold.

Cumsey dismounted in the edge of the woods and unsaddled the roan and slipped the bridle from its head. He set the horse free with a slap on its rump and then turned to study the best approach to the hotel. It didn't take him long to make his mind up, for there was no way to stay under cover and avoid some risk of being seen. The best way was often the most direct way, and audacity was his favorite calling card when it came to stealing horses.

He walked across the tracks with his rifle thrown leisurely over one shoulder, and whistling while he went. He was only halfway to the Vanderwagen Hotel when a storekeeper sweeping the dirt from his floor out the front door spotted him. Cumsey resisted the urge to run, and was relieved when the storekeeper gave a quick wave and went back to his sweeping. Apparently, the man hadn't recognized him.

That was one thing Cumsey hadn't thought through. How was everyone going to know that he was the one to steal Lot's horse? Everything about his plan required him garnering proper credit for the theft.

He wasn't a man to turn back once committed, and he walked right up to the front of the hotel and alongside the gray. The hotel dining room was easily visible through the front windows, but he saw no one there. He jerked Lot's rifle from the saddle scabbard and dropped it on the ground, then replaced it with his own. After giving the gray's cinch latigo a quick jerk to tighten it, he swung up in the saddle without using the stirrup in the fashion of a trick rider or the wild half-Indian he was.

"Hey there! What are you doing?" the storekeeper shouted at him from the store down the street.

Cumsey adjusted the split reins and spurred the gray towards the tracks. The storekeeper was in the middle of the street by then, waving his arms, but Cumsey went by him at a dead run and gave a loud, shrill Seminole war cry as he passed. The gray was a strong runner and cleared the tracks in one flying jump. He brought the horse to a hard stop, and turned and looked back at the hotel. Normally, horse thieves who were too slow in flight didn't live long enough to steal a second horse, but he couldn't resist looking back to gauge the effect of his escape.

Lot was on the hotel porch with a pistol in his hand. Cumsey took off his hat and waved it over his head in mock salute to taunt the old marshal. The sight of Lot aiming the gun at him caused him to put the spurs to the gray again. Lot's pistol boomed, but the shot came nowhere close to him. The exhilaration of the moment filled him with boundless energy, and he gave another loud war cry as he rode out of sight of the town.

Molly heard the commotion out on the street and came out of the barbershop barely in time to see Cumsey leap the tracks on the gray horse. Noodles was right behind her and almost ran into her back. He shaded his eyes against the sun and tried to see whatever it was that had caused all the excitement.

"Quell'uomo è pazzo!" Noodles said.

Cumsey pulled the horse to a stop and waved his hat, and Molly caught a flash of movement out of the corner of her eye. It was only then that she realized that Lot Ingram was on the hotel porch. He aimed his pistol at Cumsey, cursing loudly. Molly's heart skipped a beat as the gun boomed and bucked in his hand. Although Cumsey was a long ways from the hotel, it somehow seemed miraculous that Lot had missed. She watched as Cumsey rode away, apparently unscathed, and it was all she could do not to cheer for him.

"Wasn't that Lot's horse Cumsey was riding?" Pork Chop asked.

Molly looked at the gambler beside her, not realizing until then that he had come out with her and Noodles.

Noodles mumbled something that she couldn't make out. Apparently, Pork Chop couldn't understand it, either.

"I guess what you were trying to say with that jabber was what I said," Pork Chop said to Noodles. "That horse he was riding belongs to Lot."

"No," Noodles said with a shake of his head. "I say he crazy, that boy."

"Well, speak English for once so we can understand you, and not that foreigner talk," Pork Chop threw back at him.

"Minchione fetuso," Noodles said and turned for the door.

"What does that mean?" Pork Chop called after him.

"It mean you learn Sicilian if you want to know, you big stupid," Noodles said from inside the barbershop.

Molly only half listened to their argument, for she was too intent on what had just happened before her. Noodles was right, Cumsey was crazy. But he was also brazen, and that reckless daring gave her a little courage of her own.

She felt that strange feeling when you know somebody

is staring at you, and her gaze shifted back to the hotel. Lot was watching her, and the look on his face was an ugly thing.

She quickly went back inside and found Pork Chop and Noodles still passing insults. It dawned on her then that she didn't even know Pork Chop's real name. All anyone called him since she had first encountered him on the line was his nickname.

Noodles noticed her first, and he stopped whatever he was about to say and gave her a questioning look. Molly realized how truly desperate her circumstances were. The only two men who could help her were there in the room, and she didn't know one's name, and the other's she couldn't pronounce.

"Come on," she said to them with an exasperated huff, "We've got plans to make."

They followed her to the back room, and Molly poured them all a glass of gin and motioned them to the bar. She downed her entire portion, and waited for the pain in her chest to subside and for the wheeze in her chest to clear.

"You're looking awfully pale," Pork Chop said. "Maybe you ought to go lie down and let me and Noodles handle things tonight."

She scoffed at his idea. "Plenty of time for dying later. Do you still have that coach gun you used to keep behind the bar down at Canadian Station?"

Pork Chop gave a thoughtful frown while he adjusted one of the suspenders that held up his checkered pants. He was a heavy man, and if it weren't for those suspenders his belly wouldn't tolerate a pair of pants.

He went to the corner behind the table where he usually played poker. The tent walls were lined halfway up on the inside with rough planking, and he reached an arm down in the space between the wood and the canvas. When he pulled his arm back out he was holding a short, double-barreled Parker shotgun.

"How long has that been there?" Molly asked.

His only answer was a shrug.

"Can you still use that thing?"

Again, he shrugged. "What's the trouble this time? I know you, and I'm thinking you're getting ready to fight."

Molly looked from him to the Sicilian. Pork Chop and Noodles, their names sounded more like a Vaudeville stage act than men you would go to war with.

"Lot Ingram is back in town, and it won't be long until he pays us another visit," she said.

"What's got you worried?" Pork Chop asked. "He's trouble, but you always manage to handle him."

"Things have changed."

She told them of the last visit the marshals had paid her two nights previous, and of Lot's plans to all but take over her business.

"Quit standing there with your mouth hanging open and drink your gin," she said to Noodles.

"And you intend to fight him?" Pork Chop took up his own glass, but didn't drink.

"Tooth and nail." She waved at the tent around them. "It isn't much, but it's mine. And I aim to keep it that way, Lot Ingram be damned."

"Lot won't be bluffed," Pork Chop said.

"I've got no right to ask you two to help me. No right at all." Noodles had said nothing so far, but he gave Pork Chop a questioning look. The old faro dealer nodded back at the Sicilian barber.

"I want one thing," Pork Chop said to Molly.

"What's that?" she asked.

"I want to put my own roulette wheel back here," he answered.

"Is that all?"

"That's all."

"Done."

Pork Chop downed his gin, set the glass down on the bar, and then cracked open the shotgun's breech and checked that it was loaded. He snapped the gun closed again. "I'm with you."

Both of them looked to Noodles, and he held up one finger to signal that he needed a moment. He left the room but came back shortly carrying a gallon-sized metal can with the labels worn off and a piece of thin leather tied over the top to keep its current contents from spilling. He set the can down on the bar.

"You, signora Molly, you take this," he said.

"What's this?" She hefted the can, shook it, and heard a rattle that sounded like loose hardware or maybe coins.

"Three hundred and sixty-two dollars." He struggled with the English numbers. "I count it real good."

"I don't need your money, Noodles."

He shook his head to indicate she had misunderstood him, and his face twisted as he tried to find the words to explain what he wanted. "I save that money. Three years in this country, and I don't spend nothing but a little money to eat and maybe a new pair of shoes."

She had no clue where he might have been hiding his stash inside the barbershop, nor did she know how to respond to that, or what he was implying. Noodles rarely drank, wore the same two sets of clothes since she had first met him, and had slept in her saloon until recently when he had taken over an abandoned cabin on the outskirts of town.

"You take this money," he said.

"I told you, I don't want your money."

He shook his head again. "This money I save for my family . . . to pay for them to come here . . . to this place . . . this country."

"You have a family?"

"A wife and two daughters. Only money for one to take ship, and I promise to send for them." He pushed the money can toward her. "You take, and you pay for them. There is letter in can so you can send the money if I no make it."

She could easily imagine him every night squirreling away his precious few coins and counting his little hoard and doing the math that separated him from his loved ones as much as the expanse of ocean that lay between them.

"You do this?" he asked.

She looked at the funny, pitiful little man with his pants too short and standing with his hip cocked because his game leg was too stiff to stand properly. And she thought it was the sweetest gesture she had ever known and saw him as he truly was for the first time. He was willing to fight for her, and he trusted her.

"I'd be honored," was all she could manage to say, and she swiped at the wetness at the corner of her eyes.

"Well, aren't we a hand to draw to?" Pork Chop said.

Molly tapped the top of the can and looked at Noodles. "Maybe you should sit this one out. You have your family to think of."

"I stay with you." Noodles took up his glass of gin and held it up in toast. He used the glass to point at Molly and then at Pork Chop. *"Miei amici. La mia famiglia."*

"I think he said we're his friends . . . his family," Pork Chop translated.

"I know what he said." Molly wiped at her eyes again.

CHAPTER TWENTY-THREE

Morgan got a room at the Mitchell Hotel and remained in Muskogee to wait for a reply from Superintendent Huffman and for the telegraph operator's boy to return with the Creek Lighthorsemen. And yet, after a night and a full day of waiting, there was still no telegram from Huffman, and no sign of either the messenger boy or the tribal policemen he was supposed to retrieve.

The telegraph operator pointed out that the trail to Creek council house was not a good one, and any manner of things could have delayed his son. This, however, did little to help Morgan's impatience to be doing something. He didn't relish another day or more waiting on the porch of the hotel and watching the dust blow down the street or counting the number of crows that roosted on top of the telegraph poles along the train tracks.

He kept a close lookout for Ma Moon or her son, but neither showed in town. He wondered if she and her operation were already long gone. Not only did he intend to shut her tavern down, but he also hoped that if he could arrest her that she could be pressured into testifying against the corrupt marshals.

The train rolled into town shortly before sundown, and he decided he would wait no longer. If Sergeant Harjo arrived after he left, the Lighthorseman could find him in Eufaula only a half a day's ride to the south. He had no clue why Huffman hadn't responded to his message.

He paid his hotel bill and boarded the train. In less than an hour he could see the small cluster of lights that marked Eufaula directly ahead.

The locomotive hissed and chugged as it slowed, and its running gear ground like poorly oiled clockwork as the train rolled alongside the station. Morgan went out one end of the passenger car and stepped off the platform stairs before the train had stopped moving. He looked down the length of the tracks and for some reason his gaze was drawn to the powder shack where the schoolteacher lived. Her lamplight was easily visible through the little window in one side of the shack. He was about to turn away when he saw the fat gambler from Molly's place, the one she called Pork Chop, walking towards that same shack carrying some kind of bundle.

Morgan wasn't the only one to be traveling on that night. Dixie Rayburn hobbled along the wagon road from North Fork Town under the dim light of the moon. His pace was slow, and he stopped often to rest, even though it was only three miles or less from his farm to Eufaula. He had been on the road for the last two hours.

The moonlight wasn't enough to reveal the grim set of

his jaw, and the new bandages torn from his bedsheets that he wore wrapped around his middle were hidden under his shirt. However, had there been anyone to see him passing along that lonely stretch of road they could have easily told he was hurt by his unsteady gait and the way he hunched over with one hand held to his belly.

The same pale moonlight that cast him in shadows did reveal one thing. The barrel of the freshly oiled Spencer carbine he carried in his free hand gleamed like wet ebony. The same wetness shone in the reflection of his eyes when he looked up at the sky and swore for the thousandth time he was going to make it, and that the bastards who had thrown him down the well were going to pay for what they had done.

He had stopped to rest on the side of the road again when he heard the first gunshots. There were many of them. Sometime later, after he had struggled back to his feet and started once more along the road, he saw the orange glow of a fire rising above the treetops ahead, exactly where Eufaula should be.

He hobbled a little faster and clutched the Spencer tighter.

CHAPTER TWENTY-FOUR

There had been no pursuit of Cumsey after stealing Lot's horse, and he made his way to a camp not far away. It was a good, hidden spot that he had used before, and Lot had left three good blankets rolled up and tied behind the saddle that would make a decent sort of bed. But Cumsey was too restless to sleep. To compound his displeasure, he had even less love for spending a night camping than Lot Ingram did, especially when a good corn-shuck mattress and Hannah's loving arms waited for him. And a new idea came to him while he lay atop the blankets and stared at the stars overhead. This new idea struck him funny and pleased his vanity greatly. The combination of Hannah's lure and a new way to thwart Lot Ingram was enough to cause him to get to his feet and saddle the gray.

From his hideout in the dense tangle of flood debris on a little island in the middle of the South Canadian channel, it was only a short ride back to Eufaula, and within the hour he had reached the powder shack at the edge of town. He found that Hannah hadn't made it home, yet. She was probably taking supper with the Bickfords, as she occasionally did, or perhaps she was simply working late. There were times when she helped Hank Bickford out at his funeral parlor when he was preparing a body or assembling a new coffin, or when the demands of his blacksmith shop kept him from attending to his other business during normal working hours.

Cumsey had looked forward to seeing Hannah, but he wasn't especially bothered by her absence. Not while he had other things to attend to.

He lit the lamp beside the bed and pulled the thin muslin curtain closed over the window before he hunted down the stationery set she kept for writing letters and such. He sat on the floor with his legs crossed Indian fashion and Hannah's notepad on one thigh. He was a fairly literate man, but he struggled for a while over what he scratched with her pencil, for he wanted to think of just the right words that would give his latest plan the proper flavor.

Finally finished, he took the paper with his masterpiece written upon it and folded it carefully and placed it in his pocket. Satisfied with his work so far, he dug through more of Hannah's things until he found a good pair of scissors. Thus equipped, he went back outside. It was a good half hour before he finished with the scissors, but like the letter, things had to be done properly.

He led the horse away, sticking to the dark alleys and shadows, and the only time they were readily visible was when he reached the open street along the edge of the tracks. There was nothing more to give him cover other than the darkness of the night, but he ignored the danger and grinned wickedly, too caught up in the pleasure of his scheming to give a damn if he risked being found in town or worse. He led the gray to the hotel and tied it there at the hitching rail in front of the porch and closest to the front doors. The note he had written was hanging from one of the gray's saddle strings when he left the horse there.

He was almost back to Hannah's shack when he heard the train coming. The arrival of the train gave haste to his stride, as he didn't want to be caught in the locomotive's headlight beam, not when he was having so much fun. He had barely stepped back inside the shack and closed the door when the train rolled into the station. And he didn't see Pork Chop headed towards the shack, nor did he see Morgan step down off the train.

The one piece of decent furniture in the whole shoddy room was a walnut rocking chair. Cumsey had no clue where Hannah had obtained such a comfortable and fine piece of furniture, but he sat down on it and began to rock. The same wicked grin that he had worn earlier spread across his face, and he could hardly wait until daylight when Lot found what he had left for him. It was going to be a doozy.

CHAPTER TWENTY-FIVE

Ma Moon arrived in Eufaula at the same time the train did. She had her son with her and two more men besides. They had ridden all the way from her tavern, Ma astride a short brown mule, and the men following behind her on horses.

They rode alongside the train single file, and only stopped when they reached the hotel. Ma puffed on her pipe and studied the gray horse tied to the hitching rail.

"Now that's an awful thing to do to a perfectly good horse," she said.

None of the men with her seemed to have any clue how to respond once they had dismounted and studied the gray more closely.

"Must be someone's sorry idea for a joke," Ma's son managed to say, for nothing else described what he was seeing.

"Help me down off this mule," Ma said. "This here trip has set my knees to achin'."

Her son came to her side and all but lifted her from the saddle. She slapped him away once her feet were firmly on the ground and she was sure her knees would hold her up.

"You're as strong as an ox, Elijah, but you don't handle me like I'm a chunk of stovewood."

The stiffness hadn't left her, yet, and she waddled over to the gray horse to see what the bit of paper was tied to the saddle. She grabbed the paper and went up on the hotel porch and through the lobby doors, stopping only when she was beneath the great chandelier. That candlelight, combined with the lamps on the walls, gave enough light for her to make out what she held.

She was a poor reader, and her eyes weren't what they once were. She frowned over the note on the paper, and gave an ironic grunt after she had finished reading the note a second time.

Someone clearing their throat got her attention, and she looked over to find Lot Ingram and two other marshals sitting at a table on the far side of the lobby. Her initial scowl at the sight of them showed how much she disliked them, but she managed a fake grin and waddled to their table.

"I didn't figure you'd make it here until the morning," Lot said.

"My mule is a quick stepper," Ma said.

"I see you've brought along some help," Lot added, nodding at the three men standing behind her.

"Never been much help to me, but maybe you can find a use for them," she replied.

Besides her son, one of the men with her was a hatless Indian who Lot didn't recognize with a bandage around his head, and the other was a white man with a dirty face and small eyes that peered at him under the brim of his slouch hat. Lot didn't know that one, either, but he noticed the antique and enormous Dragoon Colt sagging the man's belt below his belly.

"Are they dependable?" Lot asked.

Ma flopped down in an empty chair with the three marshals, and her considerable weight made that piece of furniture creak and pop. "They've got no love for Clyde."

"Is that so?"

"Clyde buffaloed that one." She jabbed a finger in the direction of the Indian, and then she gestured at the one with the dirty face. "And he bored a hole through that one's brother. Revenge is potent medicine."

"Poor fighters, I would say," Lot said.

"My Elijah almost did for Clyde, only he wasn't quick enough to run him down," Ma said. "What happened to you, Brady? Looks like somebody took a hammer to your face."

The scar-faced marshal put a self-conscious hand to his battered nose. The swelling had gone done considerably, but most of his face was now a mess of ugly yellow and black bruises. He didn't reply to her, and only scowled his displeasure.

"How long is this gonna take?" she asked. "I don't like to be away from home no longer than necessary. Hogs gotta be fed and them Chaney boys are apt to know I'm gone and pilfer all my whiskey and raid my smokehouse."

"I intend to *arrest* Clyde as soon as he shows himself," Lot said. The way he said *arrest* made Clem laugh.

Even Ma chuckled.

Lot nodded at the men behind her. "Ya'll get your saddle horses out from in front of the porch and get back here."

Ma's chair creaked again as she shifted her weight. She

pitched the piece of paper she held in her lap on the table. "Speakin' of horses, who owns that gray tied up out front?"

Lot read the note and almost knocked the table over getting to his feet. He banged through the front doors and out onto the porch muttering profanity.

Clem took up the note Lot had left on the table and read it out loud:

Lot,

I appreciate the loan of your horse. He's a fine horse, although a little on the ugly side. I thought he could use some grooming and proper care. I think he looks fine with his new haircut. Don't you? I trust you shall take care of him, and don't be sleeping and let anyone steal him. That I would embarrass you, I'm sure, and keep me from having a little more fun the next time I need a horse.

Sincerely,
Cumsey Bowlegs

P.S. Please make the next horse you get a smoother trotter. I favor an easy riding horse. The gray is a little on the rough side.

Clem, Brady, and Ma's gang followed Lot to the porch, and stood there while he examined the gray. Cumsey's scissor work had removed the forelock between the horse's ears, and where that hair had once hung down over its forehead, it now looked as if it had been scalped. Between one end of the animal and the other, Cumsey had turned the saddle around backwards, but it was what he had done to the poor horse's tail that angered Lot most. The same scissors that had shorn the gray's forelock had cut every last hair from its tail right down to the tailbone. What had once been a fine-looking gelding now looked pitiful standing there with nothing but a nub bone sticking out of its hindquarters where it had once had a long and lustrous set of almost white hair that hung below its hocks.

A small crowd of townsfolk had gathered on the street to study the horse, and Lot knew that there was no way to keep what Cumsey had done a secret. Word would spread, and it wouldn't be long until every gossip in the territory was telling what Cumsey had done and how he had pulled one over on big, bad Lot Ingram. That was the reason the boy had done the thing. Lot knew instantly that Cumsey was rubbing sand in his eyes, and that bothered him far worse than what was done to his horse.

"That Cumsey's the drizzlin' shits," Ma observed from the porch. "You got to do somethin' with that boy, or you won't never live this down."

Lot snapped an angry look at her but held his tongue. He walked another semicircle behind the horse, and the gawkers on the street either decided to leave or fell back to give him more room. He mumbled to himself and was about to pace to the other side of the horse when he happened to look up and see Morgan stepping down off the train. Morgan wasn't the one that had mutilated Lot's horse and made a mockery of him, but Lot's rage needed a place to land.

"Get your men, Ma," Lot said. "There's Clyde."

It took Ma a bit to spy what Lot was looking at, but she finally spotted Clyde walking behind the depot. She took her pipe out of her mouth and tapped the bowl against the heel of one hand to tap the ashes out. She stowed the pipe away in her dress pocket and felt around in there until she got a hold of her pistol butt.

"I reckon you're wantin' to make that arrest, now?" she asked.

Lot drew one of his pistols and started across the street in the direction Morgan had gone. "You're damned right I am."

CHAPTER TWENTY-SIX

Morgan caught up to Pork Chop halfway to the powder shack. Pork Chop turned and looked behind him when he heard Morgan's footsteps on his heels, and it took him a moment to guess who was following him.

"Is that you, Chief Clyde?" he asked.

"It is."

"What's got you out and about tonight?" Pork Chop asked as he started along his way again.

Morgan fell into stride beside him. "I could ask you the same thing."

"My laundry needs doing, and I thought I would carry it over to Hannah's tonight rather than have to get up too early in the morning."

Morgan was about to bid Pork Chop good night when he looked up and saw again the light burning in the powder shack's window. A hunch that had been rattling around half formed somewhere in the back of his mind for several days finally took hold, and he wanted to take a look inside that shack.

"That's where that schoolteacher lives, isn't it?" he asked.

"No, Hannah does laundry with Lottie Bickford. I told you that's where I'm taking my washing," Pork Chop replied.

They were almost to the door of the shack. Morgan slid his Colt from its holster and put out his other hand to stop Pork Chop.

"What are you doing?" Pork Chop asked with some alarm.

"Quiet now."

Morgan soft-footed it the last little distance to the door. He was about to test the door latch, but decided against it and eased around the corner until he could peer in the window. There was a thin white curtain hung behind the glass, but Morgan had no problem seeing through it with the lamplight burning inside the shack. There was a man asleep in a rocking chair in the middle of the room, and that man was none other than Cumsey Bowlegs.

Morgan scolded himself for not making a closer search of the town earlier, and he wondered if Hannah was some kin to Cumsey or if the two of them were sweethearts. One of the first things he had learned as a lawman was that a fugitive most often returned to see family or loved ones, and a good way to catch them was to be waiting when they showed themselves at such places.

He went back to the door and laid a hand to the door latch, hoping the door wasn't barred shut from the inside. A gentle pull, and the door swung outward. The hinges that hung it were rusted and long without oil, and they gave a loud screech. Morgan found himself face-to-face with Cumsey when the outlaw's eyes snapped open. But Morgan was already moving forward into the room.

Cumsey reached for the Winchester propped against one wall beside his rocking chair, but Morgan's pistol barrel was already pressing against his forehead before he could lay hands on the carbine.

"I reckon you got me." Cumsey slowly lifted his hands away from the Winchester and kept them above his shoulders. "I'd appreciate it if you quit pushing that pistol of yours so hard. You're going to give me a headache."

Morgan left the pistol where it was and reached out and kicked the Winchester out of Cumsey's reach. He heard footsteps behind him and glanced that way to find Pork Chop peering through the door.

"Get in here," Morgan said.

Pork Chop did as he was told.

Morgan nodded at the bundle of laundry Pork Chop held. "Think you can find something in there that you can tie his hands with?"

The gambler dropped the bundle on Hannah's bed and sifted through it. He soon came up with one of his shirts.

"Tie his hands tight," Morgan said.

Pork Chop looked uneasy about the whole matter, but went behind Cumsey.

"You stand up real slow so that I don't mistake your intentions," Morgan said to Cumsey.

Cumsey did as he was told and put his hands behind the small of his back when Morgan gave the Colt another slight push. Pork Chop wrapped one sleeve of the shirt around Cumsey's crossed wrists and tied a double overhand knot.

"Did you tie him tight?" Morgan asked.

"Tight as I could. I imagine it will hold him," Pork Chop went back to the bed and put himself as far away from the other two men as he could.

Morgan backed away a step. Cumsey wrinkled his face

with the removal of the pistol barrel's pressure against his head.

"What next?" Most of the cockiness had left Cumsey, and he was beginning to sound worried.

Morgan backed up another two steps until he was just outside the open doorway. "You come easy now."

Cumsey was almost to the door when Morgan heard foot-falls behind him. He turned slightly and took a quick look over his shoulder and saw the shadows of running men coming towards him. Before he had time to decipher what he was seeing, someone shouted.

"Throw down your guns, Clyde! We've got you sur-rounded!" It was Lot Ingram's voice doing the shouting.

And Lot didn't wait for Morgan to throw down his gun, nor did he wait for Morgan to answer him. For the instant the shout went out, a gunshot boomed and splinters flew from the doorjamb beside Cumsey's head. Cumsey gave a cry of surprise and dove back inside. Morgan was right behind him.

Lot wasn't the only one shooting. Morgan glanced out the open door as he scrambled from in front of it and saw fire from several gun muzzles winking in the darkness. Bul-lets crashed through the open door and cut through the thin plank walls.

Morgan crawled to a corner beside the door, staying on his belly to keep as low as possible. Cumsey hooked a foot under the bed and dumped it on its side and squirmed behind it, but the bullets were coming through the shack too hot and heavy for Morgan to join him.

Something soft and heavy crashed to the floor beside Morgan and he turned his face to see Pork Chop lying there with blood all over his face and a neat little hole through his temple. The old gambler's hound dog eyes were wide open as if he found death to be a great surprise.

There was no time for sympathy or regret, for whoever was out there with Lot was determined to shoot the shack to doll rags, and Morgan along with it. Shattered glass from the window showered down on Morgan, and he knew that those outside were now truly surrounding the place. Two more bullets cut through the siding above Morgan's head and shredded the corn-shuck mattress as they passed through the bed that Cumsey was hidden behind. Morgan wondered if those doing the shooting would ever have to reload. When the lull in the firing finally came, the quiet in the room was almost louder than the gunfire had been.

He could hear Cumsey moving behind the bed, and knew that the outlaw was still alive and probably trying to free himself from his bonds.

"Are you hit?" Morgan whispered.

"I am," came Cumsey's whispered reply.

Morgan heard something dragging across the floor and saw Cumsey's hand disappear behind the bed with the Yellow Boy Winchester in his grasp.

"Keep low," Morgan whispered again. "The fools are shooting too high."

"We ain't making it out of this one, Clyde." Cumsey's voice was throaty and filled with pain.

Lot's voice carried to them once more. "Clyde, are you still with us?"

Morgan didn't answer, and he tried to determine where Lot's voice was coming from. It seemed to come from the front of the shack.

"You shouldn't have fired on us!" Lot called out again. "Didn't have to be this way."

Morgan knew that Lot was only talking for any onlookers that might be drawn to the excitement. He was building an alibi. As weak and untruthful as it was, Morgan knew that it would likely work if he wasn't around afterwards to question Lot's version of the events.

"To hell with you, Lot!" Cumsey popped up behind the bed with the Winchester belching flames.

The horse thief fanned the lever on the carbine as fast as he could, firing out the open door. He managed to get off four shots before the bullets started coming through the walls again from every direction. One of them shattered the lamp and kerosene spread across the floor as the room went black.

Morgan pressed himself as tightly to the floor as he could with his teeth gritted and his eyes squeezed shut while bits of wood and glass fell around him. The second volley aimed at the shack seemed to last longer than the first.

"Are you alive in there, Clyde, or are you just playing possum?" Lot called out after the firing ceased.

Again, Morgan refused to answer him.

"Cumsey, I didn't expect you to be in there," Lot said. "Must be my lucky day."

"You come in here and see how lucky you are!" Cumsey shouted back.

"Bring me that coal oil," Lot said to someone out there with him.

Morgan guessed that the threat of fire might be a bluff to flush them from the shack or to get them to talk, but he wasn't so sure when he remembered how Lot had set half the countryside on fire trying to roust Cumsey from a thicket.

Cumsey groaned, and Morgan wondered how severe the outlaw's wounds were.

He swallowed down the dry lump in his throat and whispered, "You still with me?"

"I am." Cumsey sounded worse than before.

The sound of running footsteps sounded from outside, and maybe it was only Morgan's imagination that made him think he heard the pale rattling against a can of coal oil.

"We've got to run for it before they set fire to us," Cumsey whispered.

"You up for it?"

"I'll manage."

Morgan tried to work down the knot in his throat again, and he let go of the Colt long enough to dry his palm against his shirt. There wasn't a chance in hell they would survive a run out that door. He guessed that there were at least four, maybe five guns outside, and every one of them would be paying particular attention to that door.

He heard someone outside moving close to the wall beside him, and he pointed his Colt at the sound and fired through the wall. He was immediately rewarded by a cry of pain or surprise, but it also started the shooting again.

For a third time the shack rattled under the barrage of lead, and Morgan was surer than he had been since the war that he was about to die. Instead of fear, a slow rage began to burn in him. Cumsey had it right. If a man was going to die he could at least go out fighting.

Someone out there had found a spot on the outside wall right above him, and they aimed bullet after bullet there. Most of those shots came so close to him that he swore he could feel the wind of their passing. The gunfire was one continuous roar as he pressed one cheek to the floor.

His vision locked on a floorboard where a bullet had knocked a chunk from one end of it, and at the same time he smelled smoke.

The pine lumber that the shack was built from was well cured, and the entire wall beside Morgan was soon in flames. The smoke became so dense that Morgan could see nothing above floor level, and both he and Cumsey were coughing.

Again, Morgan looked at the busted hole in the floor. He got to his knees. The opening was too tight to fit his whole hand, but he managed to get three fingers inside the hole. He hooked them under the edge of the board and pulled hard. Twice, his fingers slipped off the board, but he kept at it. He almost fell over backwards when the board suddenly came free with a screech of the nails holding it. He peered down into the dark void beneath the floor joists, and then he grabbed hold of another board, frantic to enlarge the hole.

He had the second board jerked loose when Cumsey threw the bed aside and charged past him and out the door firing the Winchester from his hip.

CHAPTER TWENTY-SEVEN

Business was slow in Molly's back room saloon, and it got slower when Lot's posse opened fire on the powder shack. The few customers she had went out the back door at the first sound of gunfire, leaving Molly at the bar with only Noodles for company.

"Mind things while I'm gone, will you?" she said as she went through the barbershop and out the front door to see what all the noise was about.

A small crowd of people had come from their homes and were trickling their way past the front of her shop, headed towards the tracks. She fell in with them and stopped when they did in the alley between the depot and the Whitlow and Coody Mercantile. She smelled smoke but could see nothing for the crowd in front of her. She pushed her way to the front and was sick with what she saw. Hannah's shack was on fire.

The fire gave enough light that she was able to make out some of the men encircling the shack, and she heard Lot Ingram shout something.

"Somebody help her," Molly said.

As soon as she said it she saw Hannah some distance to

her left. The young black woman was standing alone and watching the fire intently.

Someone took Molly by the elbow before she could go to Hannah's side. It was Hank Bickford who had taken a hold of her. He was a short, redheaded, pug-nosed man, who before settling down in Eufaula had worked as a horseshoer and blacksmith for the Katy from Kansas half the way across the territory with his wife, Lottie, doing laundry for the railroad workers to add to family coffers. Molly glanced at Hank and saw that he looked as sick and worried as she felt with the sight of the burning shack.

Her first assumption had been that the shack might have caught on fire accidentally, but the sight of Lot and his posse surrounding it let her know that some other trouble was at hand.

"Who have they hemmed up in there?" Molly asked, afraid to hear the answer. There was something about the fire that boded bad tidings.

It was obvious that Hank didn't want to tell her from the way he hesitated. "They've got Morgan in there."

Molly's legs went weak. She looked around her at the crowd, unable to believe that not one of them would lend a hand or stop what Lot and his marshals were doing.

"Why?" was all she could think to ask.

"Rumor's been going around town that Morgan was throwing his weight around in Muskogee, and when someone complained about it Morgan murdered them," Hank said.

"You don't believe that."

"No, but most of these here don't know Morgan like we do," he replied. "Morgan's a hard man with a reputation, and it's too easy to judge a man like him. And he's ruffled feathers and made enemies that are all too quick to believe the worst of him."

"Somebody's got to stop this."

"What's worse," Hank added, "is there are some here that are saying how Lot tried to arrest Morgan peaceably, but Morgan fired on him. And a bit ago we all heard that horse thief, Cumsey Bowlegs, yelling from inside that shack and shooting at the marshals. That looks bad. What's Morgan doing hiding out with Cumsey?"

"It's a lie. Morgan has been hunting Cumsey for days to arrest him."

Molly started to run towards the burning shack, but Hank held tight to her elbow. She thrashed and tried to jerk free, but he was a strong man.

"There's nothing you can do," he said.

Molly stopped struggling when Lot Ingram walked out from behind a tree he had been hiding behind and strutted along the edge of the firelight. He shouted something at the shack, and Cumsey yelled something back at him.

Another man came to stand beside Lot. It wasn't until he turned where the firelight lit the side of his face that Molly recognized him. It was Brady, the one with the scar—the one who had held the knife to her.

The flames were whipping high by then, and the shack's roof was on fire. The whole structure was going fast.

Brady let out a whoop. "Damn it, Lot, but you do love a good fire."

Molly spotted other men moving around the shack in the trees, and she wondered how many marshals Lot had with him and where they had come from. She knew then that there was no way Morgan was going to fight them all off, and it broke her heart. He could either come out to be shot down by Lot's men, or he could stay inside and burn.

Lot turned to the crowd watching him. "I gave him a fair chance. Tried to get him to surrender, but he wouldn't have it."

"You lie!" Molly shouted from the crowd.

The fire cast Lot in silhouette, making him seem taller than he was—a tall, thin, flickering stick man looking for her in the crowd. "Who said that?"

Several people in the crowd turned their heads towards Molly, identifying her as the culprit. However, it went no further than that, for at the same time Cumsey charged from the burning shack firing a rifle. Lot and Brady ducked for cover, and soon the whole posse was shooting at Cumsey.

Hannah screamed at the sight of Cumsey running and dodging with the whole posse trying to kill him. The shack lay right along the tracks and Cumsey's intention seemed to be to make a break for the darkness on the other side of them beyond the firelight.

He never made it. Molly saw Lot lean around a tree with his pistol extended at the end of his arm. The gun cracked and Cumsey fell to the ground and didn't get up.

The posse quit shooting and all was quiet except for the popping and creaking timber of the burning shack. The crowd waited as expectantly as the posse did for Morgan to make a run for it as Cumsey had. Not a word was said among them, for it was obvious that the shack's roof was going to collapse at any second.

Morgan never came out of the shack, and Molly knew he was gone when the roof fell inward, sending a shower of sparks into the sky. She looked away, and Hank let go of her.

"I'm sorry, Molly," he said. "I liked him, too."

"He's still alive!" someone shouted.

She whirled to look back at the burning shack, but her brief hope faded as quickly as that column of sparks floating upwards to be lost in the dark nothingness. The man who had shouted was standing over Cumsey's body.

So it was Cumsey who had survived. A horse thief made it when a good man like Morgan hadn't. She expected to cry and sob, but surprisingly she felt nothing but a sudden and exhausting weariness. The smoke hurt her chest and made her short of air, and she had to stop and sit down in front of the store. She sat there while the shack burned to the ground, and long after a limping Cumsey Bowlegs was led past her and taken to the hotel by three men holding guns on him. She remained there until most of the crowd had returned to their homes.

When she did get up she went in the back door of her saloon. She hoped Noodles had a pot of coffee made. It was going to be a long night.

She came through the door and the first thing she saw was Noodles standing behind the bar with Pork Chop's shotgun laid across it. Her eyes followed where the shotgun pointed and she saw the man sitting at the farthest table with his back to that corner of the room. The nearest lantern's light didn't quite reach him fully, and his face was hid in the shadows.

"Could you ask your man to put down that scattergun?" the Deacon asked.

Molly did nothing of the kind, and went to the coffeepot on the stove. She poured herself a mug of coffee and went behind the bar and found her only bottle of Jameson Irish Whiskey and poured a slug and then another in the coffee. She paused with the mug to her lips, studying the Deacon.

"What do you want?" she asked after a sip of the hot coffee.

"You offered me a job. Three hundred dollars you said."

The Deacon leaned forward over the table and she recognized he had changed his clothes. He was now dressed all in black, from the low-crowned, narrow-brimmed derby hat on his head to the black frock coat and vest he wore underneath it. But his eyes were the same.

"Put up that gun," Molly said to Noodles.

The Sicilian seemed to think that wasn't a good idea, and kept the shotgun pointed at Deacon.

"I said put it away."

He laid the shotgun on the bar top before him in easy reach. She went to the door and tossed what was left of her coffee outside, for she suddenly had no taste for it. Going back to her liquor cabinet she found a bottle of laudanum there. It wasn't her usual fix, but it would have to do. She felt herself getting shaky and the skin on her arms was starting to crawl and itch. She needed to be steady now more than ever. She kept her back to the men while she took a tug from the laudanum bottle, and then another.

"For my headache," she said when she turned around and saw Deacon watching her. She was instantly mad at herself for feeling the need to explain anything to such a man.

She crossed the room to him, bringing the rest of the bottle of Jameson and two glasses. She sat down across from him and poured them both a drink. He held up a hand to decline the offer when she started to push his glass to him.

"I'll pass," he said in that cat purr voice of his.

"Suit yourself," she said.

"You wouldn't like me when I drink."

"I don't like you when you're sober."

"So, Lot Ingram is giving you problems and you want me to kill him?"

She started to tell him that she had never said exactly that she wanted Lot murdered, but didn't. "You sound like that wouldn't bother you so much."

"Lot is fond of bragging about a disservice he did a friend of mine up in Missouri."

"I thought Lot was supposed to be from Texas."

"Maybe, but he claims he was in Missouri after the war."

"And this friend of yours?"

"Doesn't matter. They put thirty-three bullets in him, and that doesn't leave much to put a name to. Your own mother won't recognize you after that."

"Lot put thirty-three bullets in him?"

"Word has come to me more than once that Lot has told it that he was the one that fired the last bullet. Maybe he's bragging and that's only a lie, or maybe he really did it. Doesn't matter one way or the other. Either way, I take that as an insult. It's disrespect."

Deacon was known to talk in strange circles, oftentimes quoting Bible verses when he was having his craziest spells. Molly didn't have a clue what he was talking about, other than it had something to do with the war and the old grudges left in its wake. Most of the veterans she knew were more than willing to put that affair behind them, but the territory was full of those that wouldn't or couldn't, mostly old feudists and border partisans.

"I would think you would kill him for free." She wiped at the whiskey on her lips with the back of her hand.

"Three hundred dollars makes vengeance a little sweeter."

"All right, three hundred dollars."

He didn't answer her and stared at the whiskey bottle on the table.

"Well?" she asked.

He looked back up at her. "You make it sound so simple. I'll remind you, Molly, when you hire a killing, you own it, same as the one that does the actual deed. There's no getting away from it and no going back."

She nodded at him. "I can live with it."

He acted as if he hadn't heard her. "The Good Book teaches that all our souls are tainted with black sin."

"Save the preaching."

He reached out and tapped the neck of the whiskey bottle with one finger. "No preaching, only I remind you that there are different shades of black."

The laudanum and the whiskey were making things fuzzy, and everything he said seemed soft around the edges like the words were wrapped in cobwebs. "What are you saying?"

"I'm saying if I was you, I would pack my bags and go somewhere else."

"You aren't me."

"No, I'm a darker shade entirely." He picked up the whiskey she had poured for him and set it on the table closer to where he sat.

"Are you going to drink that or stare at it?" Molly asked.

He lifted the whiskey glass again and held it before him. "I fear we are about to make a pact that both of us will regret."

"I already regret it."

Deacon took a drink of the whiskey and gave a contented sigh.

Noodles hissed at her to get her attention. "Somebody outside."

Molly had heard nothing, but a pistol appeared in the

Deacon's hand. She turned to where she could see the door behind her in time to see Morgan enter the room. He was filthy and as haggard as she had ever seen him, but he was there. She wasn't sure she wasn't seeing a ghost.

"Behold, Lazarus," Deacon said.

Morgan looked at the gun Deacon had pointed at him, and Molly saw that he, too, was holding a pistol. The two men stared at each other for what seemed like an eternity.

"If that's for me, go ahead and use it," Morgan finally said.

Deacon holstered the pistol. "Don't believe I will."

Morgan looked at Molly. The shock of seeing Morgan alive hadn't yet left her, and she didn't know if she could have explained things, anyway.

"What's he doing here, Molly?" Morgan said as if Deacon couldn't hear him.

"It's complicated."

"I asked you what you're doing with him."

The laudanum and whiskey made her giggly. "Why nothing, Morgan. Just me and the devil sharing a bottle of whiskey."

She looked back at Deacon and found him staring at her with his burning eyes more intense than ever. And she wondered then if she wasn't right, and he was the devil after all.

Morgan went to the bar and ordered a drink, but Noodles barely had the cabinet open before Dixie Rayburn walked in from the front room. He looked even worse than Morgan did.

Dixie looked from Molly and Deacon at the table to Morgan and the little Sicilian standing at the bar. "I get the feeling I missed something."

Molly saw that Dixie was hurt, but that was the kind of night it was. She gestured at the chair beside her. "Like I was telling Morgan, it's complicated. And I imagine you've got a bit of a story to tell yourself."

She downed the last of her whiskey and swore she wasn't going to have another. It was already hard enough to think. What she needed was her bed.

She was so tired. Everything that was happening was suddenly too much, and the best thing to do was to wait until morning to sort it all out. She rose from her chair and staggered a little on her way to the door. She stopped there and looked back at Deacon. He was still staring at her. She was tempted then to tell him that she didn't really have three hundred dollars but didn't. What was it they used to say back in Ireland? Every man for himself and the devil take the hindmost.

Only now it was every woman for herself, and she finally had her edge. The only thing left was figuring out how to use it.

CHAPTER TWENTY-EIGHT

By daylight, the remains of the shack had cooled enough to sift through the ashes, and it was Brady that found Pork Chop's remains. Lot looked down at the blackened corpse with the majority of its flesh burned away to nothing but bone.

"Well, that's that," Brady said. "See that hole in his head? That's why Clyde never made a run for it. He was probably dead from the get-go."

"Where's his guns?" Lot asked.

"What?"

"I said, where are his guns?"

Brady kicked the ashes around the body and flipped a bit of burnt wood or two away but revealed nothing.

"Wherever they are, I imagine they'll be ruined," he said, misunderstanding what Lot meant.

The two marshals went back to the hotel. Brady went upstairs to check on their prisoner while Lot took a seat in a porch chair. He remained there while the undertaker loaded what were supposedly Clyde's remains in the wagon bed and covered them with a blanket. Red Molly and a young black woman were waiting for the wagon at the funeral parlor when the wagon went past him, and Lot reminded himself that he needed to pay Molly a visit to see how she was progressing with finding some whores to work for him. That Irish bitch could be stubborn, and another visit to her to remind her about how things were going to be might serve him well.

He rose and went into the lobby. Helvina Vanderwagen and her hotel clerk intercepted him.

"I will not have the help staying in my rooms, nor that other trash you have brought here," she said. "I have already lost two good customers this morning who have taken offense at your improprieties."

He guessed that she referred to Ma Moon and her son, and probably the Indian. His immediate reaction was to want to put her in her place. He had little use for uppity women, but there was his status as a marshal to behold. It wouldn't do for it to be said that he was putting coloreds and Indians in hotel rooms.

He looked the blond woman over from head to toe, not wanting to give in too quickly and enjoying her discomfort. She was a good-looking wench, but too proud. The haughty look on her face and the snide set of her mouth made him want to slap her as much as it made him want to see what was under that fancy dress she wore.

"Ma Moon isn't staying in one of your rooms," he said. "As you've said, she's helping me out with my prisoner. Your town doctor is off delivering a baby, and Ma knows a fair bit of healing."

"My hotel is not a jail."

"We have standards to uphold," the clerk added from where he stood behind the woman.

"Aren't you two a proper pair?" Lot said.

Neither of them responded to that and simply stood waiting, as if by their presence they could bend him to their will.

"You can quit worrying," he said, "I have other matters to attend to and I'll be leaving with my prisoner by midday. Your hotel can go back to normal."

"I will relay that good news along to my remaining customers." She gave him a fake little smile that he knew was meant to flatter him.

He pushed past them and went up the stairs to the room that had formerly belonged to Morgan. Cumsey lay on the bed with his bandaged leg propped up on a mound of pillows. Ma Moon was sitting in a chair by the window smoking her pipe. Clem sat at the foot of the bed and Brady stood by the door.

Cumsey looked at Lot. "Morning, Marshal."

"I see you're still with us," Lot said. "That's good."

Ma Moon took her pipe out of her mouth. "I don't know why you put me through all the trouble of diggin' that bullet out of his leg. First you shoot him, and then you expect me to doctor him. Don't make no kind of sense, you men."

"Where are your boys?" Lot asked her.

"They's around."

"I want them ready to travel. Brady, you go get our horses." Lot looked at Cumsey. "And get Cumsey here a horse."

"I don't know if that liveryman will expense us one," Brady said.

"Buy me a good one," Cumsey said. "I'm particular about what I ride."

"Any old horse will do," Lot said. "Cumsey isn't going far."

Cumsey scooted himself to a sitting position against the headboard, taking care to be gentle with his injured leg. A washbasin filled with pink-tinged water and a pile of bloody rags on the dresser were the leftovers of the surgery Ma had performed. Lot's bullet had hit Cumsey in the thigh, and it had taken her an hour to dig the bullet out.

Cumsey lifted the iron shackles that bound his wrists and looked at them as if seeing them for the first time. "You don't need these. I'm in no shape for running off on you."

Lot shook his head. "No, boy, you won't be doing any more running."

Cumsey jiggled the handcuffs and made them rattle, and he studied the other bandage covering the stubs of the two missing fingers on his right hand, the pinkie and the ring finger shot away. "I'm afraid you've ruined my good looks."

"You know what I'm going to do to you, don't you?" Lot asked.

"You're going to say you're sorry and tell me how this was all a big mistake?"

"Joke all you want to, but you know what's coming."

Cumsey's eyes darted to Clem at the end of the bed and to the rifle he was holding.

"I'm going to take you out in the woods and hang you," Lot went on. "Do you hear me, boy? We're going to ride out of here like we're headed for Fort Smith, but you ain't making it there. I'm going to find that same rope hanging from that same tree and I'm going to hang you."

"Go to hell." Cumsey refused to meet Lot's gaze and stared out the window.

"They think Pork Chop was you," Molly said once she got back from Hank's funeral parlor.

Morgan nodded at that news. He was sitting in the barber's chair letting Noodles cut his hair.

"Good," Dixie said. "That's two of us they won't be expecting."

He was pretending to be interested in a newspaper where he sat in Noodle's waiting area. She had made him eat something that morning and had cleansed his wounds and changed his bandages herself, but he still looked drawn and pale.

"So, I'm driving?" Deacon asked from where he stood peering out a window.

Morgan didn't answer him. In fact, he hadn't spoken to Deacon at all since the night before.

"That's the plan," Dixie replied to put an end to the awkward silence.

How those men could sit there doing nothing and looking so calm at such a time was beyond Molly. She had been busy all morning. Busy work kept her from dwelling on what had happened to poor Pork Chop, Dixie, and all the rest of it.

Morgan cleared his throat and waited until Dixie lowered the newspaper.

"Are you sure you're up to this?" Morgan asked him.

"You try stopping me."

She still couldn't quite get her mind wrapped around how Morgan had survived the burning shack, no matter how many times he explained how he had pulled the floorboards loose and crawled under the floor, and how the posse shooting at Cumsey had bought him the time needed to get away undiscovered. And then there was Dixie with his story about being shot and thrown down a well.

"Looks like Hank's gravedigger has dug a fine hole up at

the cemetery," Deacon said from the window. "I can see the dirt mound from here."

Morgan gave Deacon a hard look. It hadn't been that long ago that the two of them had tried to kill each other in that very tent, and the bad blood between them wasn't something that was going to go away, no more than the scars that they had given each other. Neither man mentioned their old troubles, but they had been circling each other all morning like two dogs met on the street with their hackles up and about to fight.

And Morgan didn't have much to say to Molly that morning, either. To say that he was displeased with her for bringing Deacon Fischer into the matter was putting it mildly, but what was done was done, and there was no way she could take it back, even if she had been of a mind to. It might work, yet, if the two of them didn't kill each other first.

Dixie took his Spencer carbine from where it leaned against the wall and handed it to him. Morgan passed the gun to Noodles.

"Don't try to be a hero," Morgan said. "Do what I told you to."

Noodles nodded.

Dixie stood, grimacing against the tear of his belly wound as he slowly straightened himself. He set his battered old Johnny Reb cap on his head.

"Are you ready?" Morgan asked him.

Dixie picked up Pork Chop's shotgun and gave it a grim look. "Let's go have us a funeral."

CHAPTER TWENTY-NINE

Clem, Ma Moon, and her son, Elijah, were left to guard Cumsey while Lot and the rest of his posse went downstairs to the hotel porch. Their horses were already tied along the hitch rails, ready to go, but Lot wanted to wait a little longer to see the funeral procession pass.

Brady leaned against one porch post to the side of the steps that led down to the street, and Lot leaned against one on the other side. Ma Moon's Indian and the dirty-faced white man that ran with him sat in chairs against the wall.

"Here it comes," Brady said.

The hearse was leaving the funeral parlor and coming down the street along the tracks at a slow walk. There was no crowd or attendants following it on foot, as was the usual practice. Perhaps people intended to join the procession along the way.

"Clyde sure did have a lot of friends, didn't he?" Brady said when he noticed the lack of mourners.

Lot looked off the end of the porch at Molly's barbershop around the corner and down the next street that led up to Cemetery Hill. He could see Molly standing there wearing a black mourning dress and waiting to join the funeral procession.

He waved a hand at the two men behind him to get their attention. "One of you go down there and fetch that woman. I want to have a talk with her."

The Indian was the one to get up.

"And you make sure to tell her to bring us some traveling money when she comes," Lot added as the Indian stepped off the end of the porch and headed towards Molly.

By then, the hearse had almost reached the hotel. It wasn't really a hearse, but rather a plain buckboard wagon that Bickford had painted black with red wheels. And when that buckboard came closer he noticed it wasn't Hank Bickford driving, either, but rather a taller, pale-faced man in a black suit and bowler hat that Lot didn't recognize.

The buckboard was almost directly in front of the porch, and Lot got a closer look at the coffin in the wagon bed. It was a large coffin made of red cedar and varnished to a high shine—a very large coffin.

The driver looked directly at him and stopped the buckboard. Lot still didn't recognize him, but he already had decided that something was very wrong. He noticed the holstered pistol shoved around to the driver's lap where it would be easy to reach, and at the same time the coffin lid flew open.

The rebel farmer that they had thrown down the well rose up out of that cedar box with a double-barreled shotgun, and Brady didn't even get a hand on his gun before a charge of buckshot took him in the chest. He tumbled from the porch, dead before he hit the ground.

A second charge of buckshot splintered the porch post and knocked out a front window, and it would have killed

Lot the same as it had Brady if Lot hadn't already been moving. He drew his right-hand pistol and was about to fire at Dixie when the Indian's dirty-faced buddy stepped in front of him with his own pistol raised. The driver didn't even bother to draw his pistol but cocked it where it was and tilted the holster leather and shot him in the belly.

The Indian's buddy grunted and staggered backwards. The wagon team was fighting against the ribbons, but the driver somehow managed to hold them in place with one hand. Lot got his own pistol up again. Dixie had dropped the empty shotgun and gathered a Winchester from the bottom of the coffin. Lot snapped a shot at him, but only managed to bust a chunk from the corner of the coffin. By the time he cocked the pistol again Dixie was working the lever on the Winchester as fast as he could. He was shooting too fast to be accurate, but at close range the firepower was deadly.

The one the driver had shot was already dead on his feet, but had yet to fall. He took two bullets from that Winchester that drove him backwards against the hotel's double glass doors. The hardware holding those doors closed burst inward under his weight, and he landed on his shoulder blades there on the lobby floor.

Another bullet whipped past Lot and knocked another hole in the window. Lot fired again and this time saw Dixie flinch and slump down in the coffin. Lot pivoted and ran for the open hotel doors. He was barely aware of the driver firing at him when he made it inside and dove over the register counter.

He landed hard, and when he gathered himself again he found the hotel clerk curled up in a little ball beside him with his arms wrapped over his head. Ignoring the clerk, he rose up behind that counter and looked out a window in time to see the driver getting down from the buckboard. He waited until he heard the man coming across the porch and he fired two shots through the open lobby doors to keep him at bay. Bits of glass sprayed across him as a bullet fired at his head passed through the window above and beside him. He threw another glance out at the street and saw that Dixie was sitting up in the coffin again firing the Winchester one-handed.

Lot ran again, keeping low and snapping another shot at the lobby doorway. He headed for the foot of the stairs. Ma Moon's son appeared at the top of those stairs with a single-barrel shotgun of the old muzzle-loading variety held to his shoulder. The shotgun was aimed at something behind Lot and he looked back in time to see the driver coming through the lobby doorway with his big, nickel-plated pistol aimed up at the balcony.

The driver and Ma's son fired at the same time. The shotgun blast took the driver head-on and he gave a cry of anguish and staggered across the lobby clutching his face. Lot stopped on the stairs and fired at him. His bullet struck the driver through the ribs and knocked him through one of the big dining room windows in a shattering of glass. The driver fell limply across the windowsill and remained there.

Lot looked to the balcony above him and found Ma's son lying upside down atop the last three steps with a bullet hole in his forehead. Lot was about to charge past his body when a voice stopped him. When he turned and looked back, he saw Morgan Clyde standing there.

CHAPTER THIRTY

Morgan came through a back door to the hotel that led through the kitchen. An Indian girl, the same one he had assumed was the hotel maid earlier, was rolling out piecrusts on the countertop and he motioned her outside when she looked up and saw him. She gave him one big-eyed glance and then ran past him and out the door. A long hallway led toward the lobby in the front of the building, and he had only taken a few steps when he ran into Helvina.

She took one look at the Colt in his hand. "What are you doing?"

"Go out back, now," he said. "And don't quit walking until you're well away from here."

"You're not doing this to me." She reached out to grab his gun, but he spun away from her, grabbed hold of her wrist, and pulled her past him.

She was about to turn back on him and say something else, but he put a boot against her bustle and gave her a hard push that sent her flying out the back door. He closed the door and dropped the latch.

Two other doors opened onto the hallway, and he opened

each of them. One was Helvina's bedroom, and the other was a pantry closet. He moved towards the daylight at the end of the hallway where the sunlight spilled into the lobby. He was almost there when the shooting started.

His plan had been to come on Lot and the marshals from behind, or if he was lucky, to possibly find Cumsey before the fight started. As it was, he was late, either way.

A stray bullet shredded the wallpaper beside him, and he ducked low and ran towards the sound of the gunfire. The hallway entered the lobby at one corner near the register desk. He arrived barely in time to see Lot jump from behind it and take off across the lobby towards the stairs. And he saw Deacon take the shotgun charge full in the face.

Lot was halfway up the stairs. "Here I am, Lot."

Morgan expected Lot to turn shooting, but he didn't. He stood there on the stairs with his pistol hanging at the end of his arm beside his leg.

"I thought you were dead," Lot said. "Thought I burned you down."

"You can drop it, Lot, or you can die," Morgan said aiming his Colt at Lot's chest.

Lot gave a resigned sigh and dropped the pistol, and it thumped hard as it bounced down the hardwood stairs. Morgan's attention wavered for a split second to that pistol, and that was when Lot drew his left-hand gun.

It was a slick, nervy move. and it almost worked. Almost. Lot's pistol was about clear of the holster when Morgan shot him.

Lot managed to fire his pistol once, but the round went off into the steps at his feet. Morgan shot him again, and then stepped out of the way as Lot's body tumbled downwards to land in a heap at the foot of the stairs.

* * *

Morgan thumbed the empty rounds from his pistol cylinder and replaced them with two more .45 cartridges from his vest pocket while he looked up to the head of the stairs. Cumsey was likely up there somewhere, and with him would be whoever was guarding him. One of the steps creaked under his boot as he started up those stairs.

Molly saw the Indian coming toward her and waited until he was closer before she went back inside the barbershop. When he came through the door, she was standing half in and half out of the tarp wall that divided the barbershop from the saloon. Noodles was sitting in the barber's chair with the white haircutting cape draped over him and clasped at his neck as if he were about to get a haircut.

The Indian stopped just inside the door. "Lot wants to talk to you, and he said to make sure you bring him some traveling money."

"Tell him to come himself if he wants to talk," Molly said.

The Indian looked from Molly to Noodles, and then back to her. "He said to get you, and that's what I'm going to do."

"And what if I said no?"

He started across the room, but at that point he must have seen how she was purposefully hiding her right side behind the tarp. He put a hand to his pistol butt. The Spencer carbine Noodles held in his lap under the cape boomed, and the big .56 bullet struck the Indian through the side of his rib cage and he grunted with the impact and staggered sideways until he caught himself against the wall. Noodles was working to lever another round into the Spencer, but it had become tangled in the cape when he had tried to throw the cloth free of him.

The Indian tugged his pistol free and was lifting it when

Molly stepped up to him and pressed the pearl-handled Smith & Wesson pistol to his temple and pulled the trigger.

Ma Moon paced across the room, nervous because of the gunfight going on beneath them, and nervous because she couldn't see what was going on. "Elijah, you go see what's happenin'. But take care, mind you."

Her son went out the door, slamming it behind him.

Cumsey was sitting on the edge of the bed. They had been about to go downstairs when they had heard the first gunshot. Clem was backed against the wall to one side of the window. He had his pistol leveled on Cumsey, and was taking a quick look at the street occasionally.

"I think we done played hell," Ma Moon said. "Never should have come here. Let Lot Ingram stomp his own snakes."

A gun bellowed just down the hallway.

"Elijah, you all right?" she called out.

No answer came.

"Oh, Lord," she said.

Clem jumped on the bed, kneeling behind Cumsey and pressing his pistol to the back of Cumsey's head while he watched the door.

"Oh, Lordy me," Ma said again.

"Would you shut the hell up?" Clem shouted.

A hallway board creaked not far from the door. Clem shifted a little, keeping Cumsey between himself and the door.

"You better sprout wings and learn to fly, Clem," Cumsey said. " 'Cause that's the only way you're getting out of this one."

"That you, Elijah?" Ma asked.

No answer came. A floorboard in the hallway creaked again. Clem took his pistol from Cumsey's head and fired through the door.

Cumsey took advantage of the moment and slammed his head back into Clem's face. The two of them struggled on the bed, punching and gouging. When they came to their feet, Cumsey swung with both hands and hit Clem in the head with the handcuffs. Clem fell away but recovered quickly. His pistol was swinging towards Cumsey when Cumsey ran towards the window. He didn't even slow down when he busted through the glass and sailed out of sight.

Clem ran to the window with his pistol poised to shoot down where Cumsey landed, but the door burst open behind him and he turned towards it in time to see Morgan standing there. Morgan's .45 cracked once, twice, and Clem slumped to the floor.

Ma Moon looked from the dead man to Morgan. She couldn't seem to catch her breath, and for some reason her arm was hurting so badly that she looked to see if she had been shot.

"Throw your pistol on the bed," Morgan said to her.

It took her a moment to realize what he wanted, but she finally nodded and gingerly plucked the gun from her dress pocket and pitched it on the mattress.

Morgan marched her down the stairs at gunpoint.

"Oh, Lord," she wailed when they went past her dead son's body.

Dixie met them in the lobby. His side was bloody, and he was using Morgan's new Winchester as a crutch to keep him upright.

"Are you all right?" Morgan asked.

Dixie looked down at his bloody side. "Got hit almost in the same, exact spot. Knocked another chunk out of me, but I don't think it's too bad, other than it hurts like hell. And I think I tore up something in my ankle jumping out of the wagon."

Morgan looked at Deacon's body. "The Deacon wasn't so lucky."

"No, he wasn't."

"What about Cumsey?"

Dixie shook his head and started towards the porch. "You ain't going to believe this."

Morgan pushed Ma ahead of him and followed Dixie.

Dixie hobbled down the steps and didn't stop until he was out in the street. He turned and pointed up at the broken second-story window Cumsey had leapt from. "I was climbing out of the wagon when I heard the glass bust. I look up and Cumsey's flying through the air."

Morgan saw no sign of the horse thief. "Where is he?"

"Lucky devil hit the porch and broke his fall. Even then, I thought he was dead when he hit the ground," Dixie said.

"Thought he was dead 'til he got up and ran off."

"He ran off?"

"That boy is faster on one leg than a man has any right to be on two."

Morgan grunted and couldn't help but grin. "He always bragged how fast he was. How come you didn't stop him?"

Dixie went to the porch steps and set down heavily. "Me? I'm done for the day. You go catch him if you want him. You're the lawman."

"Mind if I join you?" Ma asked Dixie. "I'm feelin' a little off."

"It's a free country," Dixie said and scooted over a little for her.

Morgan turned and saw Molly coming down the street towards him. He waited for her, but when she came to him she kept going and didn't stop until she knelt at Dixie's feet.

Morgan watched as she examined Dixie's wounds and fussed over him, and then he walked away.

CHAPTER THIRTY-ONE

A train arrived not an hour after the fight. A small group of passengers disembarked at the depot, and Morgan was sitting on the hotel porch when Bert Huffman came up the street to him. The railroad superintendent looked at the damaged hotel with a cringing expression, and was about to say something when Helvina stormed onto the porch. She spied Morgan sitting in one of her chairs and went to him and gave him a vicious slap across the face.

"You're going to pay for this," she said. "You're going to pay for it one way or the other."

Morgan fended her off long enough to get up from the chair. But whatever physical violence she had intended for him seemed spent. Now she only stood trembling and with her breath coming ragged and uneven. Her green eyes were wet with tears.

"I'm sorry . . ." Morgan said.

"To hell you are!"

"Helvina . . ."

"I'm going to get you for this, one way or the other," she said. "Maybe not today, maybe not tomorrow, but I'm going to ruin you."

She went down off the porch without giving him a chance to reply. He watched her head towards the depot.

"Quite the temper, that one," Huffman said. "I believe she meant what she said."

"Helvina usually does, and the nastier what she says goes, the more she means it."

Huffman gave the shot-up hotel another look. "I got your telegraph message."

"Little too late for that," Morgan said. "It's done."

"I take it you have already brought your investigation to a conclusion."

"You could say that."

"And I assume from this," Huffman pointed at a shattered window, "that you have done it in . . . let's say . . . your customary style."

Morgan pointed to Hank Bickford's funeral parlor. "You'll find my evidence down there."

"I was afraid of that," Huffman said.

A group of soldiers was coming from the depot house.

"Are they with you?" Morgan asked.

"Seems you don't need them now."

"Could have used them yesterday."

"It took some time to convince their commanding officer that he should get involved."

"Doesn't matter now."

"What do I tell Chief Whitley?"

"Tell him whatever you want to." Morgan gestured at the second story of the hotel. "There's a woman prisoner up there that might be worth talking to."

The soldiers were close enough by then that Huffman went to them and had a talk. Two of the infantrymen went inside the hotel to retrieve Ma Moon while Huffman came back to Morgan.

Huffman looked at the funeral parlor. "If I may ask, who is that you've sent to the local mortician?"

"Three deputy marshals and three of their posse."

"I take it that they were corrupt as we had suspected."

"You take it right."

"You know Whitley will want a report on this, and you're going to have to go to Fort Smith and explain this all."

Morgan nodded.

Huffman walked along the front of the hotel until he came to the broken front doors. The clerk was on his hands and knees scrubbing at a bloodstain on the carpet.

Huffman looked back at Morgan. "I don't doubt that she will sue the MK & T for her damage."

"I can guarantee she will." Morgan went down the steps and started along the street.

The two infantrymen who had gone into the hotel came outside.

"That woman you sent us after, she's dead," one of them said.

Huffman looked at Morgan. "Did you shoot her, too?"

"She wasn't shot," the same soldier said. "Looks like she just laid down and died in her sleep. Like her heart just quit."

Morgan went down off the porch and started along the street.

"Where are you going?" Huffman asked.

Morgan pointed towards Cemetery Hill. "I'm going to see if that gravedigger is still up there. He needs to dig another hole."

CHAPTER THIRTY-TWO

Morgan didn't get up until late the next morning, and by the time he had bathed and shaved it was near noon before he came down to the lobby. He was accosted there almost immediately by Huffman. The superintendent was carrying a telegraph message.

"I've been in contact with Chief Whitley," Huffman said.

Morgan was still too bleary-eyed and half asleep to care after staying up half the night writing a brief overview of his case and the events that had led to the shootout in the hotel— a report that Huffman had insisted be done without delay.

But he tried to give the appearance of being attentive. "Oh?"

"He seems quite pleased with your work, after I managed to smooth over some of the rougher parts of your report."

Morgan rubbed his face. "That's good."

"And there is some other interesting news. Judge Story has resigned his position on the bench," Huffman said. "I understand it that a new judge has already been appointed. A Judge Isaac C. Parker, I believe. A good republican from Ohio by way of Missouri."

"Hoorah," Morgan said blandly.

"No need to be a smart aleck," Huffman growled. "What might interest you more is that Whitley believes that he can use his influence to obtain a deputy's job for you with the U.S. Marshals office."

"I thought I had a job." Morgan tapped the badge on his chest.

"I think your talents would be far better suited to the Marshals office," Huffman said, and he gave a grin that was meant to take the sting out of the matter.

Morgan made as if to unpin the badge.

"No, I'm not firing you on the spot. Wait until you hear more from Chief Whitley."

Morgan was hungry, and breakfast was already being served in the dining area. But he didn't want to chance hanging around in the lobby any longer and encountering Helvina.

"How about a morning toddy and maybe some brunch?" Morgan asked. "I've got a friend down the street."

"I believe I'll wait for lunch and dine here." Huffman was looking across the lobby where Helvina had appeared. "Did you know she has already presented me with a bill for damages?"

"I'm sure the total was three times what they should have been."

"More like four," Huffman said. "She really is quite stunning, isn't she?"

Morgan ducked out the front door and headed towards Molly's cabin. He knocked on her door.

"Who is it?" Dixie's voice answered.

Morgan stepped quietly away. He saw that the back door leading into Molly's saloon was standing open and he went that way. He found Molly busy serving drinks to the soldiers.

She had sandwich makings on a small folding table near the stove, and he built himself one and took a seat at a corner table. Noodles brought him a beer.

Molly came over when she got the chance. "They're having the funerals today at one."

Morgan swallowed a bite of sandwich. "Stopped by your cabin looking for you."

A red flush crept across her face. "Dixie needed a place to sleep."

"I'm sure he did."

"He's hurt."

"Of course."

"You seem in a fine mood," she said to change the subject. Dixie hobbled into the room. He gave Morgan an embarrassed look and then an even more awkward exchange passed between him and Molly.

"Have a seat," Morgan said. "I'd say a man who's been shot two times in a matter of days ought to be in bed, but if you're up to it I'll gladly buy you a beer."

Dixie flopped in a chair as if his legs had taken him as far as they could. "I'll pass on the beer."

"Sleep good?" Morgan asked with a grin.

"Now Morgan, it's like this. You know Molly and I are friends . . ."

"Oh, Molly has told me everything."

"You listen here . . ." Dixie was starting to get mad. He had always had a quick temper.

Morgan held up both hands. "Peace."

"I still want to know what's got you in such fine spirits," Molly said.

"For one thing, I just heard Judge Story has resigned. It seems the heat got a little too hot in his kitchen."

"Will there be trouble over what happened yesterday?" she asked.

"I'll have to ride to Fort Smith and do a little explaining to the powers-that-be, but I doubt there will be a grand jury arraigned," Morgan said. "I don't think anyone's going to make much of a fuss about Lot Ingram's passing."

"That's good," she said. "I was afraid . . ."

Morgan noticed that Dixie put a reassuring hand on top of Molly's on the table.

"I've got other news," Morgan said.

"What's that?" Dixie asked.

"Huffman says that the Marshals' office might have a job for me."

"Are you going to take the offer?"

"There's been no offer yet, at least nothing concrete."

"Don't do it, Morgan," Molly said. "Open a business here in town. You've said you were a businessman once, and you're an educated man. I'm sure you could think of something."

"I'll think on it."

"No, you won't. You're only saying that," she said. "Hang up your gun, Morgan. There's no good end to the life you're living."

"This is what I do," Morgan said.

"And I was a whore once, but I'm not anymore."

Morgan stood. "I need another beer."

He couldn't catch Noddles's attention, for the Sicilian was too busy with the soldiers. There were five of the infantrymen that Huffman had brought with him from Fort Gibson, and Morgan found a spot between two of them and waited for Noodles to come over his way.

The light that was cast through the open door fell directly along the bar, and when it turned to shadow Morgan looked to see who was in the doorway and blocking the sun. A young man, in uniform, stood there.

The soldiers around Morgan grew quiet and straightened their postures.

"Hello, Lieutenant," the soldier to Morgan's left said. "Bet you wonder what we're doing here."

"I'm sure you're getting drunk and working on your next stretch in the guardhouse," the lieutenant in the doorway said.

Morgan squinted at the officer. It was hard to make him out with the sunlight leaking around him.

"No trouble here, Lieutenant Clyde. Just come for a haircut," one of the other soldiers snickered.

"I'm going to look away for a moment, and when I look back I expect to find all of you at the train station where you were supposed to be ten minutes ago," the lieutenant said.

He stepped aside to let his men out the door, and Morgan saw him clearly for the first time. He was tall and younger than Morgan had first guessed, a handsome lad with a fine look to him.

And he had his mother's eyes.

The lieutenant noticed Morgan staring at him. "You do realize that you're staring, don't you?"

"Hello, Ben. It's been a long time."

The lieutenant's back stiffened and he took a deep breath. "I had forgotten what you look like, but I guess I know who you are."

"Like I said, it's been a long time." Morgan stepped forward, coming closer to him.

The lieutenant took a step back. "She told me you were around when I first came to Fort Gibson."

"How long have you been stationed there?" The lieutenant didn't answer him.

"I don't know why my letters never got to you," Morgan said.

"I received them."

"I don't know what to say or where to start."

The lieutenant straightened his uniform jacket. "There's nothing to say."

"You're wrong there."

"Mother has told me how you followed her to the territory and the trouble you've caused for her."

Morgan let that lie stand. Slandering Helvina would get him nowhere. "Hear me out."

"I will do no such thing."

"I'm your father. I think you owe me that much."

"Owe you?"

"That was a poor choice of words."

The lieutenant looked Morgan up and down, and then a sneer formed on his mouth. "Indeed, it was. I have no father."

"I understand how you feel . . ."

"Then you know I want no part of you."

"I . . ."

"I must attend to my men." Lieutenant Benjamin Clyde spun on one heel in a parade ground maneuver and went out the door and left Morgan standing there alone at the bar.

Morgan had no clue how long he stood there, but it was Molly's voice that broke him from his spell.

"Give him time to think on it," she said.

"Yes, time," Morgan muttered, suddenly self-conscious

knowing that she and Dixie had overheard his conversation with Ben.

"Where are you going?" Dixie asked.

"Thought I would be there for Deacon's funeral," Morgan said.

"Wouldn't have thought you would attend."

Morgan stopped at the door. "I don't know, it just feels wrong not to go."

When Morgan was gone Molly looked at Dixie. "Now that was strange."

"His son showing up here, or him going to Deacon's funeral?" Dixie asked.

"Start with Deacon. I don't know why I told Morgan what time the services were to be held. Never thought for a million years he would want to go," she said.

"I'd guess Morgan's looking to the future."

"Future? You heard him. He'll wear that badge until they lay him low."

Dixie gave her a sad smile. "That's the future he's looking to."

Molly got up and went out the door. She shaded her eyes with a hand to her brow and looked for Morgan. She saw him after a moment. He was walking up the road towards the cemetery.

She came back and sat down, thinking about what Dixie had said. She also thought about pouring herself a drink, but she resisted the urge.

"Molly, I've been thinking," Dixie said after they had sat there in silence for a time.

"You have, have you?"

"I've got a question to ask you, but you're making it hard."

Molly looked down at the table and smiled when she looked back up at him. "You do know that you're holding my hand again, don't you?"

"Do you mind?"

"I don't. It's kind of nice."

They sat quiet again and listening to Noodles singing in Sicilian from the front room while he swept the floor. They couldn't understand the words, but somehow they fit the mood.

And outside, Morgan Clyde walked alone up Cemetery Hill towards an outlaw and a grave. It wasn't the first time he had walked that road, and it wouldn't be the last.

TURN THE PAGE FOR AN EXCITING PREVIEW!

Spur Award–Winning Author

BRETT COGBURN
The Great-Grandson of the real Rooster Cogburn

SMOKE WAGON
A Morgan Clyde Western
NEW SERIES!

LAST STOP ON THE TRAIN RIDE TO HELL

Welcome to Ironhead Station, Indian Territory, where the train tracks end and the real action begins. The hell-on-wheels construction camp is the final destination for hard-drinking sinners, gamblers, and outlaws. And woe to the man who tries to clean it up.

Morgan Clyde is a former New York City policeman and Union sharpshooter who lost everything in the Civil War. But he's still got his guns and his guts. Some folks say he's meaner and tougher than the Devil himself. Which is why the owners of the MK&T Railroad hired Clyde for one hell of a job. They plan to extend the rails through Indian Territory, connecting Missouri and Kansas to Texas. But the ornery citizens of Ironhead Station want to keep things just the way they are. They've already killed the first two lawmen who tried to tame their town. Now they've put together a welcome wagon to greet Clyde, including one half-mad preacher, one hillbilly assassin, and twenty train-robbing bushwhackers. They're laying plans to stop the railroad dead in its tracks—along with their new lawman . . .

SMOKE WAGON by Brett Cogburn

On sale now, wherever Pinnacle Books are sold.

CHAPTER ONE

Morgan Clyde stepped out of the door of the passenger car and paused on the steps, apparently unaware of, or simply not giving a damn about, the other people lined up behind him who were wishing he would move so that they could get off the train. The locomotive up the line hissed as the engineer bled off the boiler pressure, and the late winter breeze blew a cloud of steam, cinders, and coal smoke down the depot decking. Morgan squinted through the haze while he shoved a cigar in the corner of his mouth below his black mustache. His left hand flipped the tail of his black frock coat behind the Remington and Beal revolver holstered high on that hip at a cross draw, and he struck a match on the butt of the pistol and cupped it before his face, coolly studying the sprawling tent city before him over the flame.

The first thing that struck him was the noise of so many people moving about the camp: men shouting to each other or cursing wagon teams, the pound of hammers and the rasp of saws where a crew was working to raise the frame on the new depot house, and someone banging away on an out-of-tune piano down the street.

The second thing that hit him was the smell—the smell and the filth.

It had rained recently, and the one so-called street was nothing more than a mud lane running straight as a Cherokee arrow through the tents and false-fronted, canvas-roofed businesses lining either side of it. Water stood in the low places and in every hoof divot and wagon rut. And it wasn't only mud and rainwater. Horse and mule manure, dog feces, emptied chamber pots, and trash all mixed freely into the viscous soup that the street had become, until the whole camp looked and smelled like a hog pen.

The letter he had received claimed that there were, at last count, three hundred souls in the construction camp, but here it was a little past midday, and with most of the railroad crews still out working, the street was teeming with people, wading and cursing their way across or along the street. Wagon wheels sank to the hubs in bottomless ruts, and the mule teams pulling them worked hock deep with their ears flattened and their backs humped against the strain of the mud sucking everything down, down, down. Their trace chains popped each time the mules lunged forward, and the drivers shouted at pedestrians to get the hell out of the way before their wagons stalled out and became stuck.

Boards had been laid as walkways in places, but most of the boards had already sunk below the surface. Staying even reasonably clean was impossible in the shin-deep quagmire. Everyone in sight was muddy from the knees down, and some worse.

A drunk came out of one of the tent saloons and sank to his knees in an especially deep hole. The suction of the mud took hold of one of his legs, and he windmilled his arms wildly to catch his balance until he fell face-first in the street. He was soon up on his feet again, coated from head to toe in good old Indian Nations mud, and looking for the boot that had been pulled off his trapped foot. A wagonload of logs was about on top of him, and he lunged away just as the lead mules trampled whatever chance he had of ever recovering the lost boot. The wagon's driver and the drunk exchanged loud insults, but the wagon inched on toward the tracks.

Morgan took it all in with his face as hard and still and expressionless as an Indian's, his ice-blue eyes gauging the scene before him like an undertaker measuring a man for a coffin. He shook out the match and flipped it to the ground in a smoking arc.

Somebody shouted near the bare-bones frame of the new depot house, followed by catcalls and boisterous laughter from several more men near the train. A pistol cracked, and out of instinct and reflex, Morgan's hand took hold of the Remington's grip. The people behind Morgan in the doorway of the passenger car flinched and ran into each other trying to get back inside. It only took Morgan an instant to spot the culprits. A young black man dressed like a cowboy in tall-topped boots and a red silk neckerchief, and two Indians dressed much the same, had their pistols out and were shooting them into the air. They paraded up and down the depot platform like strutting roosters.

At least fifty people were gathered alongside the newly arrived train, either as passengers or gawkers from the camp. The first pistol shot quieted the crowd, and then they scattered like quail flushed from the tall grass when all three of the drunken cowboys fired a second volley. A buggy mare spooked so badly that she kicked one of her buggy shafts in two, and fell on her side and became tangled in her harness.

"Welcome to the Indian Nations, you train-riding sons a bitches!" the black cowboy shouted and took off his broad-brimmed hat and waved it in a circle above his head.

One of his companions whooped beside him, and then leaned back his head and did his best imitation of a coyote yipping at the moon. He had a pint bottle of whiskey in one hand, and his pistol in the other. "Gonna scalp me a tenderfoot before today's over."

One of the carpenters up in the rafters of the depot house flung his hammer at the black cowboy, nearly striking him in the skull. The black cowboy popped off a shot at the hammer-flinger, but the carpenter was nimble and smart enough to dodge amongst the rafters. The shot went wild, and it didn't help the black cowboy's aim that he was sloppy drunk and reeling on his boot heels. He was still peering up in the rafters with his pistol cocked and hoping for another shot at the carpenter when one of his Indian companions hissed a warning at him.

It looked like one of the railroad crews was coming up the street with its attention on the trio causing the ruckus. Every one of those railroad workers was carrying a club or a sledgehammer or some other kind of bludgeoning instrument to adjust the behavior of the men doing all the hell raising. The black cowboy forgot about the hammer-flinging carpenter, and he and his comrades began to slip away through the crowd, trying to put distance between themselves and the railroad gang coming their way. The whole episode ended as quickly as it had begun.

"You've got to be kidding," the woman behind Morgan said.

She was middle-aged, portly, and wearing a little bonnet as prim and sour as the look on her freckled, big-nosed face. Her husband, two inches shorter than her and half her weight, stood behind her in the passenger car door with a pipe clenched in one corner of his mouth. A mass of curly red hair stuck out from under the wool cap he wore.

"It'll be all right, Mother," her husband said.

"Where's the law?" She gave an indignant huff.

"There ain't no law in Ironhead Station, Mother. None at all."

"Lord, help us."

"They say there ain't no church west of St. Louis, and no God west of Fort Smith, neither," the husband added.

"Shame on you. Take that blasphemy back right now." The woman immediately slapped him hard on the shoulder.

Morgan let go of his pistol and continued to listen to the pair's conversation while his eyes followed the trio of hellions' retreat down the street. Apparently, to hear him talk, the woman's husband had been in the camp before.

"They've appointed two marshals: one a former Yankee officer, and the other a Texan. But neither of them lasted longer 'n the time it takes to spit," the husband said. "First one turned in his badge his first day on the job and caught the next train north. Had his fill of it, and was glad he didn't ride out of here lying on his back. The second one, that Texan, wasn't so smart, but he had more guts than a slaughterhouse. Lasted a whole three days before Texas George picked a fight with him and shot him dead."

"Sodom and Gomorrah is what I see. We should've stayed in Carthage," the wife said.

"We've already talked about this a hundred times if we've talked about it once. If you want to go back to Missouri, you can. It ain't like I didn't try to tell you how it was going to be."

The wife shook her head. "No, we'll stick. Can't be a family with us back home and you down here. We'll have to find a way to get by, that's what we'll have to do."

"They're always like this," Morgan said, almost as if talking to himself.

It took the man and woman a bit to realize that it was he who had spoken, so quietly had he stood before.

"Begging your pardon?" the husband asked.

Morgan exhaled a cloud of cigar smoke and turned to them. "I said, these end-of-the-tracks construction camps are always like this."

"Yep, but this one's way worse than most, and it's gonna be wild for a while," the husband answered. "That trestle across the South Canadian has things held up. They bridged the North Canadian without a problem, but this one is a whole 'nother animal. The first one they built on the south fork of the river collapsed on them, and then some of the local badmen tried to burn down their next attempt. This railroad ain't never going to get across the Territory if they don't get that bridge built, and there's more and more men packing into Ironhead Station every day—most of them the kind that you'd rather not see around."

"Is that what they're calling it?" Morgan asked. "Ironhead?"

"For now, until it catches fire, or somebody comes up

with a better name." The husband chewed on his pipe stem and made a clicking sound in his cheek. "The railroad's laid off more than half its men until the bridge gets built and they can start laying track again. Most of those they laid off are still hanging around with too much whiskey and too much time on their hands, and word's gone out across the Territory that the company is stalled out here. Every holdup artist, tinhorn gambler, whiskey peddler, and pimp and sporting woman in the Nations is either here, or on their way here to get in on the action."

"Hank!" the wife said. "Watch your talk."

The husband gave a fake grimace that was meant as an apology, but continued, regardless. "I've only been gone a week, but I already see another tent saloon that wasn't here when I left and about twice as many people."

"I know it sounds bad of me, but the Lord ought to strike this whole place down." The wife interrupted Morgan's thoughts. "Turn the whole thing to nothing but a pillar of salt and then wash it clean with a flood."

"Please don't mind the Missus. My Lottie is a God-fearing woman, but she just ain't used to all this." The husband set down an armload of luggage, and held out his right hand to Morgan. "Name's Henry Bickford. Everyone calls me Hank."

Morgan shook with him, surprised at the hard strength in the little man's calloused grip. "Morgan Clyde."

Hank Bickford pumped Morgan's hand, but leaned back as if to get a better look up at him upon hearing his name. There was a measuring and cautious look on his face, and he gathered his words carefully before he spoke again. "Pleased to meet you, Mr. Clyde."

"My Hank is a horseshoer and blacksmith for the line.

What brings you here, Mr. Clyde? What line of work are you in?" the wife asked, oblivious to the warning look on her husband's face.

Morgan reached down and picked up his single little leather valise and the bedroll he had left on the deck while lighting his cigar. Hank Bickford noticed that the bedroll was wrapped around a suede leather rifle case.

"You might say I'm a troubleshooter." Morgan smiled around the cigar, as if it took an effort for the muscles of his face, and as if it were an unnatural expression for him.

"Troubleshooter?" the wife asked. "What kind of job is that? Are you here to get the bridge built?"

"You might say that. Good day." Morgan tucked his belongings under one arm, tipped his hat to them, and started down the steps.

Hank Bickford waited until Morgan was off the train and several yards away before he picked up their luggage again.

"Seemed like a nice man for a Yankee," she said. "Although, that was kind of rude for him to walk off like that without answering my question."

Hank didn't reply to her, still watching Morgan's tall form winding its way through the crowd of people headed for the company headquarters. Lottie tightened her shawl about her neck and shoulders and stiffened beside him when she noticed a pair of prostitutes standing alongside the tracks with nothing but skimpy wraps over their underclothes, and calling out ribald jokes and loud, lewd innuendos to a group of men at work unloading equipment off a flatcar.

"Those girls sure must be hot-natured to go with so little clothes," Hank said.

Lottie elbowed him in the ribs and pulled her children close to her, hugging them to either side of her broad hips like little chicks underneath a mother hen. "This is the devil's playground if ever there was such a thing."

Hank gave her a halfhearted, worried smile, and then nodded his head at Morgan's back. "Maybe so, Mother, but the devil didn't show up until today."

"Him?"

"Yes, him. You might say hell's come to breakfast, sure enough."

"If you won't mind your talk in front of me, then remember our children."

"Sorry, Mother, but that's the pure truth." Hank's attention turned to the construction crew still chasing after the trio that had been hoorahing and threatening the train's arrival. He shook his head somberly and almost regretfully while looking over the camp, as if standing over a friend's grave at a funeral and mourning his passing. "And these poor amateurs don't even know what's coming. But they will soon enough. You wait and see. Won't be long until word gets out all through this hell-on-wheels that Morgan Clyde has come to town."

CHAPTER TWO

The railroad company had its office at the end of the platform alongside the depot house under construction, and on the corner facing the head of what passed for a main street. It was a single-story, two-room frame affair with a canvas wagon tarp for a temporary roof, and green-sawn yellow pine planks still oozing sap for siding. But however hurriedly and shoddily it was built, it did have the only boardwalk in town in front of it, consisting of a narrow ribbon of small logs laid side by side in a corduroy fashion, and a man could at least keep his feet dry. Morgan glanced at the sign over the front door.

MK&T RAILROAD OFFICE,
IRONHEAD STATION, INDIAN TERRITORY.

Two tough-looking men sat in chairs to either side of the door, and both of them had shotguns laid across their laps.

He weaved his way through the crowd on the board-walk, and nodded at the two guards. Neither of them spoke to him, but they didn't stop him from going inside, either. The front room consisted of a table piled with all kinds of ledgers and various other clerical papers, and a single chair behind it. Apparently, the clerk was gone on other business, but Morgan heard voices coming from an interior doorway to the rear of the office.

Three men stopped their conversation and looked his way when he stepped into the back room. One of them was a short, stocky, bulldog of a man, a tick past middle-age, and dressed in a tailored suit. He sat at the back of the room, reared back in his office chair with his fingers laced together over the belly of his paisley vest and his feet propped up on one corner of his office desk. Both of his jaws were covered in muttonchop whiskers, combed and waxed and sticking out like wings, and his hair was oiled and parted with perfect precision down the middle of his skull. His blue-gray eyes were like glass when he glanced at Morgan in the doorway, and an impatient frown crinkled his mouth.

Another man stood at a large set of plans and drafts-man drawings of the river bridge pinned to the wall. He was young, and unlike the man at the desk, he was dressed in rough work clothes with his sleeves rolled up to his elbows and his thumbs hooked in his suspenders. His lower body, from his canvas work pants to his lace-up boots, was covered in a thick layer of dried mud.

The third man sat in a chair at one end of the desk. He was tall and scarecrow thin, with a stoop to his narrow shoulders and a hump in his back to match a young buffalo's. Like the man behind the desk, he was dressed in a suit; however his wasn't nearly so expensive or neat. Everything about him was wrinkled and haphazard, from his threadbare jacket, to his untied string tie, to the crooked way his eyeglasses sat on the bridge of his beak of a nose.

"If you're looking to hire on, you need to come back when the clerk is in," the man behind the desk said in a tone of dismissal. He turned his attention back to the drawing on the wall, as if he had forgotten Morgan's presence already.

Morgan set his belongings down, leaning the end of the rifle case against the wall, and reached in his vest pocket and pulled forth an envelope. He crossed the room and pitched the envelope on the desk in front of the man.

"Your letter said you'd pay me fifty dollars for coming down here and looking things over, and I've looked it over," Morgan said.

"See here, we're holding an important meeting," the stooped man at the end of the desk said.

The man behind the desk held up a hand to quiet him, while he eyed the letter and then stared at Morgan as if seeing him for the first time. "Hold on, Euless. I did send for this man."

The one called Euless gave Morgan an expectant look, as if waiting for a name. Morgan ignored him and focused his attention on the man behind the desk.

"Your answering letter said you would be here a week ago." The man behind the desk had a Midwest accent that Morgan couldn't quite place—maybe Illinois, or Indiana.

"I was busy," Morgan replied. "Are you Superintendent Duvall?"

"That I am." The man behind the desk reached into a shipping crate behind his desk that served as a temporary cabinet, and pulled out a bottle of whiskey and several glasses. He set them on the desk. "Willis G. Duvall,

MK&T Railroad, at your service. This man to my left is the agent for the Creek Indian tribe, Euless Pickins."

The Indian agent nodded at Morgan. He was the odd one in the room—nervous and restless and continually shifting positions in his chair. Morgan noted how the man stared at the floor and rarely made eye contact, and how he picked at a scab on the back of one of his hands.

"And this Scotsman is my head construction engineer and foreman." Superintendent Duvall pointed at the man in work clothes standing before the bridge plans on the wall. "Hope McDaniels, meet Morgan Clyde. Mr. Clyde is going to be our new chief of police."

"Morgan Clyde!" the Indian agent blurted out before the engineer could reply. He made no attempt to hide his distaste at hearing Morgan's name.

"Care for a toddy?" Superintendent Duvall tried to smooth over the embarrassing gaff by gesturing at one of the whiskey glasses on the desk.

"Business first," Morgan replied.

"Have a seat then." Duvall pointed at a spare chair.

"I believe I'll stand."

"Are you always so disagreeable?"

"No sense wasting any of our time."

"Suit yourself." Duvall poured himself a drink and pitched a tin badge on the table before he leaned back in his chair again. "You start today."

Morgan didn't even look at the badge, much less pick it up. "We need to sort out a few things first."

"Go ahead." There was impatience in the superintendent's voice.

"One hundred and fifty dollars a month," Morgan said.

"You never told me you were trying to hire this man," Agent Pickins interrupted them again.

Superintendent Duvall made another dismissive wave of his hand at the Indian agent. "Let's hear the man out, Euless."

"I hire my own deputies, and you'll pay them seventy-five a month," Morgan said as if it were only he and the railroad superintendent in the room. "I won't hire more than two of them."

"Your price is too steep. That's half again what you quoted me in your reply to my letter."

"You get what you pay for," Morgan said. "And I quoted you that first price before I had a chance to look this camp over. I've seen it now, and I think it calls for a premium on my services."

"I suppose this is negotiable?"

"Those are my terms, take them or leave them," Morgan said. "Normally I get a cut of the fines, too, but this place won't be here long enough to set that up."

"This is preposterous. You've no right to hire a marshal," Agent Pickins said. "This isn't a real town, nor will it be according to the terms the railroad has promised the Indian tribes."

Superintendent Duvall pulled a folder from his file cabinet while the Indian agent was talking. He slapped the file down on the desk and thumbed it open, donning a pair of spectacles so that he could inspect the documents within it. "Morgan Clyde: Two years as a New York policeman. Quit at the start of the war to join up with Company A, 1st United States Sharpshooters, Berdan's regiment. Decorated for valor at Malvern Hill and Gettysburg. Marshal of various cow towns: Sedalia and

Baxter Springs. Last known job, U.S. Deputy Marshal for Judge Story's federal court out of Van Buren, Arkansas."

"I don't need your report to know of this man's reputation . . ." Agent Pickins tried again, but wasn't allowed to finish.

"Euless, I'll remind you that we're all gentlemen here, and that there's little that you can add about this man that I don't already know." Duvall gave the Indian agent a sharp look and then closed the folder and slapped it with the palm of his hand like a judge's gavel in a final verdict. "The Pinkerton Detective Agency put this dossier together for me as a favor."

Morgan leaned over and rubbed his cigar out in the tin ashtray on one corner of the desk. "What else does that file of yours say?"

Duvall laced his hands together over his belly again and met Morgan's hard look. "Among other things, it says you killed two men in Baxter Springs, and then another while you were working for Story's court. Says you're a damned hard man who's too quick to shoot to suit the tastes of most of your employers. I heard myself that Judge Story fired you for shooting and wounding a prisoner who claimed his hands were shackled at the time of the incident."

Morgan ground the cigar more firmly into the ashtray, unaware that he was crushing the stub of it. "Somebody's a damned liar."

"Maybe, but if I didn't believe most of this report on you wasn't accurate, I wouldn't have sent for you. My job is to get this railroad to Texas, and yours will be to see that none of these secesh sons of bitches and renegade trash that have been holding up my trestle job get in my way again." Duvall leaned forward until his face was closer to Morgan's over the desk. "You can sweet-talk them, kiss them, rock them in a baby cradle, or you can shoot every last living one of them between the eyes for all I care. This line has got to make it into Texas by the first of the year, and I want some by God law and order in this camp."

"You should have discussed this with me first," Agent Pickins said.

Duvall held Morgan's stare a brief instant longer and then turned to the Indian agent. "It's my company's money that's going to pay this man, and what do you care if I hire a railroad policeman to handle my camp?"

"Your line runs on Indian land, and as a duly appointed agent to the Creek tribe . . ."

"My line runs on a right-of-way granted to me by the federal government." Superintendent Duvall turned to the engineer at the bridge drawing. "What do you think, Hope? It's your bridge."

"Something has to be done." The engineer already seemed to have lost interest in the conversation and he was studying the diagrams again.

"There you go, Euless," Superintendent Duvall said. "Two votes to one. You've now been consulted with."

"I agree we need a peacekeeper, but this man's little better than an outlaw himself," Agent Pickins said.

"You be careful before you go any farther with that line," Morgan said quietly.

"I will not be bullied by the likes of you." The Indian agent looked defiantly at Morgan, quickly adjusting the wire-rimmed eyeglasses on the bridge of his nose, but only managing to leave them more askew than they had been before. "We have no need for another ruffian in this camp."

"I'll not warn you again." Morgan turned slowly to face the Indian agent, and the tone of his voice had changed.

Superintendent Duvall cleared his throat. "I don't think striking a federal Indian agent and a man of the cloth will help your reputation any, Clyde."

Morgan frowned at the Indian agent, as if reassessing the man. "Him?"

"I'm an ordained Methodist minister," the Indian agent said, straightening a bit in his chair.

"Euless used to run the Ashbury Mission school for the Indian children, and he was appointed agent to the Creeks not long ago," Duvall added. "He and his Indians have been howling to Washington about my right-of-way being granted without their approval."

Morgan grunted. "You've heard my terms. Agree to them, or give me my fifty dollars for coming all the way down here."

"And here's my final offer," Duvall answered. "Seventy-five dollars a month for you, and fifty dollars a month for your deputies. Have we got a deal?"

"Pay me my fifty dollars, and I'll be gone." Morgan turned to McDaniels, the engineer, while Duvall opened the safe behind his desk. "That's quite a bridge you're building."

McDaniels nodded absentmindedly, and it took a bit to pull his attention from whatever he was thinking on. "Yes, yes, it's a real corker. We made a good start on it once, but the first design was all wrong and the pylons didn't hold and the whole bloody thing collapsed. And now we've got other problems."

"Such as?"

The engineer shared a look with his superintendent, and only continued when Duvall nodded at him. "It seems some of the rough element in camp don't want the railroad to progress past here. Somebody tried to burn the bridge down two weeks ago."

"They're fine with making their profit right here, aren't they? And I'm guessing you've got a few saloon owners and a bunch of others that like having all the sheep they can fleece congregated in one herd."

Again, a look was passed between the superintendent and the engineer, but like before, the superintendent showed his agreement with a simple nod of his chin. "There's a bad mob of outlaws down in the thickets along the river. Not only do they cause problems in camp, but they robbed one of our wagon trains coming overland with supplies from Fort Smith two weeks ago. And the worst thing might not be all the criminal sorts, but the fact that I'm having problems getting all of my men to show up for work because they're drunk and laid up in one of those tent saloons."

Duvall held out Morgan's money. "My offer still stands."

"No deal." Morgan took the mix of paper money and coins and counted them before shoving them inside his pocket. He pointed at the safe behind the desk. "Is that why you've got the guards out front?"

"Rented Pinkerton agents. I keep a little money on hand, but we wait to bring in the payroll from Kansas City each month."

"Must be worse than I thought."

"You aren't the only peace officer for hire."

"No, but I'm the only one that's here." Morgan gave a curt tip of the brim of his hat and turned and went out the door.

"Abrupt, isn't he?" the engineer said when Morgan was gone.

"A difficult bastard, for sure." Superintendent Duvall scowled at the door.

"You should count yourself lucky that he didn't take your offer," the Indian agent said after Morgan left.

Duvall didn't answer him, and swirled his whiskey around in its glass and continued to stare at the door.

Agent Pickins knocked a bit of grass off of his rumpled coat and took up his hat from the rack on the wall. "Mr. Duvall, if you don't get this camp under control, I will be forced to take action. You know that the sale of intoxicating spirits in the Indian Territory is against the law, as well as the fact that you are basically setting up a town here, rather than the station you originally promised."

"My right-of-way grants me the roadbed and every alternate section of land alongside it."

The Indian agent scoffed. "Save that for those that don't read the newspapers. News travels fast, even way out here, Duvall. No matter what you say, Congress has revoked all but your roadbed rights. You know it and I know it. Much of your so-called grant has been deemed unconstitutional and illegal, and was never agreed to by the tribes."

"It is still being discussed. Damned lawyers." Duvall threw down the last of his drink and poured himself another one. "Shysters and crooks and liars, every one of them."

"Unless Congress changes its mind, your authority extends nowhere beyond the narrow strip surveyed to lay your tracks."

"Say what you mean, Euless," Duvall said with color flushing his face. "Don't beat around the bush if you are going to threaten me."

Agent Pickins willed himself to lift his eyes from the floor and meet the superintendent's hard look head-on. "I'll go to the Board of Indian Commissioners, or Office of Indian Affairs if I must. My brother . . ."

"Yes, we know all about your brother, the great senator from the state of Vermont, and how you got your job. You've thrown his name around more than enough."

Agent Pickins shoved his hat on his head so hard that he dented the crown, and stormed out of the room.

"That Clyde is an independent, surly devil, isn't he?" Duvall said to the engineer when the Indian agent was gone.

McDaniels chuckled. "I think that's putting it mildly. Kind of reminds me of someone else I know."

Duvall propped his feet up on the desk and poured himself another glass of whiskey. "That's a shame. I think he might have been mean enough to pull it off."

"We need that man. You should have paid his price."

"I'll be damned if I'll be held up by an overpriced badge packer with too high of an opinion of himself. No, he can work for what I've offered, or I'll find us another man for the job."

"And then what? What happens while we wait for you to find someone else? The camp's getting worse every day," the engineer said. "From what I hear of Clyde, he's a fair man, even if he has a reputation for being a little too willing to use his gun."

"To hell with Clyde. We don't need him."

"That was some of Texas George Kingman's mob out there shooting things up. He's supposed to have more men coming in any day. Most of his men are secesh, and they're talking it up big that no bloody Yankee railroad is going to come through their country."

"I said I'll hire us someone else. Maybe get the Lighthorse down here like Useless Pickins has been suggesting."

The engineer was too serious to laugh at Duvall's nickname for Agent Pickins, and the superintendent had said it too many times in the past for it to have any humor left, even on a better day. "The tribal courts don't have any jurisdiction over white men, and those Lighthorsemen won't bother themselves with mixing in our business. Not with Story's crooked court ruling against the tribes every time they go to trial. You know this."

Duvall downed his whiskey and threw the glass across the room, busting it against the far wall. "First, I've got the board members, politicians, and every bondholder breathing down my neck, and now I'm hearing it from you. Build your damned bridge, and leave the rest of it to me."

The engineer put his back to his boss, acting like he was studying his drawing again. He kept his back to him when he spoke again. "You didn't tell Clyde that Bill Tuck was in camp," the engineer said. "I hear Clyde killed Tuck's brother-in-law up in Baxter Springs."

"Let him and Bill Tuck kill each other if they want to. We've got a railroad to build."

Visit us online at
KensingtonBooks.com
to read more from your favorite authors,
see books by series, view reading group guides, and more.

Visit us online for sneak peeks, exclusive giveaways,
special discounts, author content, and engaging
discussions with your fellow readers.

Sign up for our newsletters and be the first to get exciting news
and announcements about your favorite authors!
Kensingtonbooks.com/newsletter